Readers love
LOUISA MASTERS

The Bunny and the Billionaire

"Looking for a story that's the very definition of sweet romance? Here it is."

—Scattered Thoughts and Rogue Words

"I really really loved this one and very much recommend it."

—Diverse Reader

"The bottom line is that this book was incredibly entertaining."

—Just Love: Queer Book Reviews

The Athlete and the Aristocrat

"…a good book. Laughter, a few tears, and happy ones too. A good read."

—Love Bytes

"Would definitely recommend to readers who enjoy billionaire romance, or sports/athlete heroes."

—Joyfully Jay

By LOUISA MASTERS

O Hell, All Ye Shoppers

DREAMSPUN DESIRES
#43 – The Bunny and the Billionaire
#73 – The Athlete and the Aristocrat

JOY UNIVERSE
I've Got This

Published by DREAMSPINNER PRESS
www.dreamspinnerpress.com

I'VE GOT THIS

LOUISA MASTERS

Published by

DREAMSPINNER PRESS

5032 Capital Circle SW, Suite 2, PMB# 279, Tallahassee, FL 32305-7886 USA
www.dreamspinnerpress.com

I've Got This
© 2019 Louisa Masters

Cover Art
© 2019 Reese Dante
http://www.reesedante.com
Cover content is for illustrative purposes only and any person depicted on the cover is a model.

Trade Paperback ISBN: 978-1-64405-475-8
Digital ISBN: 978-1-64405-325-6
Library of Congress Control Number: 2019904442
Trade Paperback published September 2019
v. 1.0

Printed in the United States of America
∞
This paper meets the requirements of
ANSI/NISO Z39.48-1992 (Permanence of Paper).

Once again, for Becky Johnson,
who insisted this book was worth it when I was ready to give up.
Don't tell her how right she was!

AUTHOR'S NOTE

JOY UNIVERSE is obviously fictional, but I don't think it takes much effort to guess what it's based on. Disclaimer: I have never run or even worked at an entertainment complex of that size, and freely admit there's probably a lot I've got wrong. I hope you love it anyway.

CHAPTER ONE

Derek

I JUST can't help it—I sing loudly to myself and the cars around me as I drive to work. Well, considering the speed traffic is moving at, it's unlikely anyone in those cars can hear me, but I like to think that maybe I'm brightening someone's morning with my off-key warbling along to the radio. Everyone should be as happy to face the morning as I am.

Admittedly, I have a pretty great life. I'm thirty-seven and have great parents who live far enough away that I don't have to see them too often. I'm also financially independent, with friends around the country—the world, actually, thanks to my employer's propensity for hiring talented people from around the globe—and generally get along with everyone. I can recognize the good things about myself—and the not-so-good things, but why would I want to tell you about those? Let's call it confidence. I'm confident in myself. And that means that most mornings I wake up happy to face the day.

Some people hate their jobs. Not me. I've worked damned hard since graduating college, and now I'm in the enviable position of being an assistant director at the second-largest entertainment complex in the world—the *youngest ever* assistant director. For those of you who don't know, that's Joy Universe, a resort and theme park complex in southern Georgia, not far from the Florida state line. JU has four theme parks, twenty-six resorts and three campgrounds, and a shopping and entertainment village that rivals anything on offer anywhere else.

The downside? The complex is pretty much in the middle of nowhere, except for the town that was established to provide housing and services for staff. It's called Joyville, and is now a thriving small city, actually beginning to attract residents who don't have any connection to JU—although, as a long-term resident myself, I don't know why. Still, the University of Georgia recently decided to build a campus in Joyville, so I guess it'll keep on growing.

I'm just turning in the entrance of the JU complex when my phone rings, cutting off the musical talents of whatever pop star the radio was playing. I flick a glance at the in-dash display.

Fuck.

It's Dimi, my assistant. He's an ambitious overachiever, so he usually beats me to the office, despite the fact that I get there at seven thirty and he's not required to start work until eight. The point is, he knows exactly when I'm due to arrive, so the only reason for him to call is if there's an emergency.

I'm just about to hit the button to accept the call when sirens shatter the morning calm. A peek in the rearview mirror shows two police cars, lights flashing, tearing around the corner from the highway. They zip past me as I answer. "Are those sirens for us?"

"Murder at Tiki," Dimi says tersely.

Double fuck.

A horn blares through the speaker, and Dimi swears. He's in his car, probably headed from the office to the resort. We don't get deaths too often, let alone murder—on average less than five deaths a year in the whole of JU, which considering how many million people visit each year is pretty amazing. Most of the deaths are from natural causes—like heart attacks—or accidents because people don't follow safety instructions. Only twice in the history of the complex, which is fifty-seven years, has the fault for a death been found to lie with JU. Murder is even less common—in the last ten years that I've been working here, we've had one. Our security in the parks and the village is intense, and in the public areas of the resorts too, but there's only so much we can do in the guest rooms.

"I'm five minutes away," I tell him, hanging a U-turn. It's a lie, or would be normally, since Tiki Island Resort is halfway across the complex from where I am now, but I don't plan to adhere to the posted speed limit. Thank God it's early and there's not too much traffic on the complex roads. "Tell me what you know."

"Not much, sorry, Derek," he says. "Resort housekeeping got a call about thirty minutes ago from one of the deluxe bungalows, requesting a linen change, so they sent a housekeeper over. We're not entirely sure of the details from that point, because the night manager says she's hysterical, but apparently there's blood everywhere, a dismembered body on the bed, and another guest acting like nothing's wrong."

Fuck fuck fuck. Could this get any worse? Our housekeepers for the deluxe bungalows are pretty unshakable. They see a lot of weird shit, because those rooms go for over a thousand bucks a night and rich people can be eccentric—hence the reason nobody batted an eye at the request for a linen change before seven in the morning. But a dismembered body… yeah, that could freak out even the most jaded housekeeper.

"Is the situation contained?" The road is completely clear, so I press down on the accelerator. Our security team actually monitors the roads for speeding drivers, since guest safety is one of our highest priorities, but security should already be aware that we have a grisly murder on our hands and will likely not stop me from getting there as soon as fucking possible.

"As much as it can be. The housekeeper hit her panic button and got the hell out of there. Security found her about twenty feet away, hiding behind a tree. They say she was pretty composed when they first got there, but then fell apart. They've got eyes on the door and have quietly evacuated the guests on either side—thank God it wasn't a standard room."

Hell, yes. Standard rooms at Tiki are in long buildings and share walls with each other, whereas the deluxe bungalows are completely separate and actually have about fifteen feet of space between them. If this had happened in a standard room, JU policy dictates that security would have had to evacuate the entire building—fifty rooms, and up to two hundred guests. A nightmare.

I turn down the side road that leads to Tiki and one of my other resorts. Dimi's car is about a hundred feet ahead. "I'm behind you," I tell him. "See you soon." I disconnect the call.

So what exactly do I do that I love so much, even on a day that starts with a murder? Well, JU is divided into five administrative districts, four of which include parks and a bunch of resorts. The fifth also has resorts, but instead of a park, it includes the village—which is officially called Joy Village, but we just call it the village. We're real creative like that. Each district is managed by a JU assistant director—that's me. They tell us the districts are of equal importance to JU, but that's bullshit. Mine, I'm happy to tell you, is the most profitable. I look after six resorts and Planet Joy itself, home to Joy Bear, the space-traveling cartoon bear that started the whole Joy Incorporated crazy journey. Joy and her zany spacefaring friends can be seen every day at Planet Joy, along with a variety of other characters and experiences Joy Inc. has developed over the last fifty years.

That's what the marketing brochures say, and my team and I do our damndest to make it true. Especially when shit goes wrong.

My phone rings again.

Quadruple fuck.

The director.

I answer immediately. "I'm about a minute from the resort, Ken," I tell him, because of course he knows what's going on. Anytime the police are called, an alert is sent to his assistant. Calling the cops because of murder would have had her interrupting him no matter what time it was or what he was doing, even if it was his sacrosanct weekly golf game—which thankfully isn't today.

"What do you know?" he demands. He doesn't like negative headlines associated with the complex, and murder tends to be the most negative of all.

I run down the situation quickly, finishing just as I turn into the Tiki driveway with a little too much speed and pull the car to a stop right behind Dimi and the police cars in the forecourt. "I'm at the resort—I'll call you back as soon as I have more information." That isn't exactly the truth. I'm planning to call him back when I can tell him the situation has been resolved. Hopefully that will be soon, or else he'll be calling me again.

He hangs up without answering—such charming manners—and I leave my car, tossing the keys to the valet because I know there's a busload of guests due from the airport soon. I wonder if the cops will let us move their cars? I catch up to Dimi quickly, and we stride together into the lobby, where we're met by the assistant manager, Carol, who looks a bit frazzled. She's technically not even supposed to be on shift yet—hell of a way to start the workday.

"Derek, thank God! This way." She races toward the north door, and Dimi and I jog along with her.

"Do we have the guest information?" I ask, and she fumbles in a pocket and pulls out a sheet of paper. I frown, because I was expecting her to say it had been sent to my virtual inbox. The JU staff app on my smartphone means that all information can be flagged for my urgent attention right from any computer terminal hooked up to the intranet—which is all of them.

Dimi takes the paper and flashes me a glance that clearly says he's on it. We've worked together long enough that he knows I'm thinking about staff refreshers on properly using all the tools available to us.

He reads aloud from the paper as we run past the main pool. At this time of morning the lifeguard is not yet on duty, so it's pretty much deserted. "Peter and Kylie Rutherford, married, repeat guests, and members of the Forever Joy vacation club. There's no past incidents on file. Both late forties, in on April 20 and due to check out tomorrow. Deluxe dining plan for both of them, and they've charged several bottles of high-end wine to their account, as well as a considerable number of purchases in the parks and the village."

There's a crowd around one of the deluxe bungalows up ahead. What looks like most of the resort's security team, the night manager, the not-yet-on-duty resort manager, and four cops. We skid to a halt among them.

"Gentlemen, you can't be here," one of the cops says, but Link, my manager, looks so relieved to see me, he's on the verge of tears.

"This is our assistant director," he tells the cop.

"Derek Bryer." I offer a hand. "What are we doing here?"

"Officer Higgins," the cop says, shaking my hand briefly. "The plan is to break through the door and neutralize whoever's on the other side. Do you have the guest information? The assistant manager was going to get it."

I frown again, because any of the security or management employees standing around would have been able to access the guest profile from their JU-issued tablets. The cops shouldn't have had to wait. Dimi hands Officer Higgins the printout Carol gave us, then pulls out his tablet and taps at the screen, probably making notes about the staff training I'm going to insist on. I turn to Link.

"Where's the housekeeper who found the body?" The answer had better be that she's in the staff room with one of our staff EMTs, and a doctor and a counselor on the way. "Oh, and what's her name?"

"It's Maya. She's over there." He points about fifty yards away, where a middle-aged woman in a housekeeping uniform is sitting on one of the benches the resort has scattered around for guests to sit and enjoy the scenery. I mentally add management training to my list. Sure, Link's shaken up, but dealing with a crisis is something he's been trained for, and there's a process for a reason. At least there's an EMT with her.

"Do you need me here, or can I go talk to her?" I ask the cop, and he shakes his head.

"She's pretty shaken up. We couldn't get anything out of her," he warns me, but I wave him off and shoot Dimi a look. He nods, and I know he'll monitor the situation and call me over before any action can take place.

I approach the bench slowly, making sure to make noise as I walk. No way do I want to scare a woman who just found a dismembered body. Also, no way do I want to be dealing with a lawsuit because of her trauma. JU is going to do everything possible to make sure she can sleep at night.

The EMT looks up. "Derek's here," he tells the woman softly, and she turns her head to look at me. She's shaking, and her eyes are red-rimmed and puffy.

"Hey, Maya," I say, speaking just as softly as the EMT, whose name tag says Pat. "Shit start to the day?" I hold my breath, wondering if maybe that was crossing a line, but she huffs a watery laugh. "Can I sit?" I give her the control in this situation—something I learned in one of the *many* management seminars I've been on.

She nods, and I perch on the bench beside her. "Is there anything I can get you?" I start, raising an eyebrow at Pat. He shakes his head slightly, telling me that Maya's basically okay and doesn't need to be taken to the hospital. Maya is looking at her hands in her lap, but she answers me.

"I just want to go home."

"Yes," I assure her. "I don't think it's a good idea for you to drive, though, so we're going to have a car take you, and someone will bring your car back to you. First, I'd really like it if you let the doctor see you—she should be here soon." She'd better be here soon. If it turns out that Link and his team haven't called her, there is going to be a serious management reshuffle at the Tiki Island Resort.

"I spoke to her on my way here," Pat says. "She'll be here any moment."

"Well, in that case, why don't you and Maya head back to the staff room? You'll probably meet her in the lobby. As soon as she's seen you, you can head home. Take the rest of the week off, with pay, and we'll have a chat with you later about when you think you want to come back to work."

Maya sniffles, then nods. "Thank you," she whispers.

I reach out to pat her hand, but stop, hovering midair. Who knows if she wants to be touched right now? "Don't thank me. I'm so sorry this happened to you. We're going to do anything you need to make you feel comfortable at work again."

She grabs my hand and holds on tight, giving me a tearful look. I squeeze her hand. This has to be so hard for her—I mean, a dismembered body? Really?

Crap. The cops are going to want to talk to her.

"Maya," I begin hesitantly, "the police are going to have questions for you." Her grip tightens, threatening to bruise. "I'm going to tell them you've left, whether you're still here or not." The pressure on my hand lessens, and blood rushes back to my fingers. "Hopefully they'll be so busy today they won't come to you at home, but they will eventually want to talk to you. They don't know anything about what's happened." Yeah, pretty sure *that* was crossing a line, but probably not as much as what I'm about to say. "Is there anything you can tell me that I can pass along, maybe get you a reprieve?"

Her nails are digging into my skin, but I figure I deserve it. She takes a deep, shaking breath.

"She opened the door in her nightie," Maya whispers, her voice shaking. "I couldn't see into the room, but it was dark. She told me she needed the bed changed, then went into the bathroom. I walked into the room and went to turn on the bedside lamp. It was... sticky." Her voice breaks, and Pat frowns.

"Maya, you don't have to say anything else," I assure her. The rest seems pretty self-explanatory, really. She nods again, and I tip my head at Pat.

"Come on, Maya, let's head back to the staff room. I'll make you a nice cup of tea while we wait for the doctor." He helps her up, and I squeeze her hand one last time before I let go.

"I'll check in with you later in the week, Maya, but if there's anything you need, just call." I pull a card from my wallet, one of the ones with my cell number on it. "Call me direct." She takes it and clutches it to her chest, and Pat leads her away toward the main building.

I watch them go for a moment, then jog back over to where the cops seem to be preparing to break into the bungalow. They've been joined by a few more of their colleagues, which I assume is the reason this is taking so long.

"Did she say anything useful?" Officer Higgins demands. I don't love his tone, but I guess he needs to know.

"She's been deeply traumatized, Officer." I keep my voice level. "The door was opened by a woman, I assume Mrs. Rutherford, who asked Maya to change the bed and then went into the bathroom. The lights weren't on when Maya went in, but she turned on a bedside lamp—she said it was sticky, I assume with blood. I don't know if the lamp is still on."

The officer grunts, and I make a mental note of it. I'm not that impressed with him—for one thing, I just sent his only witness away, and he doesn't even seem to have noticed. Dimi taps at his tablet, probably making an actual note. It's kind of scary the way he and I think so much alike. I probably won't be able to keep him as my assistant for too much longer—he needs to be promoted soon, or he'll be headhunted away from JU. Losing him will be hell.

The officer sighs and looks at his watch. "We wanted to wait for the detective to arrive, but he said not to, so I guess we better get in there."

Yeah. Definitely not impressed.

Things move pretty quickly after that. I'm glad, because the later it gets, the more guests will be wandering around. Carol has pulled herself together enough to go and get a master key for the bungalow, so the cops don't have to actually break down the door. They stand there in all their gear, counting down with their fingers, and then swipe the card. The lock disengages, they shove the door open, and they're bursting into the room with shouts of "Police!" and "Hands up!" I wince and glance around to see if the noise attracted any guests.

Within a few minutes they have Kylie Rutherford in handcuffs and are escorting her out to the cars in front, while yet more cops arrive, one who quickly takes charge, and some with tackle boxes full of equipment. Someone is here from the medical examiner's office, too, I guess to remove the body parts, since it's pretty clear Mr. Rutherford is dead. Unlike the suites in the main hotel building, the bungalows are open-plan, and I manage to sneak a peek through the door before the cops usher me away. It's gruesome, and I wish I'd managed to restrain my curiosity. Even though I knew he was dismembered, I was still expecting to see a body. I'm not going to be able to look at raw meat for a while—just thinking about it turns my stomach.

Dimi is totally on top of things, as usual, and has given orders to the valets to direct the cops to the resort's west parking lot, which is not only closer to the bungalow and more convenient for them, it's also not at the front entrance of the resort. It's very bad for business when guests arrive and see a half dozen police cars parked out front. He's also talking to HR about getting Maya whatever services she needs—a counselor, for one thing.

I gather Link and Carol together. I've already sent the night manager home with a reminder to schedule a session with one of our staff psychologists. "Right," I tell them. "Today is going to be a shit day. Do I need to call people in to cover for you?"

Link gulps and looks me in the eye. I hope he knows that if he tells me he's not up for dealing with this, I won't fire him. Maybe give him a less stressful job, though. My resort managers need to be able to deal with anything, and it's not like he was the one to walk into that room.

"I'm fine," he says. "I can work today. We've already relocated the guests who were in the nearest bungalows. They've been upgraded to executive suites in the main building, and their stay has been comped."

I nod approvingly. True, those guests really haven't been inconvenienced, but we want them telling their friends how amazing their stay was, not that they were roused from sleep because someone was murdered.

"I'll call in one of the off-duty concierges to act as liaison with the police and ensure they have everything they need," he goes on. "And make sure that security set up a manned barrier around this area. I'll put on more staff to deal with guest questions, too, and… and… and all the guests will receive a free drink at the resort bar tonight."

I clap him on the shoulder. "Good idea. Make sure all the staff know not to talk about this—the official line, whether to a guest, their family, their friends, and especially to the media, is that there was a situation, the police were called, and any questions are to be directed to them or the media office. Got it?" Fuck, the media will be all over this. I can't believe they're not here already—how am I so lucky?

Link and Carol nod, and I decide they can probably handle things. "Call me if you have any questions or anything comes up that might *possibly* become a problem later. We need to stay on top of this. The bungalow will probably be a crime scene for a while, so have someone rearrange reservations if necessary—no guests are to stay in this area until you have my go-ahead." I smile, although it's the last thing I want to do. We may end up having to tear down this bungalow. People can be weird about rooms that were the scene of grisly murders—and other people don't want to stay in them.

Link and Carol nod, seemingly buoyed up and ready to take on the challenge of the day. As they head back toward the main building, talking quietly, I pull out my phone and call Ken.

"Derek, you'd better have damn good news after making me wait so long," he tells me, and I take a breath.

"The police have arrested one of our guests, who has allegedly murdered her husband." I rush on, not wanting him to dwell on that. "The scene is secure, and not too many guests have realized yet that anything is going on. The cops will be here for a while, though, and we've taken steps to ensure guests are disturbed as little as possible." What else does he need to know?

"Is this going to look bad for us?" he demands.

"No." At least, I hope not. "I don't know why she killed her husband, but at this stage it looks to be something between the two of them. We were just unlucky that she chose the resort as the scene of the crime. The staff have been very thorough in ensuring all guests are happy." That's true, anyway. Well, except for Peter Rutherford, poor bastard. And Ken really doesn't need to know that my staff need refresher training on how to cope with an emergency. That's for me to take care of.

"Okay. Kim is waiting for your call. I want a full report by noon, and updates until this is resolved."

By "resolved" he means when JU is completely freed of any connection to the police or the murder—which will be a while, with the way legal proceedings go. He won't actually read the reports, anyway—his assistant might, but in general anytime Ken requests shit like this, it's because he wants to cover his own ass. But that "okay" is the important part. The rest is just routine boss douchery.

"No problem." I make sure to smile so it will show in my voice. He hangs up. Yeah, that's how he always ends calls—total douche, right?

I call Kim, the chief media liaison, next. There are a few alerts on the JU app, indicating my attention is needed, but no red flags, thank God. The rest can wait—it's not like my morning isn't completely fucked, anyway.

"Derek, talk to me." Kim is one of my favorite people at JU. She's no bullshit, no-nonsense, and because my district rarely causes any problems for her to deal with, she's always happy to go out of her way to help me. With her backing, we've had some really spectacular media coverage of events at Planet Joy and my resorts.

"Babe, I got a dead man who was chopped up by his wife, and a housekeeper who's gonna have PTSD," I tell her bluntly, trying not to dwell on what my words actually mean. Work first.

She sucks in a breath. "They said murder, but… what do you mean, chopped up? You're exaggerating, right?"

I deliberately don't close my eyes, not wanting to see that image again. "Kim, I wish I was. I got a look into that room, and I'm pretty sure we're gonna have to bulldoze it, because there's blood everywhere. The dead man was in pieces, piled up on the bed. I'm gonna be sleeping with the light on for weeks, and I knew what to expect."

"Right." She shifts directly into superhero mode. "No one talks about this—not to their spouses, friends, priests, and sure as hell not the media."

11

"Done. I've reminded the manager, but I'll have Dimi send a memo to all staff and nudge the manager to reiterate it in the morning meeting." Speaking of Dimi, he's coming toward me, moving fast and with an *oh shit* look on his face.

How many fucks am I up to now? Oh, right. *Quintuple fuck.*

"Great. I'm calling the police now to see what they'll tell me, and I'll talk to legal too, see if someone there knows anyone they can lean on. If anybody gets anything out of the cops on site, pass it along ASAP, yeah?"

"Got it," I tell her, now slightly distracted.

"As soon as the cops give me the all clear, I'll issue a statement to the press. It won't say much. In the meantime, do you have the resort guests under control?"

"Yes. Management here is on it, and I'll be overseeing things personally." I hope. Unless whatever has Dimi so freaked is going to take over.

"And HR is looking after the housekeeper?"

"Yeah, Dimi spoke to them already, and I'll follow up in a bit. I'll also check in with her." Dimi comes to a stop beside me.

"Emergency," he says quietly.

Sextuple fuck. What could be more of an emergency than this? "Kim, I gotta go. Something's come up. We keep each other in the loop, yeah?"

"You bet. Talk later." She ends the call, presumably off to work her magic, and I turn my full attention to Dimi.

"What?"

He sucks in a deep breath. "We have no performers for Planet Joy today."

Fuuuuuuuuuuck.

CHAPTER TWO

Derek

"SO WALK me through this," I demand, glaring at the phone in the Tiki conference room Dimi and I have commandeered. "Because I don't understand how none of our performers can be available today."

"It's not none," Mandy in the entertainment office says, her voice tearful. "There are thirty-seven of them who are fit to go."

"Thirty-seven!" Fuck, this is not good. "Mandy—" I stop and take a deep breath. This is not her fault. I'm not going to be the asshole who yells at her for something that's not her fault. "Okay, tell me what happened."

"Well, last night after the last performance, they all decided to go out for sushi."

I close my eyes. Yeah, I know where this is going. "All of them?" We have nearly one hundred and fifty performers working in the park on any given day, between all the official stage shows and "impromptu" performances.

"Yeah. They even called the people who'd already gone off-shift or weren't working yesterday. It was going to be a fun bonding thing for them."

More like a fucking circus.

"How did they even find somewhere that would feed them all?" Dimi asks. "That's a lot of people to serve at once without any notice."

I can almost hear Mandy's shrug. "They drove out to the coast. There's a sushi festival going on, apparently."

Is she for real? The coast is a two-hour drive. How can I be this unlucky, that all my performers decided at nine at night to drive for two hours so they could have sushi from fucking food trucks?

"Right. And then they were all struck by food poisoning? I assume we're talking food poisoning here, and not that giant aliens landed on the road and crushed all their cars as they were driving back?" Irritation colors my tone, and I force myself to sit back and take another deep breath. Dimi, across from me, glances up from where he's been tapping at his tablet. He turns it to me, displaying the headline on a news site:

SUSHI FESTIVAL STRUCK BY SALMONELLA

Of course.

"Never mind," I interrupt Mandy, who's telling me all about the horrific salmonella outbreak that has hospitals at the coast overflowing with victims. "Did all our people make it back here, and are any of them in need of medical assistance?" I assume that since it's made headlines, the relevant government departments are aware.

"HR is checking into that now," she assures me. "But I think everyone got back well before symptoms started—we only got the first call an hour and a half ago."

I glance at the clock. We're in big trouble; the park opens in twenty minutes, and the first show is scheduled for thirty minutes after that. "We'll talk later about why I'm only hearing about this now," I say grimly. "What are our options?"

"You were dealing with a murder!" she exclaims. "I thought I should—"

"Mandy, our options?" Yes, I sound like a dickhead, but you can't imagine the disaster it will be if we have to cancel all the stage shows for even one day, much less until everyone is back on their feet. How long does salmonella poisoning last, anyway? *Please be just a few hours.*

I don't like my chances.

"Okay, so the absolute minimum number of people needed to run all the performances is one-twenty," Mandy says. "You have thirty-seven, which is why I've been scrambling to find another eighty-three. We've decided to cut entertainment personnel across all four parks to the bare minimum, which means we can lend performers from the other parks to you until this is over."

The massive weight on my chest eases. "Phew. Wow, okay, great. Why didn't you just lead with that?" We'll still need to cancel a couple of shows this morning while everyone goes over the choreography and other shit, but that's waaaay better than canceling everything for days. I smile at Dimi, then stop when I see he still looks somber.

"Because some of the performers from the other parks also went to the festival," Mandy tells me. "Not many, but some. So that only gives us sixty-one. We're still twenty-two performers short." She hesitates, and I get the feeling this is the part she *really* doesn't want to tell me. "I think we need to cancel the impromptu performances," she says in a rush.

I shake my head, even though she can't see it. "No. No way." What the hell? Is she crazy? Part of the magic of visiting Planet Joy is seeing Joy and her friends racing through the park as they chase after the space bandits who stole what-the-fuck-ever from who-the-hell-cares. Or the evil supersoldiers from *Galactic Wars* herding prisoners, who then break free and fight back. And most of all, *not knowing when or where it's going to happen.* We get the best feedback about the impromptu performances, and they're the cheapest to run—no sets, no crew, no staging, minimal crowd management.

"Derek, it's the only option," Mandy pleads. "It's just for today and tomorrow. I've already spoken to agencies in Jacksonville and Atlanta, and they've promised I'll have dancers here by noon tomorrow. They can be up and running for Wednesday morning, but I just don't see how we can run all the shows until then."

"Think outside the box," I tell her firmly. "There are dance schools in town, right? Call them and see if they have any senior students who want a couple days' work and a golden résumé opportunity. Make it clear that we only want skilled dancers." Fuck, even to me that sounds lame. Joyville is not a big town; we might get three or four dancers out of it, if we're lucky. This is when being in the middle of nowhere really *sucks.* Where the hell am I going to find twenty-some professional dancers—

"Fuck me!"

"That goes against corporate policy," Dimi says dryly, but he's smiling. "You've had an idea."

"The village has how many shows playing right now? Six?" I can't believe I didn't think of this earlier.

"Seven, I think," Mandy says. "We'd have to check with events. Why—" She breaks off abruptly. "Derek, I don't think that will work. Those dancers are committed to their shows. Plus, we have no authority over them."

"So let's ask nicely." Really, what the hell? For someone who's in charge of the entertainers, she doesn't seem to have a creative bone in her body. "It's Monday, right? Most of the shows don't have performances on Mondays. So we have a bunch of dancers with a day off who might be interested in earning some extra cash and two free lifetime park passes each." Mandy still hesitates, and I throw an annoyed look in Dimi's direction. He shrugs. "Mandy, I'll handle this myself. You make sure the—" I pause to do some fast addition. Mental math was never my strong point. "—ninety-eight performers we have are at the park and rehearsing ASAP. I'll cancel this morning's shows, but they'll be starting again at noon. I'll get you the extra twenty-two dancers for today and tomorrow—make sure there's someone ready to show them the ropes."

"Derek, I really don't think—"

"Make it happen, Mandy. I'm not canceling the impromptus for two days." I put extra steel in my voice, even though I'm not actually sure I can pull off my side of the bargain.

She sighs. "Fine. I'll let you know if we run into any other problems." She ends the call, and I grab my phone.

"Dimi, find me some dance schools in town." I scroll through my contacts for Toby from events. "And follow up with HR to make sure all our people are okay."

"Got it." He's working away on his tablet—I wouldn't be surprised if he's already found the dance school information.

"Toby speaking," a voice says in my ear, and I switch my attention to the call.

"Derek, Toby. Listen, I need—"

"You want to postpone this morning's meeting," he interrupts. "I'm not surprised, with the murder and all, but, Derek, we needed to have this meeting yesterday. We can't—"

"Nope, not why I'm calling." I interrupt him in turn. "Although it's something we might need to consider. I've got another issue." I run down the details quickly and explain my plan. To say he's dubious is putting a positive spin on it. In the end I break into his hemming and hawing.

"Toby, I'm working against the clock here. All I need is for you to present my offer to the director or stage manager or whoever of each show and ask them to pass it on—*urgently*—to their performers. I'm offering triple the usual rate"—which is pretty damn good—"plus two lifetime park passes to every dancer who's willing to work today and tomorrow. I guarantee they can have the easiest roles too. Whatever it takes to get them to agree."

"They might be able to help you today," he concedes, "since none of the shows are running tonight. But tomorrow will be a problem. There's no matinees on a Tuesday, but the first show is at seven thirty. The performers would need to be cut loose by late afternoon."

"I will make sure they are." We'll do split shifts or something and make sure we have enough staff performers for the evening shows. I make a note of it in the JU app, and send it to Dimi's inbox.

Toby sighs. What the fuck is it with everyone and sighing? "Okay, I'll call around."

"Great! Thanks, Toby. Tell anyone who's interested to call Dimi— you got his number, right?"

"Yeah, I got it. Listen, Derek, don't get your hopes up, yeah?"

God, what is with all the Debbie Downers today?

"I won't," I lie. "Hey, just in case, make it quadruple the usual rate, and four lifetime passes each." It's gonna cost me a fuckton, but the important part is that guests never know there was a crisis.

He sounds shocked as he agrees and says goodbye. I look at Dimi as I hang up—he's just ending a call himself. "You good to manage this?"

"No problem," he says confidently. "Sometime this morning, can you come down to the park and meet them? Show them how important they are."

See, this is why I happily approve massive bonuses for Dimi every quarter. He thinks three steps ahead, and he's *always* on his game. Not like some of the other people I've spoken to today. "Sure, good idea. Any luck with the dance studios?"

He nods. "There are three in town. One woman said her students are all too young and inexperienced, but the other two seemed keen. They promised to call their students now, and if anyone's interested, I should hear soon."

"Good." I stop and take a deep breath. I do that a lot, you'll have noticed. It's because the act of taking in a breath and letting it out gives my mind time to settle and releases tension. Another trick I learned in a management seminar. "So we have a new plan for today. I'm going to call Don"—the Planet Joy park manager—"because he's been trying to reach me for the last fifteen minutes, probably to freak out, and let him know what's going on. He can handle the logistics around canceling this morning's shows. Let's do a giveaway of some kind to distract people— he can sort that out too, something free to every pass holder." Dimi and I both make notes, him on his tablet, me on my phone. "Then I'm going to talk to Link and make sure he has everything under control here. I'll go check in with the cops and call Kim back, see if she has any news for me, check in with legal, and then I'll run back to the office and see if there's anything important happening there—and get the team up to date and delegate out the stuff we were supposed to be doing this morning." More notes. "In the meantime, you get the dancers sorted and follow up with HR and medical about our performers and Maya. I'll meet you at the park, in the rehearsal studio, at ten forty-five to meet the dancers, and then we should have just enough time to make it to the events and marketing meeting at eleven thirty. I'll revise the schedule for the afternoon as we go."

"Sounds like a plan," Dimi says, and his phone rings.

Chapter Three

Trav

I'M JUST getting back to my room from the resort gym when my phone rings. I answer it quickly, not wanting to wake Kevin, my roommate. Sure, it's after nine—barely—but when you work in show business, it's not uncommon to sleep late in the morning. I'm kind of the odd one out that way—I can't sleep later than seven, no matter what time I go to bed. In my partying days that led to a lot of exhausted mornings.

"Hello?" Caller ID tells me it's Rick, our producer.

"Trav, good morning. I have a proposition for you. Want to earn some extra cash?"

I raise my eyebrows, even though he can't see me, and step back out into the hall. Well, it's actually a covered outdoor walkway. The resort Joy Universe has put us in doesn't have interior hallways.

"Sure, as long as it's legal." There are some things I won't do, and dancers get a lot of hinky offers.

He laughs. "Completely legal. I know you too well to offer anything even slightly shady. There's been a salmonella outbreak at a festival on the coast—"

"Yeah, I saw the news headlines." I've had bad sushi before and can commiserate. "But, Rick, gotta be honest, I'm not interested in traveling two hours each way."

"That's fine," he assures me. "You wouldn't have to. Turns out, a lot of the performers here at Joy Universe went to the festival last night, and now they're scrambling to find enough people to keep their shows going today at Planet Joy."

I sit on one of the steps leading down into the perfectly manicured garden. Perform in a hokey stage show probably based on a cartoon aimed at kids? Not exactly my dream job.

"I don't know, Rick—"

"Look, there's no obligation—they've asked us to spread the word, and that's what I'm doing. But they're offering a decent pay packet, lifetime passes to the parks, and the work's not hard, man. The way it was explained to me, the shows are thirty minutes each and run every hour and a half. They've canceled this morning's shows and have agreed that anyone who helps out will be cut loose in plenty of time for tomorrow night's shows at Joy Village, so it's like six hours' actual performing over thirty hours, plus some rehearsal time this morning. And I've been assured that you can have the easiest roles—who knows, you might just have to wear a mushroom costume and do the cancan."

I laugh, because, come on, mushrooms doing the cancan? That's funny. "How much are they offering?"

He tells me, and my heart speeds up. Seriously? That's a nice chunk of change for relatively little work. In fact, I would almost feel guilty accepting that.

No, I wouldn't.

Yeah, okay, I wouldn't. And lifetime park passes? Those would make great Christmas gifts for my sister's family. Joy Universe is *not* cheap, but they could stay at the campground, or if they want to splash out, at the resort I'm at—it's supposedly only three-star, but it's the nicest three-star I've ever seen.

I must've hesitated too long, because Rick starts talking again.

"Don't worry about it, Trav; there's no pressure here. I'm calling through the cast list, but if you see anyone, mention it, yeah? These guys are pretty desperate, and this is their Hail Mary."

I'm curious. "Why are they so desperate? I mean, it can't be the end of the world to cancel the shows for a couple days."

Rick snorts. "That's what I figure, and so does Toby in events planning who called me, but the guy in charge of the park is adamant. Toby says he's all about the guests getting what they pay for, and part of that is live shows, blah blah blah."

Aww. Now that I can get behind. This guy must be a real sweetheart, to prioritize all the potentially disappointed little kids over his bottom line, because the pay he's offering is going to cost a mint.

"Okay, sure. I can do it. I didn't have other plans for the day anyway. Might be fun."

"Really? Great!" Rick sounds surprised, but quickly gives me the details of who to call and tells me they need me ASAP—which I'd kind of guessed. I end the call and head back into my room to wake Kevin before I call this Dimi guy. Kev's always strapped for cash, so once he's awake enough to understand what I'm telling him, he'll jump at this chance.

TURNS OUT Dimi is one of those superorganized people who plans the life out of everything, down to the last detail. I call him while Kevin is waking himself up in a cold shower, and after he thanks me profusely, he tells me he's sending a car to pick us up in ten minutes, and what shoe sizes do we wear, because while the costumes are designed to be adjustable, the shoes aren't.

I drag Kevin out of the shower and jump in myself to wash the gym sweat off, and then we scramble to get to the front of the resort, where sure enough, a couple of black cars are waiting.

"Are you here for us?" Kev asks one of the drivers, who is kitted out in slacks and a Joy Universe polo shirt.

"Are you the dancers for Planet Joy?" the driver counters.

"Yep," I announce.

He nods. "We just have to wait for a couple more. There are eight of you coming all up, so I gotta fill the car. But you can get in, enjoy the air-conditioning."

Kev and I slide into the back seat. I have no idea what kind of car this is—should have checked the badge—but it's surprisingly roomy. I wasn't looking forward to being crammed in the back seat, but three of us will be comfortable back here.

Within a couple minutes, a guy and a girl join us. I don't know them personally, but I recognize them as performers from one of the other shows currently at Joy Village. We share pleasantries on the fifteen-minute drive to Planet Joy, where we're whisked in through a back entrance and ushered to a rehearsal studio.

Dimi is waiting for us there, along with another thirteen dancers from the shows at Joy Village—I wave at the ones I know—and six nervous-looking teenagers.

"Thanks for coming, everyone. You're real life savers, and because of your assistance, thousands of little kids aren't going to be disappointed today." He hands out forms for us to fill in so we can get paid, and then another one so we're covered by insurance, and we take five minutes to complete them before he hands us over to the entertainment staff. "You've all got my number—feel free to use it anytime. I'm going to make sure payroll do a special run so you get paid by Thursday instead of having to wait for the regular pay cycle next week. If you need anything this morning, I'll be in that office"—he points—"making calls, and our assistant director, Derek Bryer, will be in later to thank you personally. He was determined that the show go on, and that's only happening because of you."

Wow, talk about laying it on thick. Still, he's not wrong—we are all here to do them a favor, and there are thousands of little kids who would be disappointed if the shows needed to be canceled. My parents brought my sister and me to Joy Universe when we were kids, and although the rides were fun, we could have just gone to the Six Flags that was literally eleven hours of driving closer to our house for those. What we actually came for was the experience of seeing our favorite characters up close and personal.

Dimi disappears into the office, and we're quickly assessed by the park's entertainment supervisor, who luckily didn't go to the sushi festival. I'm still not sure how so many performers were taken down by food poisoning—that's a long way to go for sushi, when Joy Village has three sushi places open past midnight just a ten-minute drive away.

It turns out the teenagers are students from local dance schools, and while they're actually pretty good, it's clear they don't have a lot of performance experience. Even though we professionals were promised the easy roles, none of us complains when the very easiest are assigned to the kids. Nobody wants an accident on stage due to inexperience. We're all soon sorted into roles—I'll be playing the wisecracking, badass (in a G-rated way) sidekick in a thirty-minute adaptation of the animated feature film *Space Reivers*. It could be a lot worse—Kev will be wearing a mouse costume for his Planet Joy dancing debut.

We're shuffled off for costume fittings so the seamstresses can make emergency alterations while we rehearse. A lot of performers hate being fitted, but it's one of my favorite things to do. What most people don't realize is that the person kneeling at your hem with a mouth full of pins is *listening to everything you say*. If there are two people being fitted at once and chatting, or if you're on the phone, they hear it all—and like everyone in show business, even the modified kind here at Joy Universe, they like to gossip.

So do I.

While Laura, my new best friend, is pinning me into a pirate costume, I spend the next ten minutes or so subtly grilling her for information. The other seamstress, who's working on one of the still-terrified teenage girls, chimes in periodically. I quickly find out exactly how the whole salmonella shambles occurred, along with the fact that most of the dancers here today are actually supposed to be working at the other three parks (which means the food-poisoning fallout is much worse than I thought), but because Joy Universe policy is to rotate dancers around the parks instead of permanently assigning them to one, and the last rotation was only a few weeks ago, most of them are familiar with the shows we need to perform.

Then I steer the conversation to the boss, the guy who is so adamant the show "go on." I mentally roll my eyes every time I hear that, by the way. It's way overused.

"Derek?" Laura says, sitting back to critically study my pants. "Derek's awesome, as long as you follow the rules."

"Oh?" I aim for casual. A rule follower, eh? I like this guy already, especially since he also seems to care about the people visiting the park, and not just profit. Although I suppose happy visitors lead to better long-term profit….

"Yeah. He likes things done a certain way, and he has really high standards. He's always open to suggestions and ideas, but he doesn't like people to get creative in front of the guests unless he's approved it first. Can't really blame him for that—the last time it happened, we got sued."

Hmm.

"Anyway, he's the best AD JU has. If you follow the rules and meet his standards, he always signs off on bonuses at the highest percentage.

That's why everyone loves rotating through Planet Joy. He's tough, but super fair."

"Did you know," the other seamstress—I didn't catch her name—chimes in, "I called Maylee before to see how she was feeling, and she said Derek authorized HR to pay the insurance co-pay for anyone who had to be admitted to hospital with this food poisoning."

Wow. That's pretty generous, considering how much this puts him out. It's actually too generous, really. What's the guy's angle?

"That's nice of him, and must have cost a lot," I venture.

Laura shrugs. "He's always doing stuff like that. It's not easy to keep talented performers, to be honest. There's not much night life in town, and it's a pain in the ass to get anywhere interesting or exciting from here. Staff turnover among the actors and dancers is pretty high—they come to gain experience and some résumé fodder, and then move on. Derek is all about keeping people here so we don't have to spend money training new ones." She gets to her feet. "You're all done, hon. Let me help you out of that, and you can head back out and learn your choreography."

The shows are pretty simple, relying more on the characters and the narrative to wow the kids than anything too fancy in the way of choreography and acrobatics, and I have it mostly down when there's a stir near the entrance. The group I'm rehearsing with stops, and we all turn to see what's going on.

Dimi is by the door, talking to a man. The man is tall, built, blond, and it looks like he has light eyes, though I'm too far away to really tell. His skin is tanned; his smile is white and blinding. He's bold, brash, vibrant, his energy filling the massive rehearsal studio, and the way people turn toward him, orbiting in the force of his charisma, makes me envision him as a sun.

I dislike him on sight.

"Oh, Derek's here!" one of the staff performers says, her face lighting up in a smile.

Derek? This is Derek, the assistant director everyone has been talking about all morning? The man who insisted on finding extra dancers so none of the shows would be canceled, and then paying us a mint? Who is paying his staff's medical bills? Who is apparently loved by all?

I sigh.

If Derek were an actor in a teen flick, he'd be the high school jock hero. In a college flick, the frat boy hero. It's wrong to typecast people by how they look, I know this, but it's not just his physical characteristics— he has the aura. The "center of the universe" aura. Although his looks aren't exactly anything to sneeze at, all boy-next-door action-hero perfect. For fuck's sake, he even has a square jaw and cheekbones you could cut glass with.

Why do I care? He reminds me of every jock who made my life miserable in high school, every fraternity guy who made me feel like a loser in college. Because I was the shy, nerdy gay boy who was into musical theater, and that made me a target.

So I get nervous around popular men with head-turning charisma.

I brace myself because Dimi is bringing the man around, introducing him to those of us who don't normally work here, and soon I'll have to meet him and pretend shaking his hand doesn't give me flashbacks.

That's not fair, because seemingly he's a good guy who does good things. But emotion isn't logical, and in my experience when a universally liked, charismatic guy is nice to me, he's working an angle for self-gain.

Finally they reach me. "And this is Trav," Dimi says. I'm actually pretty impressed that he remembers all our names. We met once, for like five minutes, and there were more than twenty of us. Dimi seems like a pretty cool guy—good-looking too, and only a couple years younger than me from the looks of it. Not like a certain unnamed person who is clearly *much* older than me.

I ignore the voice in my head that says Golden Boy looks to be early thirties, max, and smile at Dimi, then turn to Golden Boy. If the smile turns slightly forced, nobody seems to notice. "Trav Jones," I say, offering a hand.

"Derek Bryer. Thank you so much for doing this, you're really saving our bacon. If there's anything you need while you're here, give Dimi a call and we'll take care of it. Not just today and tomorrow, but the whole time your show is running." He gives me a megawatt smile, and the knot in my stomach tightens.

"Thanks." I'm pretty sure he notices now that my smile is pasted on, because he blinks and the blinding smile dims a little.

"Not at all," he says smoothly, then seems to hesitate. Is he waiting for me to say something else? I wish he'd just move on so I can get myself back together. "If you like, you can have my number too. I'm at your complete disposal." The smile he gives is a little toothier than before. Fuck, should I be gushing over him like some of the others were? I can't, I just can't right now. I need time to prepare so I can look past the Golden Boy aura.

"That's not necessary," I tell him. I meant it genuinely, I swear, but somehow it comes out sounding like I don't want his phone number polluting my phone, and I just want to die. A little silence falls around us, and I'm getting surprised looks from the other performers, who clearly all adore this man. I have to work with them for the next two days, so a little damage control is in order. "I mean, thank you for the offer, but it's fine." I look away, take a tiny step back. I'm so uncomfortable right now. I'm sweating like crazy, my heart rate is way up, and I just know my face is red. Why won't he go away and let us get back to work? I can't help it; I fold my arms across my chest.

Dimi puts a hand on Golden Boy's arm, and they turn away for a moment, murmuring to each other. I seize the advantage offered and take a couple of deep breaths. It's a technique one of my acting coaches taught me—the act of pausing and breathing gives your mind and body the chance to release tension and reset. Could I maybe slip away while they're distracted, or would that be rude?

By the time they turn back, Golden Boy's mouth open to say something, I'm ready to end this, and the only way to do that is to seize control.

"I'm sorry." I jump in before he can speak. "I—I think I mustn't have gotten enough sleep"—lie—"and I've never worked at a theme park before, so I'm a bit… flustered." Crap, that has to be the lamest excuse ever. I push on. "I'm, uh, going to go get a drink." Yeah, that's no better.

He flashes that megawatt smile, and *flashback*. Disdain curdles in my belly. *Fake*. I need to get away.

"No problem, Trav," he says. "We're all under a lot of strain today. I'll let you get back to your rehearsal, and I'll drop in later today to see how things are going." He makes solid eye contact with me as he says that. "I'm going to take Dimi with me now"—he raises his voice so everyone in the room can hear—"but he can still be reached by phone."

They leave then, and the supervisor calls a five-minute water break. Kev makes his way across the room to stand by me.

"Dude, what the fuck was that?" he asks incredulously, and I can only shake my head.

CHAPTER FOUR

Derek

As Dimi and I walk out to our cars, I'm completely off my game. What the hell was that? Why did that guy act like I was a leper? I suck in a deep breath, then another. He looked at me like I was about to mug his wheelchair-bound grandmother.

"You okay?" Dimi asks tentatively.

"Fine," I snap. Then take another deep breath. "Sorry. Feeling a bit sensitive. Did that Trav guy have something against me, or what?" I'm not used to being treated like that. People *like* me, goddammit! I work hard to make them like me.

Dimi shrugs and stops next to his car. "Don't know. I can't imagine what could have made him act that way. He seemed pretty together this morning, and the updates Pete has given me have all been positive—he said Trav was actually helping the more inexperienced dancers. Maybe he's just having an off day, like he said."

I grunt, then wish I hadn't. Attitude adjustment needed *right now.*

"Okay," I say after another deep breath, which seems to take better effect than the others. "We're going to be late if we don't get moving. I'll meet you back at the office for the meeting with events and marketing, and then we can have a quick lunch while we work out everything else. I'll have Gina order something. Sound good?"

"Like a plan," he affirms, and we split up.

The whole way back to the office, I'm flustered. I try to put that Trav guy's obvious... what? Dislike? Contempt? Whatever it is, I try to put it behind me, but I just can't let it go. What the hell? I've never met the guy before, but he acted like he knew me and didn't think I was worth his time. And the worst part is, before he opened his mouth, I was actually perving on him. I mean, he's seriously my type—only an inch or so shorter than me, lots of muscle but in a lean way, ash-brown hair,

28

green eyes, and skin so fair it's practically translucent. Plus, he has that air about him, like he doesn't know how absolutely fucking awesome he is. I was honestly thinking about maybe waiting until he finished working for me and then asking him out—and then he opened his mouth, that full, soft-looking mouth, turned that gaze on me, and that thought went by the wayside.

Which is a real shame, because if I picture him in the moments before we started talking, just the image of him standing there in loose cotton pants and a tank top is enough to get my motor running.

I pull into the office parking lot and park in my spot, right up near the door. Time to turn the motor off, unless I want to face some embarrassing moments in the office.

We have a meeting with events and marketing today to plan out next year's schedule for entertainment at Planet Joy and the resorts. Yes, I know it's not even May, but that's how things roll in entertainment. We actually should have had this meeting a couple months ago, but the two departments—which work so closely together that I tend to think of them as one—got caught up with a huuuuuuge crisis in one of the other parks about planning permits and licensing not being up to date for a couple of the shows and one of the rides. When the dust cleared on that one, the park had to *close* for three days—the *whole* park—and both the park manager and the AD for that district were looking for new jobs.

Shit like that doesn't happen in my district.

I make it through the door into the conference room booked for the meeting with literally seconds to spare, after a lightning-fast pause at Gina's desk to grab the file I need and request that she organize lunch for Dimi and me. Everyone else is waiting, with varying degrees of interest and sympathy on their faces. By now, all the JU staff will be aware of the shitstorm my morning has been—first a murder, then over a hundred critical staff absences.

They're not going to see me looking frazzled, though. No fucking way.

I flash a smile and take my seat. "Sorry for the delay, everyone. We've had a lot going on today." I say it sardonically, rolling my eyes, and of course the four people from events and marketing chuckle. Dimi just grins. He knows my policy about faking till I make it—this is a highly competitive industry, where even most of your friends won't cry too much if you fail. No matter what happens, we always remain cool. Even if we're sweating buckets.

"No problem, you made it," Toby says. "And great idea to ask the dancers from the village to help out."

"Thanks" is all I say. *No thanks to you* is what I want to add. "Shall we get to it?"

The meeting was originally scheduled for an hour and a half. The idea was for the events and marketing—you know what, I'm just going to start calling them evarketing. It's so much easier. They really should be one department, anyway—people to give me and Dimi a top-level overview of what they have planned, and then we'd take away a detailed plan to review with the park and resort managers, with another meeting, this one four hours, scheduled for next week to go through every single item in the plan. Except right off the bat, I have a problem with their ideas. They're just a rehash of everything we're doing this year, and that's not good enough. A lot of families come annually, and they expect a magical new experience every visit, not the same old, same old. The last thing we want is for them to stop coming.

Obviously Toby and Elise—the head of marketing—aren't thrilled when I point this out, and so the meeting drags on as I tear their plan to shreds point by point. "I know you guys can do better than this," I conclude. "Last year was spectacular, this year even better. And they were completely different from each other."

"There are only so many new ideas out there," Elise protests, and I nod sympathetically.

"Right, but Joy Inc. will have twelve new feature films released this year, and I know there are another eleven scheduled for next year. Why aren't we capitalizing more on those?"

"None of the other ADs had any problem with their plans," Toby snaps—defensively, because I've made a very good point, and he knows it.

"They will have when Ken sees the schedule—and when next year rolls around and the guest feedback rating drops. And anyway, I don't care what the other ADs thought. This is my district, and that's just not good enough for my district."

"Your district has had a murder and a major staffing catastrophe in the space of hours." From the look on her face, Elise regrets making the bitchy comment, but it's too late.

"That's right," I agree. "Two catastrophic events that are completely outside my control occurred this morning. And yet the disruption to routine and guests has been minimal—which it wouldn't have been if I hadn't pushed my staff and the entertainment and events teams just as I'm pushing you now. Find me something fantastic for next year. We have a meeting scheduled for next week, so let's keep it and plan to get things locked in then. You can send me ideas to discuss at any time between now and then. And just a word of friendly advice—if the plans for the other districts are like this, see if you can spruce them up a bit. Because when these go to Ken for final approval, he's going to send them back, and then you'll be starting from square one."

THANKFULLY, GINA ordered sandwiches from my favorite deli in the village for lunch, because anything else would have been cold by the time Dimi and I retreat to my office to eat, forty-five minutes after that meeting was *supposed* to end.

"Was I a prick?" I ask him, and then take a huge bite out of my turkey sandwich. I'm absolutely starving—it's nearly two, and I haven't had anything, not even coffee, since breakfast, which was before seven. This day has been a complete nightmare.

He shakes his head, mouth full of food, then finally swallows. "No. That meeting was a total waste of our time, especially today. They have to know Ken would never approve the plan—it's basically this year's but with the dates changed. Hell, on one of the pages, I saw the old date."

Yeah, I saw that too. I nod. I know I was right, but it's nice to have the affirmation. I wasn't my usual chirpy self going into that meeting, and I don't want to have taken my bad mood out on people who don't deserve it.

Lucky we didn't have that meeting before I had to ask this morning's favor of Toby, though.

"Right," I say, putting my sandwich down, then picking it up again immediately and taking another bite. I chew and swallow fast. "The team seems to have managed everything here okay this morning. Have you had a chance to check the memos on the board?" I'm referring to the virtual notice board in the staff app, of course. Anything that the whole team needs to know can be posted there, and each member will get an alert to check it. Those alerts can't be cleared unless you actually click into the memo on the board and check the box at the bottom to say you've read it, which the author of the memo is advised of—a great way to prevent notices from being lost in inboxes.

"Yep. It looks like they've got it all covered. My inbox is clear of all red and yellow flags, but I still need to go through the nonpriority stuff." Dimi shoves some chips in his mouth. He's got to be just as hungry as me.

I grimace. I don't even want to think about the state my inbox must be in. My phone alerts if I get anything red or yellow flagged, so I'm on top of those, but last time I had a look, the rest was out of control.

It's going to be a long night.

"Good. Gina said there have been a few press calls that managed to get past the switchboard, but they've just been transferring them through to the media department. They were going to hang up but decided that might lead to some of those stupid 'Joy Universe could not be reached for comment' statements." I can't help but be proud of my team. They think shit through and act in the best interests of JU and all of us.

Dimi swallows a huge bite of his sandwich and grins. "You're going to have to promote Gina soon. She's outgrowing her job." I agree, and the same can absolutely be said of him. That's the problem with hiring really great people and training them properly. They get too good for the job you hired them for, and you lose them—and have to start again. "I called Link while you were talking to Gina. The cops seem to be finishing up, or at least most of them have left. They said the area will be closed off as a crime scene until further notice, though, and ask that we have security monitor it to keep guests out."

"No problem." It's not like I'm going to set up an exhibit and charge guests a fee to visit. "I think it's best if we have Kim and Jeff from legal do all the talking with the cops. When I check in with Link later, I'll remind him not to promise them anything—they can direct all requests to legal or us."

Dimi wipes his hand on a napkin and taps on his tablet. "Pete's been sending me updates all day via the app. He says the shows reopened at noon as planned, and so far everything is going well. No problems."

Well, that's a huge relief. I gotta admit, I had some doubts that my plan would work. Not *big* doubts, but little niggles. It seemed to be going well—except for that Trav guy who dislikes me *for no good reason*—but you never know, do you?

I smile confidently. "Great. I'll head down to the park later and check in personally."

Dimi looks surprised, as well he should. There's no real reason for me to do that, and I sure as shit don't have the time. He doesn't say anything, though, and I rush on in an attempt to distract him. "Have you heard anything else from Don?"

When the park opened this morning, Don and his team were ready with vouchers for a free small popcorn and soda from our snack carts for every guest who entered between opening at nine, and noon, when the shows recommenced. Honestly, the guests who just come for the rides wouldn't even have noticed the shows weren't running, but it's better to just issue a blanket "apology." It didn't cost that much, either—concessions are one of the most overpriced things in our world. It does mean that we need to place a huge reorder immediately, though, or we'll run the risk of running out of popcorn and flavored corn syrup next week. I flick quickly to the supply part of the app and see that Don's concessions manager has already created the order, and Don's signed off on it. It's just waiting for me to approve—that's not normal procedure, by the way, but because it's not a regular order, there are hoops to jump through. It helps to prevent theft.

"He left me a message while we were in that meeting. It wasn't urgent, just letting me know that everything seems to be okay, and that the number of complaints about the shows being canceled this morning were fewer than we expected. I haven't called him back yet."

"I'll call him." I make a note on my phone. I have a tablet, just like all the other senior staff, but I prefer to work with my phone. It fits in my pocket. My tablet doesn't, and before I gave up on trying to use it, I used to leave it everywhere. "Or I'll check in with him when I go down there." I wince internally. *Good one, Derek, remind him of the completely unnecessary visit to the park you're planning. He's not going to wonder why at all.*

To be completely honest, *I'm* not entirely sure why I'm going. It has nothing to do with that guy who doesn't like me, even if he is my type and most people like me.

"I'm going to call Maya when we're done here." I doggedly move on. "What's the word from HR and medical?"

Dimi scrunches up the bag his sandwich was in and tosses it in the trash. "Doc Stacey says Maya has a mild case of shock but is otherwise physically fine. She prescribed a low-dose sleeping tablet and arranged for one of the staff counselors to visit Maya this afternoon." He looks at his watch. "They should be there now. Maya will see the counselor for as long as she needs to. HR have flagged in her file that even after the usual five free sessions per year are up, she won't need to pay the co-pay. They sent her flowers." He makes a slight face, and so do I. We can do better than just flowers.

"What about food? She's got a lot on her mind right now, and probably doesn't want to cook. Can we have catered meals sent to her for the rest of the week? Enough so she can have family and friends eat with her."

Dimi makes a note. "Easy. I'll call Tiki and see if any of her coworkers know her favorite restaurant."

"Good idea." I really am going to have to find another job for him. It's days like this that truly make that stand out.

"I've also been having HR send me updates on our performers—the staff ones, not the fill-ins."

I throw my rubbish in the trash can and lean back in my chair. "How are they?"

He grimaces. "As I understand it, in a lot of really disgusting discomfort. Nobody is critically ill, though. Three needed to be admitted to hospital for IV fluids due to dehydration, and from what I've been told, that number may increase over the next few hours. Medical are sending some of the EMTs around to everyone's houses to check on them and make sure they're getting care if they need it."

I blink. "Really? That's not procedure," I point out. "It's a great idea, and totally necessary, but it surprises me that medical—or HR—even thought of it."

He flushes. "They didn't. Um, I told them it was your request." There's an uncertain expression on his face, which makes sense because if "I" requested this, it will be charged back to my cost center—which has already taken a lot of hits today.

A grin spreads across my face. "Spot on, Dimi. Good job."

He *almost* sags in relief but catches himself just in time. "Thank you. Er, I think that's it. Oh, Mandy from entertainment sent a message. We'll definitely have performers here from Atlanta and Jacksonville by noon tomorrow, and she's working with Pete to set up training and rehearsals for them in the afternoon. The plan is for them to take over the evening shows, which will mean no need to do split shifts tomorrow."

Win. Things are finally going my way. "Fantastic. Okay, let's get back to it. We'll review tomorrow at eight, and hopefully everything will go right between now and then."

Dimi heads back to his desk, and I log on to my laptop for the first time today. The first thing I see is a message from Grant.

Heard about your fubar. Let me know if you need me to carry anything.

I can't help but smile. Grant is one of the other ADs, and probably the colleague I'm closest to—in fact, I think you could say we're friends. He got promoted to the job after the last AD—the one who fucked up earlier this year—got kicked out. He should probably have had the job to begin with when it opened a year ago, but the gossip Dimi found out for me was that HR opted for the other guy because they were worried having two gay ADs would "send a message."

I know. Completely fucked, right? The other guy was just as qualified, and although his employment record wasn't quite as stellar as Grant's, he'd been at JU longer, so officially there was no cause to question his promotion. You know, until he completely dropped the ball, screwed the pooch, or whatever other lame cliché you want to use. The unofficial reason Grant didn't get the job is especially stupid because JU has always had a really great diversity policy—after all, our recently deceased founder, Edwin Joy, was a gay black man. He didn't come out until late in life, but he always made damn sure that his company was as inclusive as he could make it.

Grant's a genuinely good guy—case in point, today is his first day back after two weeks' vacation, and the last thing he needs to be doing is taking on any crap from my district.

Actually, on that note....

I pick up my phone and call him.

"Hey." He answers immediately. "You need a drink yet?"

"Hell yeah, but I'm holding off until I get home." I chuckle. Truth is, I'm kind of scared to have a drink, just in case something *else* goes wrong. I need to be in full possession of my faculties right now. "Welcome back."

"Thanks. I thought things were crazy in my office after being away, but then I heard about yours, and suddenly it seemed like a spa retreat in here." Someone murmurs in the background. "Derek, can I call you back?"

"No need—I just wanted to ask if you've seen your events and marketing plan for next year yet. They had the meeting while you were out, didn't they?" I remember that because Grant complained several times about evarketing's lack of flexibility to schedule the meeting. In the end, he reluctantly agreed to let his team handle it, subject to his final approval, of course.

"Not yet—I'm probably taking it home with me tonight. Or I'll get to it tomorrow. Why?" There's a note of dread in his voice. He knows what's coming. This is not the kind of thing I'd just casually call to ask him.

"Bump it up the list, buddy, because you're going to want to call Toby and Elise once you start reading it."

He groans, thanks me, and says he'll call later in the week. Before I disconnect, I hear him telling someone to push back his next meeting.

Right. What's next?

IT'S AFTER six before I've cleared my desk enough to head over to the park. I'm just telling Gina to leave—total workaholic, that woman, would probably stay all night if I didn't chase her out—when Toby comes around the corner.

"Derek, you got a minute?" He looks kind of sheepish.

"Sure, walk with me. I gotta get to the park. Gina, I mean now, not 'in a minute,'" I tell her sternly. She grins, but I know she'll head home.

Toby and I start walking toward the main door to the parking lot. It's not a short walk because this building is only three floors but has to house all the administrative and support staff needed for JU—which, as I'm sure you can imagine, is a fuckton.

"I just want to apologize," he starts, and my estimation of him rises again. It takes guts to be up-front about being wrong. "You were right about the plan. The truth is, we got so caught up in the dramas earlier this year"—no need to say which dramas; I've just had a murder and a massive staffing crisis on the same day, but that *still* can't compare to having to *close a park*—"and the plans slipped off the priority list. By the time we got back to them, we were running way late and… well, you know."

"Yeah." I make sure to sound sympathetic. I think Toby's an idiot for letting that happen, but fact is, people can make mistakes, and I'm going to need to work with him in future. I need him to not hate my guts. "I know how quickly things can spiral out of control." Cue self-deprecating laugh. "And, buddy, you know I wish I hadn't had to be such a dick today, but…." I let it trail off, because I don't need to reiterate how utterly crap the plan was.

"No," he says firmly, "you were completely right to call us on it. Ken would never have approved it, and if Grant had been here for his meeting, we would have already been revising before you even heard about it." Another sheepish look. "He saw it this afternoon, and his reaction was almost identical to yours. It was real quiet in his team's offices too."

I can imagine. Not only did his team tentatively okay that plan, they failed to raise any concerns with him. If something like that had gone to my team while I was on vacay, I would expect them to call me ASAP, no matter where I was—Aruba, Africa, or the moon.

"Well, it's done now. You guys are gonna have a tough enough time trying to come up with a new plan this week without me making you rehash it. Let's put it behind us," I say firmly. "I appreciate that you took the time to apologize, though."

He flashes me a smile as we reach the elevator lobby. Normally I'd take the stairs—it's only two flights, and every time I use them is a couple minutes less doing cardio at the gym—but taking stairs two at a time is not conducive to conversation.

"So why are you headed to the park?" Toby asks. "Not another problem?" He hits the call button for the elevator.

"Nah, I just want to check on things, make sure it's all running as smoothly as I've been told—mostly just be visible to the staff. Plus, I may have told one of the fill-in performers that I'd check in." Shit. What the hell made me mention that?

"Oh?" The elevator arrives, and in the fluorescent glare of the lights as we step in, Toby's eyes gleam. "Something there?"

I force a laugh. "Hardly. The guy hated my guts."

Silence. I glance over to see surprise on Toby's face.

"He hated you?" he asks finally. "I didn't think anyone could hate you. I mean, this afternoon I wanted to smack you in the face and poison your coffee, but I still didn't hate you."

I take that in, make a mental note not to accept coffee from Toby anytime soon, and shrug. "Well, the second we were introduced, he was all attitude. Dimi says Pete's reports about him were all glowing, and nobody else seemed to have problems with him, so…." It's even more depressing when I spell it out like that. Some random guy I never met couldn't wait to get away from me.

"What's his name?" Toby's nose is almost twitching, he's that keen for the gossip. Oh well, I'll throw him a bone. Who cares, anyway? Maybe it will make people like me more if they think someone hates me against all reason.

"Trav Jones." Shit, did I say that too fast? Should I have hesitated, maybe pretended I didn't remember?

Toby gasps. Actually gasps.

"*Trav Jones?* You have Trav Jones performing at Planet Joy in some hokey kids' show?"

The elevator doors open, but I hesitate. I know I haven't lived in New York for ten years, but I still get up there occasionally, and I try to keep up with all the latest Broadway hoopla. After all, we eventually get all the hit shows in the village, so if I don't know what's taking Broadway by storm, how will I know what I need to see? And so if Trav is so noteworthy, why haven't I heard of him before?

"Do you know him?" I ask. Shit, has living in backwoods Georgia totally disconnected me from the world I used to know?

"Not personally," Toby admitted, "but I've been meaning to go over and introduce myself since I heard he was coming with *Day Dot* from New York. A few of the shows he's been in have come down here, but he's never traveled with them. He's… he's one of the backbones of Broadway."

Wow. I mean really, *wow*. That's a hell of a statement, considering the range of amazingly talented actors and dancers on Broadway, and even more so since Trav didn't look to me to be older than twenty-five.

"I haven't heard of him," I admit, feeling completely lacking. "I thought I knew of everyone who's been in a starring role in a decent show during the past thirty years." Yes, I've been geeking out over theater since I was that young.

We're just standing in the lobby now, the few people who are still around just flowing around us as we talk. I have to get to the park, but I'm not missing this insight into the guy who hates my guts.

"He hasn't been in a starring role." Toby drops that bombshell as if it was nothing, as if he hadn't just called the guy *one of the backbones of Broadway.*

Right. I don't have time to stand around chatting so Toby can drip-feed me information and get his own gossip fodder.

I flash a smile. "I guess I need to get up to New York again soon, catch up on what's happening. Oh well, I gotta get going—I'll talk to you later, yeah, Toby?" I'm striding away before he can even answer, tossing a wave over my shoulder.

My car is right near the door, so I barely have time to get my phone out of my pocket and open the web browser app before I reach it. I type in Trav's name, adding "Broadway" for good measure, hit Search, and then toss my phone on the passenger seat and start the engine.

I'm not looking until I get to the park.

I back out of my parking spot and head toward the lot exit.

I'm not.

There's no traffic coming, so I pull onto the road and head in the direction of the park.

I'm really not.

I get maybe halfway there before I cave.

Okay, it's a little less than halfway. I've driven this road enough times to know exactly where the halfway point is, and I haven't reached it yet. But I can't wait any longer. I pull over, put the car in park, and snatch up my phone. Technically there's no stopping anywhere on the complex roads, so I only have a little while before security comes to move me along.

Wow. Trav's got more hits than I would have expected for someone who's never had a starring role. Several are links to articles about shows he's been in, but there are also a bunch of entertainment sites, and what looks like a fan site.

I click into a site for a reputable New York media outlet specializing in theater. It leads me to an article called "Behind the Scenes with Trav Jones," and I skim avidly. It's actually an interesting piece, giving a basic profile (he's twenty-seven, so I wasn't too far off with his age), talking briefly about his upbringing and education (he's actually a New York native, like me), before going on to discuss the roles he's been in.

None of them are starring. They're all support roles... but good ones. Meaty ones. Interesting sidekicks. Funny best friends. The villain's wisecracking henchman who turns good in the end. And from the notations beside each role, he's been critically acclaimed—as much as supporting actors on Broadway are. He's even been nominated twice for a Tony for Best Featured Actor in a Musical.

There is a short Q&A section where Trav and the journalist talk about the roles he liked best and his ambitions for the future. Trav was fairly generic there, saying he wants to portray a wide variety of characters and explore all the flexibility Broadway has to offer.

But it's the last few paragraphs that interest me the most. The journalist gives a short editorial on Trav:

To many who haunt Broadway's every premiere, Trav Jones is a familiar figure. I know I've seen him in many shows, and every time he has delivered a performance beyond what could be expected of the role.

At the beginning of his career, I and my friends told each other, "This guy is going places." We fully expected to see his name in lights within a few short years. So why hasn't it happened yet?

It's not due to lack of opportunity. Though it's not a widely known fact, Jones has turned down, at the time of this article, three offers for leading roles—that I can confirm. The actual number is rumored among Broadway insiders to be more than double that. Why, we ask, would an actor not want to be a Broadway star? Jones isn't saying. In fact, when I asked, he smiled and changed the subject.

Whatever the reason, while it has denied us the pleasure of seeing Jones bring his special brilliance to a starring role, it does ensure great reviews for several otherwise lackluster shows.

I stare at my phone, completely bewildered. Seriously? The guy's been offered leading roles on Broadway and *turned them down*? I wonder briefly what the roles were, but that's not important. This guy is a real conundrum.

I'm just clicking into the fan site when someone taps on my window. It's security. I roll it down.

"Sorry, sir, you can't— Oh, hi, Mr. Bryer. I didn't realize it was you. Um...." The young security guy looks nervous. He's not supposed to let anyone park on these roads, but he clearly doesn't want to tell me I have to move.

I smile at him. "You can call me Derek. Don't worry, I'm going—I know I shouldn't have stopped."

His return smile is relieved. "If you have to check a text or something"—he nods to the phone in my hand—"I guess another minute won't hurt."

Shaking my head, I toss the phone back on the passenger seat. "Nope, it's all good. I've got to get to the park anyway. You have a nice night."

He steps back from my car. "Will do, sir. You too."

I give him a minute to start walking back to his car, and then pull out onto the road. I still don't know why Trav Jones hates me, but I now know that in addition to being extremely attractive and (according to other people) a really great guy, he's supremely talented.

And there's something odd going on with him.

CHAPTER FIVE

Trav

I HAVE to admit, this job is kind of fun.

The role lacks the sophistication of anything I've done before (well, in my professional career, anyway. There are some self-written amateur roles in performances I put on with my cousins when we were kids that might compare), but since it's pretty much a ninety-minute animated feature film chopped up and rearranged into a thirty-minute stage show, I can't really complain. It's an intense thirty minutes, but the audience is always great—the kids totally get into it. And then I have an hour to chill before the next performance. I've done four already today, and one more is left before I finish for the day.

Can't complain, really.

I deliver my next line and follow it up with a camp flourish, which isn't technically part of the choreography, and an ad-lib. The kids seem to love it, based on the cheers and laughter from the audience. The guy playing the lead, who's one of the staff performers, gives me a wry look, but plays off the improv. I'm nearly distracted at one point by something going on in the wings but force myself to stay focused. Whatever it is, it can wait until after the show.

Soon we're taking our final bows, and then running into the wings while the curtain comes down and the amphitheater starts to clear. I've got big plans to get some food before the next show—just a salad or something, since I have to dance again soon, but I can't wait any longer to eat.

It's a real shock to see Golden Boy waiting backstage. There's already a crowd forming around him, staff and fill-in performers and crew who want just a second of his attention, just a moment to bask in his radiance.

Ease off, Trav. Deep breaths.

I need to be professional. I've worked with people who make me anxious before; hell, show business is full of people with buckets of charisma and giant egos and little to actually back them up. I can schmooze and fake smile with the best of them—well, mostly. I can definitely put on a show of liking this guy for the less than twenty-four hours remaining until I never have to see him again. Especially since we're unlikely to run into each other again during those hours. He's an assistant director, right? That sounds important. He's probably got tons of other shit to be doing instead of hanging around here.

Right. So why's he hanging around here? Oh crap, is this *my* fault? Is he here because I wasn't suitably worshipful?

Jesus, Trav, you're an actor. Why couldn't you act impressed by him?

I quickly shimmy out of my costume and hand it over to the wardrobe people. They'll do a check for anything that needs to be repaired before the next show, but it should be fine. Then, in my street clothes, still in full makeup—it's not worth taking it off and reapplying between each show, so we just get touched up—I head in the direction of the backstage door. It leads directly into the staff-only area of the park (and wasn't it a kick to get to see that) where I can go to the cafeteria for some food.

"Trav!"

Crap. So close. At least it isn't Golden Boy. I turn to face Parker, who's playing the lead pirate in our little extravaganza.

"Hi, Parker. What's up? I was just going to get a snack."

Parker smiles at me, all glossy black hair and sparkling brown eyes. He's a total hottie, and perfect for the lead role—he's also one of the few staff actors here today who is supposed to be here, one of the lucky ones who didn't get sick. "I just wanted to ask what made you think of adding that bit just now," he says.

Uh-oh. Am I in trouble? There can be a lot of sensitivity about newcomers adding different flavors to existing roles, and I really don't want to step on any toes.

"It just seemed to fit at the time," I venture cautiously, trying to judge his mood. He's smiling, but in an industry of fake smiles and *acting,* that doesn't necessarily mean anything.

He laughs and claps me on the back. "Chill, dude. I thought it was awesome, definitely fit the show. I was just wondering because there's an amateur theater group in town that could really use some help."

Oh. Well, that's not what I expected.

"I don't know that I have time to take on another role," I begin, but Parker's already shaking his head.

"Nothing like that. The cast is all amateurs, all locals—what they need is someone to consult on blocking and choreography. There are a bunch of us here from JU who volunteer, but now with so many people down for this week, it would be great if you could help out. Even if it's just this week, if you don't want to commit the whole time you're here."

I hesitate. It sounds like a lot of fun, to be honest, and I do like noodling around with choreography and stage blocking. But do I want to build connections to the people here at Joy Universe?

That sounds awful, doesn't it? Like I don't want to make friends. But friends are hard work, and I've always kept my circle small, confined to people I know I can depend on and who I don't mind having depend on me.

Parker notes my hesitation, and a touch of disappointment flashes in his gaze. "Hey, you're busy. No worries. Just thought I'd ask."

He starts to turn away, and I blurt, "No, wait." My sister always tells me that I have to seize opportunities and take chances. This is something different for me, even if it's right up my alley. "I was just thinking about the logistics. Is it a daily commitment?"

Parker grins. "Hell no! None of us could handle that. Right now it's twice a week for an hour, for whoever can make it—obviously we all have different schedules here at the parks. As the show gets closer to opening, things get busier, but everyone is really understanding about what we professionals can commit. We're really only there to offer advice and guidance—they do most of the work themselves."

I make up my mind. "That sounds great, Parker. I'm only here until the end of July, but I'd love to help out. Thanks for thinking of me." I offer a hand to shake; I don't know why—it just seems the thing to do.

Parker shakes it heartily. "Great, that's great! You're going to have a blast—it's so much fun, and everyone is super cool."

"Who's super cool?"

I close my eyes. Crap. I've only heard it once before, but believe me, I'd recognize that voice anywhere. It's like summer sun on wine grapes—heady and sweet.

When I open my eyes, Parker is giving me an odd look, but he quickly transfers his gaze—and a welcoming smile—to the person behind me.

"Hi, Derek," he says cheerfully. "We were just talking about the theater group in town."

Golden Boy comes up beside me. He has a friendly and interested expression on his face, and I can't stop myself from wondering if he practices it in the mirror.

Friendly, Trav. Friendly and polite. Or at least polite. At least I'm not on the verge of falling apart just from his presence, like this morning.

"They do some great work," Golden Boy is saying. "Are you interested in seeing a show? I don't think there's anything on at the moment—they're in rehearsals for this summer's season."

"Trav's going to consult," Parker tells him, and I want to kick him for sharing even the most trivial piece of information about me.

Golden Boy is nodding. "Choreography, right? I saw that little extra thing you did. The crowd loved it."

He was watching the show? I smile weakly. "Thanks." I should say something more—Parker's looking at me strangely, as if he's remembering my weirdness with Golden Boy this morning—so I add, "I'm surprised you know the show so well."

Oh hell. That came out completely wrong. What is *wrong* with me? When did I lose the ability to converse like a human being? I add quickly, "It speaks well of your dedication to your staff and the park." I snap my mouth shut. Now I sound like a condescending, pompous ass. I can feel my cheeks getting hot, which means they must be fire engine red. I blush really easily, a nasty side effect of having fair skin.

Parker and Golde— You know what, I need to start calling him Derek in my head. If I don't, you can bet your ass I'm going to slip up and call him Golden Boy out loud. So Parker and *Derek* both have those annoying oh-how-sweet expressions people with nontranslucent skin get when they see me blush. I grit my teeth and suck in a deep breath in an attempt to calm myself, but unfortunately, annoyance is also one of the things that can set off a blush, so it's unlikely the color's going to fade anytime soon.

Whatever.

"Anyway," I push on, determined to get the hell out of this hellish situation, "I need to grab a snack before the next show, and they'll be expecting me back to fix my makeup soon. Parker, see you in a few. Derek"—*yessss!* Total win—"nice seeing you, and thank you again for this opportunity. It's been fun." I toss in a smile for good measure, inwardly congratulating myself, then without waiting for either of them to reply, I stroll as casually as I can manage toward the door. I am *so close*—literally just steps away—when someone comes up alongside me. I don't even need to look to know who. His sun-god presence announces him.

"Trav, can I walk with you?"

I don't think I could ever get used to the sound of his disembodied voice. At least when I'm looking at him, I can brace for it. No fair that he has a voice like that.

"Sure," I say, because it's rude to say no, right? And I'm trying to make up for my shit-tacular scene this morning. We push through the back door and head toward the cafeteria. I watch Gol—Derek from the corner of my eye. He's smiling and waving at people as we pass, like he's royalty or something. *Douche.*

Then I notice that he's actually waving *back*. People are waving at him first. Shit. I made a snap judgment—a *wrong* one. Thank God I didn't say anything out loud—that would have been a hard one to come back from, especially since I haven't exactly been friendly so far.

We're nearly at the cafeteria, and he still hasn't said anything to me. I have absolutely no idea why he wanted to walk with me. Does he eat at the cafeteria often? Why? I mean, the food's not terrible, but it's not brilliant either, especially compared to some of the other places here at JU. I can't imagine wanting to come here if it wasn't the closest, cheapest option—oh, and by the way, Dimi fixed things so those of us filling in eat for free at the cafeteria. I felt a little guilty about that at first, but not for too long. Even with the discounted dining plan that was set up for us while the show is running, food at Joy Universe is *not* cheap.

Wait, if Dimi fixed it, does that mean Derek did?

I open the door just as his phone rings. He makes a face. "I have to take that—too much has happened today to ignore it. I won't be a second." He waves me inside and pulls his phone from his pocket.

I stand there, I'm sure with a stunned look on my face, as he answers the call and takes a few steps away. Is he… expecting to eat with me? Like does he think I want his company or something?

Fuck.

I scurry inside and over to the salad bar. Maybe if I scarf my food down quick—which I kind of have to do anyway, because time is flying by—I'll be done before his call ends. It's not like I can hang out and wait for him—I've gotta be back for makeup soon.

I grab a salad and glance around. There are a bunch of people I met at rehearsals this morning sitting at a table in the corner. I decide to crash the party. Maybe if I look like I'm super busy with my new "friends"—even mentally I choke on the word—Derek won't bother coming over.

What the hell can he want from me, anyway?

I stroll over to the corner and smile when two of the people there look up. "Hey. Mind if I sit here while I eat this at the speed of light?"

That gets me a laugh, and a general reshuffle to free up a space at this end of the table. "Sit, enjoy what little time you have," one of the women coaxes, patting the chair. I put my salad, which is not an exciting one, if you were wondering, on the table and plant myself, making eye contact and murmuring a greeting as I pick up my fork. The conversation continues around me as I begin wolfing down leaves and vegetables. Eating that fast is probably going to give me indigestion, even if it isn't heavy food.

I'm about halfway through when one of my tablemates waves and smiles at someone across the room. "Hey, it's Derek. Do you think he knows what's going on with everyone else?"

One of the guys—Steve? Sam? Pretty sure it was an *S* name—shrugs. "Dunno, but we should ask him." He waves, too, and calls out. "Derek!"

Are you fucking kidding me? *Seriously?* This has to be some kind of giant cosmic joke, right? Like, these people remember the idiot I made of myself this morning, and have decided to play a practical joke on me… right?

Except they're all smiling and looking expectantly behind me, and dammit, I can *feel* him getting closer.

What's with that, anyway?

"Hey, everyone," that voice says, and even though this time I was kind of expecting it, it still affects something deep inside me. It's not fair that he even has a great voice. I shove some veggies into my mouth so I won't have to join the chorus of greetings.

"Have a seat, Derek," the woman beside me—Karen? Katie? Damn, I suck at names—insists, and then *she shifts down, leaving the seat empty.*

So of course Derek sits in it.

Next to me.

Where I can't avoid him.

I eat more lettuce. In fact, I concentrate so hard on that lettuce that I miss whatever question they ask him.

I don't miss his answer, though, because he's saying it in his stupid great voice.

"Mostly everyone is going to be fine. Five people are currently in the hospital, but only for IV fluids. There are no other health issues. We sent the EMTs around to everyone's house to make sure there weren't problems, and a lot of people are already starting to feel better. Well, the vomiting has stopped, anyway."

Oh, right, the sick performers. I make appropriately sympathetic noises (I *am* sympathetic, by the way, because being sick totally sucks. I just sound like a spoiled, whiny preteen diva) and open my mouth wide to fit the last of my salad. Done. That's it, baby, I'm outta here.

I shove back from the table, plate in hand, flash a bright grin, and declare, "Thanks for letting me join you, folks!" *Folks?* Oh my God, what the hell? "Gotta get back for the last show. See you all tomorrow?" I aim the smile around the table. Maybe it doesn't quite make it to Derek, but that's only because tilting my neck that way would be awkward. I swear, it *would!*

And then I'm gone. I pause only long enough to leave my plate at the bussing station, and I'm out the door, walking as fast as I can manage without looking like I'm running away.

Because that would be rude.

THE LAST show of the day is over before I know it, and I'm glad. Sure, it's relatively easy work, but it's been a long day, and tomorrow will be even longer, because in addition to the five performances during the day before the agency dancers take over from the five o'clock show onwards, I'll be back to my "day" job tomorrow night.

I don't regret this, though. It'll be a tough week with no day off, but this has been fun, and a great experience. And, hey, now I'm going to be consulting on amateur theater. Stepping outside my box, and all that shit. My sister will be so proud.

"Trav," someone says just as I finish cleaning off my makeup. I look up to find Parker standing beside me with S-guy from the cafeteria.

"Hey." I stand and run a hand over my hair. I wear it pretty short, but it's still kind of manky from the modified helmet I've been wearing today—space pirates, remember? I make a slight face at S-guy. "I'm really sorry, but I can't remember if it's"—crap, gotta pick some *S* names—"Steve or Seth."

He grins. "It's Sam, actually."

Well, fuck. I grimace. Wasn't I thinking it was Sam, in the cafeteria? "I'm sorry," I start, but he just laughs.

"Don't worry about it. There are a lot of us here, and we can't expect you to remember all our names."

"Right." I give him a relieved smile. "You're all done for the day?"

Parker claps him on the shoulder. "Sam was doing impromptus today. Those finish up before we do—I'm actually not sure why. Marketing probably has a reason. Anyway, I was just telling Sam that you're going to give Joyville Amateur Theater a hand this season."

I turn my attention back to Sam. "You're involved too?"

He nods. "Yep. There's about half a dozen of us performers, plus two of the crew, a set designer, and Laura from costumes. You might have met her, actually, because she was supervising the fittings here this morning."

Ah yes, my gossipy new BFF. "Sure, I met Laura. She seems really cool." That gets me instant approval, I note—clearly Laura is a favorite. *Note to self, be extra nice to Laura.*

"Anyway," Sam goes on, "I was just kind of curious.... You seemed in a bit of a rush to get away when Derek joined us at dinner, and then there was this morning...." He trails off, and I inwardly groan. That's my cue.

I wrinkle my nose. "You mean this morning when I made a complete ass of myself?" I ask self-deprecatingly.

"Yeah, then," Parker deadpans. Right, they both seem to be on my side—or at least not against me—but who knows how long that will last? *Don't be an ass about Golden Boy, and you won't have any problems.*

Derek. I meant Derek.

I sigh. "I don't know what to tell you. I didn't mean to sound like an ass. The words were all normal in my head, but they came out all wrong." I tilt my head and pretend to consider it. "It was the tone, I think? But I didn't mean to sound that way." It's kind of true. I *felt* that way, but I didn't mean for anyone else to know.

They exchange glances. "Yeah, but it kind of seemed like you had something against him," Sam ventures. "And that's weird. Because, dude, Derek's like the best AD in this place. Rotating through Planet Joy is the highlight of my year. Sure, he's tough and, man, does he expect us all to work hard, but if you meet the targets, he *always* pays the quarterly bonuses in the top percentile. And he gives other bonuses, too—if the park has a great day, everyone gets rewarded."

"And he actually comes out here to talk to us," Parker adds. "At least three times a week we see him walking around the park. Sometimes it's all official and he'll have Dimi and Don—that's the park manager—with him, and other times you gotta look twice to realize it's even him, 'cause he's got a hot dog in one hand and he's standing in line for one of the rides."

He must see the surprise on my face. "Oh, he doesn't actually ride them," he assures me. "He just likes to stand in line and see what the guests are saying, and how long it takes—and if there are new people on shift who might not recognize him, he watches how they're interacting with the guests. I don't know if he knows we know he does it, though."

I follow that sentence to the end—barely—then shake my head. "Look, I don't even know Derek. I will admit that something about him pushes my buttons all wrong, but it's not him personally, because I've barely even spoken to him—and when I did he was completely professional, even though I probably didn't deserve it. I have to admire that about him." I manage not to choke on the words, because it's true that he was professional in the face of my almost-rudeness this morning. The guys don't need to know that part of me doesn't think it was genuine.

Although it could have been. I need to start being fair. Nobody's had anything bad to say about this guy, so maybe he's the genuine article. He's probably not like the guys who used to bully me, even if he does remind me of them. Maybe he's really... perfect.

No, that can't be right. Nobody's perfect. The guy's got flaws, no matter how well he keeps them hidden.

Truthfully, I don't think I care enough to find out what they are. Even if he's a genuinely great guy, that perfect sun god façade drives me insane. I like my guys with their flaws right out in the open—as evidenced by my most recent ex-boyfriend—not hidden by an exterior that requires worship.

It's all moot, anyway, since I'm not likely to run into him again.

I smile determinedly at Parker and Sam, who seem to have bought my whole I-don't-hate-Derek spiel. "So, tell me about this amateur theater. When and where?"

"Right now, Saturday morning at nine and Wednesday evening at seven at the community center in town," Sam tells me. I bite my lip.

"I can do Saturday, as long as I'm back by twelve thirty for the matinee show. Wednesday night, no way." Is that going to affect whether they want me? I'm surprised to find I'm actually disappointed at the thought of not consulting. Huh.

But Sam shrugs, and Parker shakes his head. "That's fine, Trav. We all come and go depending on our schedules here."

"They'll be adding another day in a few weeks," Sam puts in. "It doesn't matter to us which day, since we all rotate through a seven-day schedule, but if you have a preference, you should mention it."

I feel kind of bad about being so unsocial with new people all my life. Are people always this nice when you put yourself out there? Is this what my sister has been talking about for so long?

Then I remember some of the dickheads I've had to deal with and shunt that idea aside. Maybe some people are nice and welcoming, but you can never be sure who they'll be.

But these guys are being super nice, so it's worth making an effort to be nice back. "Monday is good for me," I volunteer. "We always have Monday off. Or mornings—even if we have a matinee, I'm usually not needed until lunchtime. But I bet most everyone works during the day, right?"

They both nod, and I shrug. "I should probably get down there and meet everyone and see if they actually need more help before I start mentally rearranging my schedule." We laugh, and then *I yawn*.

Because that's the kind of socially inept imbecile I am.

Parker snorts. "Big day, huh? We'll let you get finished up here and head home. Hey—where are you staying? I never even thought of that. Do they put you up in apartments in town, or something?"

"Come on," Sam jeers before I can answer. "There aren't that many short-term rentals in town. When they build the college campus, they're putting in a ton of housing, too."

"We're not staying in town," I interrupt. "JU assigns each show a block of rooms at a couple of the resorts for the duration of the show, since there's not a lot of options out here. If we want alternative housing, we have to find and pay for it ourselves. I'm at the Shire Hamlet." The resort is really pretty cool. It's been designed to resemble a quaint English country village—only on a pretty big scale.

"Lucky you're not at the Tiki," Parker says, and he and Sam exchange glances. Ooh, gossip.

"Why?" I ask in a hushed tone.

Sam leans closer. "Murder," he says, tone equally hushed. Then he grimaces. "It's not a secret. The local and national news were both broadcasting about it earlier. But policy is not to talk about shit like that."

"I'm pretty sure the news would tell me more than you just did," I tell him. Murder? Wow.

"Probably," Parker agrees. "It's not like we know anything, anyway. The resort staff might know more, but Derek would have locked them down. No way will any of them spill anything and risk pissing him off. So all we know is what the police told the media—some woman 'allegedly'"—he makes air quotes—"murdered her husband by chopping him up, and the housekeeper found him."

I know my eyes widen, because I can feel the strain. But... *wow.* "That poor housekeeper!" Also, Derek? Golden Boy's been dealing with a murder today? Huh, I kind of feel bad for him now. Maybe I should try harder to be nice. Not that I'll ever see him again.

"Yeah, that's gotta be rough. She won't be sleeping well for a while," Sam commiserates. "Anyway, are you taking the shuttle back with the guests, or do you want a lift?"

Ah... I hadn't actually thought about that. This morning Dimi had us picked up, but how are Kev and I supposed to get here tomorrow? We need to be at the park before opening, and the shuttles obviously don't run then.

"A lift would be great," I tell him. Then another thought occurs to me. "Um, how far is it to Joyville? Is it... walking distance?" I'm pretty sure that's a pipe dream, and the incredulous looks on two faces prove me right.

"It depends on what you consider walking distance," Parker says. "And whether you like walking on the shoulder of the highway."

Well, fuck. "It might be a problem for me to consult, then." My tone is genuinely regretful. "I don't have a car." I live in New York, for pete's sake. What would I need a car for in the city? And here at Joy Universe there are shuttles everywhere. Guests park their cars when they arrive and basically don't even look at them again until they leave. I didn't think I'd be leaving the complex, because it has pretty much everything—and Joyville, the only place around for miles, is reputedly not that interesting.

"That could be a problem," Sam admits. "But let's not borrow trouble. Maybe we'll think of a solution."

"Trav?" Someone calls me from across the room, and I turn. Pete's looking for me, and I wave to get his attention, then turn back to the guys.

"I'll be back. If I'm more than ten minutes, just go without me, and I'll get a shuttle." I get affirmative responses, and cross to see what Pete wants.

"Are you ready to go? There's a car waiting for you," he tells me. "I'm supposed to tell you it will pick you up tomorrow morning, as well. Talk to the driver about the time, but you need to be here by eight."

Okay, that's one problem solved. "Thanks, Pete. I'll just tell Parker and Sam I'm going." I've half turned away when he catches my arm.

"Trav, you did a great job today. Was everything okay from your end?"

I smile at him. Sure, I'm doing him and his bosses a favor, but it's still always nice to be praised. "Yeah, this is a lot more fun than I expected. I thought today was great."

He smiles back and lets go of my arm, and I go to say good night to my new friends.

Boy, will I have a lot to tell my sister when I call her this week.

CHAPTER SIX

Derek

BY MIDAFTERNOON on Tuesday, I'm beginning to believe the crisis is over. There's still a lot of fallout to deal with—not least of which is one of the security staff at Tiki apparently taking bribes from guests to sneak them into the "forbidden area" around the "murder cabin"—but the major calamities seem to have ended. I'm no longer getting phone calls every five minutes from people on the verge of meltdown. Dimi actually had time to sit and drink his coffee while going through emails, instead of sipping while zooming around the complex. It seems like everything is going to be fine.

Don't get me wrong. We're still dealing with more than the usual crap. We have over a hundred people out on sick leave, and although the temp dancers have arrived and are currently being trained up by Pete, with the watchful, if not useful, supervision of Mandy from entertainment, they're not my regular people, they're not familiar with working at Planet Joy, and they're not going to deliver up to the standard I usually demand. It's a blow to me that the guests who will be here this week won't get the usual Planet Joy experience.

Yeah, I know. I need to get over myself. Chances are, nobody will know the difference.

I also still have an active crime scene at one of my resorts, and I had a meeting this morning with the detective in charge, Jeff from legal, and Kim to try and sort out what the hell we're going to do. All Detective Gooding would say is that they'll try to wrap up the scene as soon as they can, and that things are proceeding.

That's super helpful, right?

I followed that meeting up with a discussion with Dimi and Link about whether we need to demo the bungalow. At the moment we're undecided, but I think it's probably going to happen. There's too much morbid interest in the site. If Tiki was a small independent hotel, we could play up the murder to attract clientele who actually want to stay in a room where someone was gruesomely murdered, but that's not what the JU experience is about.

At some point today I need to squeeze in a follow-up call to security. When I got the phone call at three this morning from Tiki's night manager, I honestly didn't know what to expect—in that hazy just-woken state, I actually feared the ghost of Peter Rutherford was wreaking havoc. Hearing that a security guard was charging guests ten bucks each to sneak them into my no-go zone, and in the case of one particularly intrepid couple, past the police tape and into the bungalow, woke me all the way up—and sent my blood pressure through the roof.

"I don't know if I need to call the police or not," my night manager said. "I thought it might be best to run it past you first."

I'd assured him it was, then called the head of security on his cell and woke him the fuck up while I put on pants.

By the time that was dealt with, a new security officer brought on shift, and the trespassing guests sternly but politely told to keep to the public areas of the resort, and advised (not by me, because I didn't have a freaking clue) that criminal charges can be laid for interfering with a crime scene, which includes entering one without permission, I was so wide awake there was no way I'd get back to sleep.

So I didn't bother. Instead I went to my office and cleared out my inbox. When Dimi arrived at seven (seriously, he got there a full *hour* before his required start time), I was caught up on everything I'd had to overlook yesterday and ready to tackle the day.

The pot and a half of coffee helped.

As a result, today wasn't the clusterfuck it could have been. Sure, I'm dragging a bit now, but I won't be scrambling to catch up for the rest of the week. Right now, Dimi and I are going through every single element of our two crises: what happened, what actions we've taken, the results, and what still needs to be done. Mostly now we just need to keep on top of other people, make sure they're doing their jobs. It's a big relief, because it means making phone calls rather than having to take on mammoth tasks ourselves.

Although we do have a meeting scheduled with accounting for tomorrow. We've authorized a lot of unexpected large expenditures in the last two days, and although I know we can cover it, the bean counters always freak out and demand a meeting to recheck the budget when… well, I was going to say "when stuff like this happens," but nothing like this has ever happened in the history of JU, so let's just make it "when we spend up big without consulting them."

"Anything else?" I ask Dimi, who's tapping away in the app, checking items off on his list and making notes. He looks up.

"Yes, but it's not work-related."

My stomach sinks. Fuck, he's going to leave. I knew it was coming, but I thought I'd have another position ready for him, so I could at least keep him here at JU.

Wait… wouldn't his resignation be work-related?

Maybe I'm jumping the gun.

"Sure, what's up?" I make an effort to sound casual and encouraging. *Let me be your mentor and friend. Don't even think of leaving.*

"You know how I'm part of Joyville Amateur Theater?"

I grin. "Of course. I come to every show you guys put on. You do an amazing job." It's completely true. For an amateur group in a tiny town in the middle of nowhere, they're beyond exceptional.

"Thanks." There's a slight flush of pink on Dimi's cheeks. "Um, you know how a bunch of the performers from here at JU usually lend a hand with planning?"

"Yeah, you've menti— Oh hell, is this food poisoning going to hold up your rehearsals?" That would really not be good, although I'm not sure there's anything I could actually do to help with that. I know quite a bit about theater, but only from the audience perspective.

"No, no, nothing like that. Or if it is, we don't know it yet," he added, a hint of wry humor in his tone. "It's just that Parker, one of our consultants, called me this morning to say he's found someone else to help out—for the short term, at least."

It's not like Dimi to dance around the point like this. His efficiency has always been one of his best traits. I'm not sure what he's leading toward, but hopefully it will all come clear soon.

"Oh?" I venture, mostly in an attempt to prompt him onward.

He sighs. "I'm sorry, I'm doing this all wrong. The person Parker found is Trav Jones, the performer who was kind of rude to you yesterday."

Oh. "Oh." Am I beginning to sound like a broken record? *Wait, didn't I already know this?* "Now that you mention it, Parker—well, I think it was Parker. Dark hair, brown eyes, tall?" I have a lot of people—literally tens of thousands—working in my district, and the ones in the parks rotate. I try to get to know as many as possible but memorizing all their names and faces is beyond me. Dimi nods, though, so if it wasn't Parker, it was someone who looked like him. "Yeah, Parker actually told me last night when I checked in with Pete at the park. From what I've heard, Trav is a very talented performer. This is a good thing, right?" I'm still not clear on what Dimi wants. Does he dislike Trav? That's not the impression I got—he was a bit surprised, sure, but Dimi's generally a fair and even-tempered guy.

Like me.

"Yeah, it's good," Dimi assures me. "Uh, after the—issue we had yesterday morning with Trav, I looked him up. Just in case. He's a great performer, and he knows the business. He'll be a huge help. So you're not still annoyed at him?"

The sudden change in direction gives me whiplash. "N-no. No, I'm not still annoyed. He's entitled to not want to be my best friend." As annoying as that is. "And I spoke to him briefly last night too." More briefly than I would have liked, to be honest. The guy has a habit of slipping away when I want to talk to him—although exactly what I was going to say, I'm not sure. Even though I'm super curious about his career history, it's not like I could've just asked him about it out of the blue.

Dimi looks relieved. "Good. Have you sold your car yet?"

Okay, if I had whiplash before, I don't know what I've got now. "My car?" Even I can hear the confusion in my voice. I bought a new car last month, and that left me with a perfectly good five-year-old, immaculately kept car to sell. The dealer offered a trade-in, of course, but I wasn't happy with the terms so I decided to sell it privately. I keep meaning to take some photos and advertise it online, but... well, my schedule is kind of brutal, and every time I remember I have to do it, I'm in the middle of something else. "Um, not yet."

"That's what I thought. Can Trav rent it from you?"

I blink. "Come again?" Did he just ask if Trav could rent my old car?

"Trav doesn't have a car," he explains. "He's from New York. He didn't bother to rent one here, because the performers are bussed between the village and their resorts for rehearsals and performances, and we have shuttles throughout the complex for pretty much everything else. But if he's going to help with the theater—"

"He's going to need to be able to get to Joyville," I finish, finally understanding. "Sure, he can use my car, no problem. He doesn't need to rent it, either, as long as he takes care of it and pays for gas." Am I being too trusting? *Hang on....* "He does have a driver's license, right?" A lot of New Yorkers don't bother—the only reason I got one is because my dad isn't a native New Yorker, and he insisted.

Dimi looks stumped. "I don't know," he admits. "I never thought to ask. I'm not sure if Parker did, either. I'll find out," he promises. "Thank you, Derek. I've already talked to a bunch of the others from the theater, and we're all excited about the help Trav will be able to give us. It would be a real pain if we had to set up a schedule to pick him up and drop him off all the time."

"Not a problem," I assure him. "The car's just sitting there. Maybe I'll stick a For Sale sign in the back window and someone will see it while Trav is driving around."

Dimi thanks me again and then hurries out, leaving me to contemplate the secret I've been deliberately ignoring all afternoon.

Last night, I wanted to talk to Trav, and I don't know exactly why. There's something about him that draws me. Sure, part of it is that he's pretty much my exact physical type. And yeah, I'm honest enough with myself to admit that my ego is also contributing—as a rule, people like me, and it bugs me that he instantly did not.

But there's more to it than that. I saw him on stage last night. Okay, it wasn't for long and the role wasn't exactly the kind that earns a Tony nomination, but his performance was electric. After seeing him, I totally understand what Toby meant when he called him one of the backbones of Broadway. He was compelling, and if he could be compelling as the sidekick to a space pirate in the abridged stage-show version of an animated movie aimed at six-to-twelve-year-olds, I can only imagine what he would be like in a role with substance.

So why doesn't he want one? Sure, he's had some great parts, but with his experience, he should be in starring roles by now—and according to that article, the only thing holding him back is him. Why would a professional performer who worked like a dog to get through the ranks on Broadway *turn down* leading roles?

He's an enigma, and he fascinates me. I've only spoken to him twice, and neither of those conversations were exactly deep and meaningful (nor hinted at a deeper connection), but for some reason, I've spent more time thinking about him in the past thirty hours than I really had to spare.

Which is why I got myself a ticket to Trav's show tonight.

I want to see him perform again, but more, I want to see him again. It's not uncommon for me to go backstage after a show. The AD in charge of the village doesn't actually like theater—philistine—and never attends any of the shows, whereas I go pretty often. I consider myself an ambassador of sorts for JU—it's not always fun for people who are used to night life to come out to the middle of nowhere, and I like to thank the performers, sometimes hand out some park passes or discount vouchers for the restaurants. Nobody will think it's odd for me to be there tonight. It's entirely ordinary.

Even if it's not.

And now I have an excuse to talk to him: the car. We have to sort out details, right? At the very least, I should ask if he has a valid driver's license.

WHEN THE curtain comes down for the final time, I stay in my seat for a few moments as the people around me gather their things and begin the process of inching their way out of the auditorium.

It was a great show. Not one of my favorites, but definitely one I liked and will recommend. Solid plot, interesting characters. A little bit funny, a little bit solemn.

But hell, Trav is brilliant. I thought so last night after *Space Reivers* but seeing him in a decent role just hammers it home. *Why* doesn't he want a leading part?

Sighing, I get up and make my way toward the stage. There's a discreet door on the left side that leads back to the dressing rooms. It's manned by a security guard, of course, but she recognizes me and opens the door to let me in.

"Evening, Derek," she says, smiling.

"Hi," I reply. "How's your week so far?" I don't know her personally, but security staff rotate through all the parks and resorts the same way the performers do, so she'll have worked for me at some stage.

"Good," she tells me cheerfully. "Better than yours, I'll bet."

I laugh. "That wouldn't be hard this week. Have a good night."

She closes the door behind me, and I head in the direction of the main dressing room, which is really just for show. None of the actual dressing gets done there, but it's where VIP ticket holders can meet the cast after the show. I'm not sure if there were any VIPs in tonight's audience, but the cast and crew usually use that room as an informal lounge anyway.

Sure enough, when I get there, I find quite a few people milling around in varying states of undress—hopefully that means there are no VIPs here—chatting, stretching, and just generally hanging out. Most are out of their costumes already, and some have even already cleaned off their makeup. I scan the room, mostly looking for Trav.

"Can I help you?" A man comes up beside me. His tone is polite, but he looks slightly wary. He's a little older than me, I think, but in good shape and good-looking.

"Probably," I say, flashing him my megawatt grin, the one I use on guests who are causing trouble. I offer my hand. "I'm Derek Bryer, one of the assistant directors here at Joy Universe. I watched the show tonight, and thought I'd come back and say hello and pass out some free dinners." I pull a stack of meal cards from my pocket. Each card entitles the bearer to a free meal (conditions apply) at one of the nominated restaurants.

"Oh, that's nice of you." The wariness drops away, and he shakes my hand. "Rick Carter. I'm the producer. So, did you enjoy the show?"

"I sure did. You've got a great production here, and some very talented performers." This is a great opportunity to do some digging. *Cue rueful smile.* "You've probably heard about the staff trouble I had yesterday. Several of your performers here helped me out."

Sure enough, Rick's eyes light up with his smile. "Oh, sure! Trav and Kev, and I think Melia, right?"

"Right," I agree, because fortunately those names are all familiar, not just Trav's. I had to sign the order for the special pay run this morning.

"That's pretty bad luck," he commiserates. "I mean, how often do all your performers go out together, anyway? To get hit by food poisoning... I can't even imagine the odds."

"I *know!*" I'm a little more emphatic than I really need to be, because before I fell asleep last night, I was actually wondering how the hell to even calculate those odds. "If it were part of a movie plot, critics would call it unrealistic."

Rick laughs and claps me on the back. "Come and meet some of the cast. They'll be thrilled to get those freebies." He guides me over to the nearest group, and for the next forty-five minutes I make amiable small talk with cast and crew alike, handing out cards for free food and asking them their thoughts about performing in the village. Several people get up the nerve to ask me about the murder—I don't think they know it happened in my district, they're just seizing the opportunity to ask someone who works for JU. I keep my answers vague, although really, I don't know much more than what the police have already released, and since I'm already struggling with the image of dismembered limbs that pops up every time I close my eyes, there's no way I'll risk making it worse by discussing it.

I steer the conversation away from the murder to the resorts themselves. I've never actually bothered before to find out how events works out where to lodge the show people. All I know is that I'm required to keep a certain number of standard rooms at my three-star resorts available, to be charged back to the village's cost center at a discounted rate. I was told that it doesn't matter which resort the rooms are at, and that the number required can be split across the resorts, so that's what I had my team do. It's not really surprising, then, when I find out that the performers and crew for *Day Dot* are staying at three different resorts— one of them mine. I take the opportunity to get some feedback—after all, it's not often I can be totally candid with guests, but because they're here to work, this is my chance to drill down on details.

The whole time I'm making mental notes for the resort manager (and planning a surprise reward for all the staff, because the feedback is *good*), a small part of my brain is tracking Trav. I located him across the lounge about five minutes after I arrived, and since then, as I slowly circle from group to group, some of my attention is always on him. It would really suck if he left before I got to him.

What almost sucks worse is that I'm so very aware of his presence, and he seems completely oblivious to mine. I mean, come on! He hasn't even glanced in my direction.

Finally, *finally*, Rick leads me to the group Trav is with.

"Everyone, this is Derek Bryer, one of the executives here at Joy Universe. Derek, meet Syl, Paul, Hamish, Denise, and you know Trav, right?"

I smile and nod at everyone, then meet Trav's gaze head-on. "Yeah, we've met. Thanks again for your help, Trav. I spoke to Pete earlier, and he said the agency guy they've got now doesn't hold a candle to you." It's completely true, but most of the reason I say it is to see if— Yep. There it is, that fire-bright blush.

Who knew a blush could be such a turn-on? Seriously, I've seen people blush a million times, whether it be from embarrassment, pleasure, anger, or anything in between, and it's never affected me the way Trav's blushes do. I want to strip off his clothes and see if that vibrant red covers his whole body. I want to lick his flushed skin and see if it's as hot as it looks.

I want to stop thinking about this right now so my hard-on subsides before someone notices it.

"You're welcome," Trav mutters. "It was more fun than I expected."

I decide to give him a reprieve. "I'm glad. You all"—I widen my focus to the rest of the group, who seem divided between looking curiously at Trav and suspiciously at me—"put on a great show tonight. I just wanted to come and tell you how much I enjoyed it, and to hand out these." I offer the freebie cards. One of the women—Syl, maybe?—takes one.

"What is it?" she asks, then looks at it and her eyes widen. "Oh, a free meal? That's so nice of you. Thank you."

The others reach for cards also. "It's a small token of our appreciation. We're really glad you're here," I tell them. They all murmur thanks, a little bit more welcoming now—it's amazing how free stuff can make people like you—and I'm quickly drawn into conversation about the nightlife in the various cities the show has played in over the past six months since they left New York.

Soon people start to drift away, and I check my watch. It's just after eleven, which is probably not that late for the performers, but I've been up since 3:00 a.m. and I'm definitely feeling it.

Not that I'm going to let that stop me from finally talking to Trav. I wait for a pause in the conversation he's having with Rick, and then smile right at him. "Trav, can I have a quick word?"

He looks a little uncomfortable, but nods. "Sure. I'll see you guys tomorrow," he tells Rick and Syl, the only two left in the group, and then follows me toward the door.

I take a deep breath. This is it. Ostensibly, I'm here to talk to him about the car, but I decided earlier tonight (read: during the show when his performance magnetized me so much I had to fight an erection) that I'm also going to find out once and for all why he dislikes me. Because he does, even though he's been trying to hide it.

We make it to the hall, and as we stroll toward the stage door, I start. "I was talking to Dimi today, who was talking to Parker—"

He snickers, and I stop. Fuck, what did I say?

"Sorry," he apologizes. "I didn't mean to interrupt. It's just... for a second, it all sounded so high school."

I have to laugh. "Yeah, it does, doesn't it? You've got no idea what this place is like—a hotbed of gossip and feuds and politics, just like a soap opera. Or high school." It's totally true. We're an incestuous miniature society, where everyone knows everyone else, what's going on in their lives, and likely has slept with most of their coworkers.

That's one of my few firm rules: no sex with coworkers—or guests. There's so much potential for complication, especially with me being in such a position of authority, and I've seen it all go horribly wrong for my colleagues who don't have a similar rule. Since Joyville is mostly populated by people who work for JU, I've had some really lean times over the years, sexually speaking. In fact, my last actual relationship was before I left New York. Since then, it's just been the occasional hookup when I'm on vacation.

On the plus side, Trav didn't sound disparaging with that comment, just amused. Time to push forward?

"Anyway, Dimi and Parker activated the secret squirrel message system—" Trav laughs, and I take a second to enjoy the sound. "—and I found out that you need a car."

Trav sighs. "Yeah. I called a couple of rental places this morning, but even with a long-term rate, the price was scary, considering I'll only use the car a couple times a week. And because the rental places are all at the airport, it doesn't make sense to hire only when I need the car—I'd have to get out to the airport to pick up the car every time. The only other option is for someone to come and pick me up, and that's just not practical, or fair to them." He sighs again. "I guess I could buy a car." It sounds dubious, and I can't blame him for that. Buying a car, even an old banger, just for a few months so he can drive into town a couple times a week is a ridiculous expense.

"Not necessary," I say cheerfully. "The reason Dimi mentioned it to me is because I can help you out. I haven't got around to selling my old car yet, and it's just sitting in the garage, desperate for some love. Wanna borrow it?"

He stops walking, and his whole face lights up. Seriously. You'd think I just offered him a hundred-million-dollar winning lottery ticket. I turn toward him, and something in my belly flips. Indigestion?

No.

Lust. I really like having him look at me that way.

Damn it.

"Really?" he asks, almost breathlessly. "I mean, are you sure?"

"Absolutely," I assure him. "I keep meaning to list it for sale, but I haven't had time. It'll be good for it to be driven, even if it's not every day." He's grinning now, his mouth stretched so wide it's probably uncomfortable.

"Thank you." He grabs my hand, half shaking it and squeezing. "I didn't realize how excited I was about consulting for the theater until I ran into this transport problem and thought I'd have to pass. Thank you so much. I can pay rent."

I want to squeeze his hand back, but I'm scared if I do, he'll let go. His hand is warm and callused, and it feels really good in mine. I shake my head instead. "Nope, that's not necessary. Like I said, it's just taking up space in the garage. Keep it gassed up and take care with it, and we're good. Oh, you've got a valid driver's license, right?" I'm assuming he does, since he wouldn't have thought to rent a car without one, but best to ask.

"Yeah, of course." He seems to realize we're just standing there holding hands, and he flushes and lets go. *Man, that blush!* "Uh, this is really great of you, Derek. I-I want to say again how sorry I am for being weird yesterday."

And if that's not the perfect opening for phase two of my plan, I don't know what is.

"It's fine." I have to handle this perfectly. I'm not likely to get another shot. "We got off on the wrong foot. Actually, I wanted to ask… did I do anything? It just seemed like you"—how to put this?—"took an instant dislike to me, and I wondered if it was—"

"No." He interrupts me, which is good because I'm not sure exactly how I was going to end that sentence. "No, you didn't do anything. Um, I was actually predisposed to like you. Everyone here has good things to say, and I thought it was really great that you were willing to go above and beyond to keep the shows running."

I don't say anything, because what the hell can I say? If he was predisposed to like me, what was our little… confrontation about? Wait, does he mean *like* like? Is this some sort of playground-crush thing, where a kid is mean to the one he likes to get their attention?

Has JU actually become high school?

I must be wearing my confusion all over my face because he hurries on. "It's just…. God, this is going to sound so stupid, and shallow. I'm not shallow, I swear. But you look like the boy-next-door jock frat hero, and that pushes a lot of not-great buttons for me. So when I saw you, it kind of brought up some bad feelings."

What the ever-loving *fuck*? He judged me based on my appearance?

Don't get me wrong. That's happened to me before. A lot. But usually I'm not found lacking.

I'm trapped between being offended and confused, and the fact that his face is getting redder and redder as he tries to explain is adding a healthy dose of lust to the situation.

"Okay," I interrupt. "Let me get this straight." He subsides into silence, looking utterly miserable, and I want nothing more than to make him smile. *I've got it bad.* "For reasons I can only guess at, you don't like the way I look, and you reacted badly to that despite the fact that I'm not—" Fuck, how to finish this sentence. "—that bad a guy?" *Lame.*

He cracks a smile, the blush subsiding a little. "If someone were to give me a piece of paper with everything I've learned about you since I got here written on it, but I never actually met you, I'd say you're a really great guy."

I take a minute to think about that. On one hand, it seems like a nice compliment, but.... "So you don't like the way I look?" Should I be offended? Or just write it off to personal taste? Or both?

"You know you're hot," he says bluntly, and his cheeks are red again. "But... it's not your looks, exactly. More your manner."

Now I'm truly offended. I work damn hard to be friendly and approachable, even when I don't want to be. I'm about to end this conversation, and our acquaintanceship, but Trav's still talking.

"You were popular at school, right? Played football or something?"

"No," I say shortly. He raises an eyebrow. "Lacrosse," I admit. I don't comment on the "popular" comment, because it seems like bragging. Plus, given the subject we're discussing, I don't think it would weigh in my favor.

"Did you play in college too?"

I nod reluctantly. "A lot of people play sports," I defend, and he gives me a patient look.

"And I'll bet you were in a fraternity."

Am I supposed to feel bad about this? I played sports and I was in a fraternity, and people liked me. So were a lot of other people.

"Look, Trav, I don't—"

"I was bullied. A lot. By the popular jocks at my high school and college. Most of them were in fraternities too."

I close my mouth. I never bullied anyone, but I'm ashamed to say I knew some of my friends did. Not when I was around, because I made it pretty clear how I felt about it—my parents had strong opinions that they passed on to me—but I probably could have done more to make sure it wasn't happening.

"I'm not saying you're a bully," he tells me earnestly. I can see embarrassment and something else—shame, maybe?—on his face. He can't meet my gaze. "But you have a lot in common with the people who did. I sometimes find it hard to deal with people who have a certain charm and charisma. That's my problem, not yours, and I'm really sorry I took it out on you yesterday. But I hope this helps you understand why I did."

I just stand there like a lump. The truth is, my looks and charisma have opened a lot of doors for me over the years. I've worked damn hard to keep those doors open and to develop the opportunities they gave me, but I'm not stupid—I know people with less charm and who aren't as good-looking sometimes don't get the same welcome I do. The world can be a shallow place, for all we protest that it isn't.

The silence draws out as we stand awkwardly in the hallway.

Trav swallows. "So… uh, I'm glad I got to explain. I, uh, I'll see you around." He turns away and continues toward the stage door.

What am I doing? I haven't been able to stop thinking about this guy for the last thirty-six hours. Am I really going to let him walk away just because my feelings are bruised—over something he's apologized for and I don't really even have a right to be upset about?

"Trav!" I jog after him. Luckily he hasn't gotten far, and he stops to wait for me. "Have you eaten?"

He looks surprised. "Uh… no. I usually have a light snack before the show and then supper after."

"Great. Come and have supper with me." I can still feel the exhaustion of the day dragging at my body, but my mind is energized, and I'm willing to sacrifice sleep for a little longer.

"Are you sure?" He seems wary, and I get it. He probably wasn't expecting me to react to his confession with a request for a date.

"Yes." I make my voice firm, and then flash my megawatt smile. He takes a step back, and I tone it down. "Sorry. Force of habit. Yes, I'm sure. I really want to go out for a meal with you."

He's still a little suspicious. "You're not offended by what I said?"

"I'd be lying if I said my ego isn't a little dented," I admit. "But you're entitled to your feelings. Things happened to you to make you feel that way, and I can't expect all that to disappear like that." I snap my fingers for emphasis. "I can only hope to show you that I'm not like the people who bullied you."

He studies me for a second more, then nods slowly. "You're right. Derek, I'd love to have supper with you."

CHAPTER SEVEN

Trav

I'VE LIVED in New York all my life, and I'm no stranger to great restaurants. There have been times I've saved for months to afford a single meal at an outstanding eatery, and other times I've gotten amazing food from an inexpensive deli—or street vendor.

The restaurant Derek takes me to fits the category of outstanding. Not because it's fancy—it's not. Derek's wearing what seems to be his work uniform of dress pants and shirt (the shirt's blue, by the way, and it almost perfectly matches his eyes. He probably chose it for that reason), though he's taken off his tie and opened his collar, and I'm in jeans and a polo. I'm actually lucky I spilled coffee on my sweats while I was at the resort before the show tonight, otherwise I'd be wearing those, and that would probably be a bit too casual.

So no, the place isn't fancy. It's nice, with tablecloths and elegant place settings, but the lighting and décor set the mood for comfortable and casual rather than stiff and formal. The staff are friendly and professional, which is what I've come to expect from all the staff at Joy Universe, and the food is to die for. The restaurant is in one of the five-star resorts, and although I'd been told it's a great place to eat—which it is—I hadn't tried it because it's expensive and I've got no problem admitting I'm tight-fisted with money. I don't mind splashing out on occasion, but the occasion hadn't yet arisen since I arrived at JU.

I guess tonight is the night, though. God knows, I owe Derek a meal at least, after everything that's happened and with him lending me a car. That sounds wrong, like I'm only here in this fabulous restaurant having a wonderful time with a good-looking, intelligent, witty, amusing, kindhearted (are you getting the picture yet?) man who's made me laugh more times than I can count since we arrived because I feel like I owe

70

him. I don't. I mean, I *do*, but that's not why I'm here. I'm here because of all the reasons I listed a second ago.

Yeah, there are still moments when I have to push aside an instinctual reaction that screams for me to *get away from him*, usually when he turns the charm on heavy, or uses that I'm-on-duty-being-a-super-guy smile. For the record, I like his real smile better, the one he gave me while we were talking about places to eat in New York and discovered that we both love the same Indian takeout place. Turns out we actually grew up not far from each other.

Around us, the staff are cleaning up. The music's been turned off, and they're setting tables for tomorrow, silverware clinking as it's laid out. It's after midnight, the kitchen closed a while ago, and we're the only people left. I'm actually pretty sure the kitchen was on the verge of closing when we arrived, and the only reason it stayed open was because of Derek. I would feel guilty about that, but from the way the hostess and our server lit up when they saw him, they were more than happy to work a little late if it was for him. The chef came out of the kitchen to sit with us and chat as we decided what to eat, and ended up telling us to leave it with him. The result was nothing short of fabulous.

I lean toward Derek and lower my voice. "They really love you here."

He leans in too and also lowers his voice. "This resort is part of my district—I'm their boss. They have to love me—or at least pretend to." He winks to show he's joking, then looks around. "I guess we better let them finish up and get home, though."

Sitting back in my chair, I watch him as he smiles over at our waiter and calls out cheerfully for the check. The boy and the hostess hurry to get it ready.

"I don't think that's it," I say, and he turns his attention back to me, his smile that gorgeous natural one that makes me feel warm all over.

"What's not it?"

Wow, it's really hot in here all of a sudden. "Uh, I don't think they love you just because you're their boss." I look him right in the eye as I say it, hoping he gets what I'm trying to say. Derek has a lot of natural charm and charisma, and I can see how that would draw people to him right away, but it's not superficial. After only an hour of conversation, I can honestly say he's supersmart, funny, and actually really sweet. I also get the feeling he's hiding something behind the fun, charming golden boy façade he puts up—but of course I could be wrong. An hour is just an hour, after all.

His smile fades slightly, and his Adam's apple bobs as he swallows hard. We stare at each other. Part of me is wondering how my feelings about him could have changed so much in such a short time. I know my initial antagonism wasn't really to do with *him* so much as what I assumed he represented, but given that it was less than two days ago, and right now I'm desperately trying to stifle daydreams of future dates and cozy evenings chatting and making out in front of the TV, it still seems like a big leap.

Especially since I'm not even sure if this was really a date. Maybe he was trying to prove a point that he's not like those guys that bullied me? Maybe this was just intended to be a friendly meal, and he's not actually interested? It's not like I'm anything special.

The waiter—his name is Tom—comes over with the check, and Derek and I both reach for it, then freeze.

"I'm paying," I say firmly. "It's the least I can do."

Derek eyes me for a moment, then turns to Tom. "Can you give us a sec?"

Tom obediently retreats. I watch him go. "You didn't need to send him away; this isn't complicated. I'm paying."

He meets my gaze steadily. "I didn't want to discuss it in front of anyone. I said before that this place is like high school, and I wasn't kidding. That means we all gossip like retirees playing bridge"—I grin, because that's pretty funny—"and there's already going to be talk because we're eating together after our slightly rocky start—which everyone already knows about and has blown out of proportion. I didn't think they needed details."

He's right. I'm a pretty private person, and given the chance, I'd rather not have people discussing the details of my life.

"Thank you," I say quietly. "You're right, of course. But I'm still paying."

He raises one perfect dark-blond eyebrow. "I invited you," he points out. "I'm not in the habit of asking men on dates and then letting them pay."

My heart soars, and a giddy feeling takes over. It *is* a date! It's all I can do to keep the stupid smile off my face. "We'll split it," I offer, reaching for the little folder. Because I literally can't remember if I've ever let a date pay for my dinner.

Is that sad? Thinking about it now, I feel like maybe it's sad. Shouldn't *someone* have bought me dinner at least once? Not let me insist on paying?

I yank the leather folder out of Derek's reach before he can grab it, flip it open, and blink at the total. That can't be right....

"This is…. It's about half of what it should be." I saw the prices on the menu. Did I add wrong?

"Employee discount" is all Derek says. I don't look up, but I can feel his eyes on me, and I scan down the itemized check. The item prices look right, but—oh, there it is. The discount line.

"Wow, that's some discount," I say stupidly, then wince. When I glance at Derek, he looks faintly embarrassed.

"The best restaurants around here are part of JU," he defends, "and the staff apply the discount automatically if they recognize me."

I purse my lips. "Do they ever *not* recognize you?" It's a rhetorical question, and he seems to get that, because he doesn't answer—though he does flush a little. It's really cute to see him flustered.

Because of me.

Right. He's done all the running so far, even in the face of animosity— maybe it's my turn to stick my neck out.

I push the folder across the table to him. "Okay, you're right. You invited me, so you can have this one. But on our next date, I'm paying."

Our gazes meet. "Our next date?" There's a note of… something in his voice that brings back the giddy feeling.

"Yeah." I rack my brain. Dinner is the most obvious option, since he works during the day, but my job makes going out for a meal at a decent hour tricky. I have Monday nights off, but I don't want to wait that long to see him again. "Lunch," I blurt. Fuck, I have the matinee show four days a week. The only days off are Monday, Tuesday, and… "Thursday." A pang of disappointment strikes that it won't be tomorrow, but maybe it's better this way.

He smiles, the good smile, the one I like. "Lunch on Thursday," he repeats.

Something occurs to me. "You'd better tell me if there's a place we need to avoid."

The satisfaction on his face fades a little, and he shrugs, pulls out his wallet, and slips a credit card into the check folder. Tom is there instantly to grab it, and as soon as he leaves, Derek says, "Pretty much anywhere we go around here, there's likely to be someone who recognizes me. And if we want to go further afield, then lunch on a weekday isn't the best idea." He seems almost tentative, and it's so different from the man I've seen so far that it pisses me off.

"Nope, it's lunch on Thursday. I'll sort something out," I tell him firmly, and he visibly relaxes. I hate that he was unsure, but at the same time, it makes me feel really great that he was so concerned about dating me.

Wait. That sounds wrong. He wasn't concerned about *dating me*; he was concerned that I would be unhappy with the logistics of dating him.

I think.

I'm still turning the concept over in my head as we walk out to the valet stand at the front of the resort. The restaurant must have told them we were coming, because Derek's car is waiting. I slide in and switch to thinking about the logistics of our next date.

"What time is good for lunch?" I ask as he pulls the car out of the resort forecourt and heads down the driveway to the road.

"On Thursday? I have to check my schedule, but I think one. Is that cool with you?"

I shrug. Thursday mornings we have a rehearsal, and then nothing until the evening performance at seven thirty. "One's fine. Why don't I give you my number, and you can let me know for sure?"

He grins at me. "Can I use your number for more than just confirming dates?"

Heat climbs up my neck and floods my face, and I know I must be red. Christ, I've always blushed easily, but I spend more time red-faced around this guy than anyone else I can remember. "Maybe." I meant it to sound flirtatious, but it comes out sounding more like a parent who means no, but doesn't want to say it for fear of incurring a tantrum.

What the hell is wrong with me? I'm no Casanova, but I'm not a reclusive virgin, either. I usually have a pretty good dating life. I know how to flirt.

I pull out my phone. "What's your number? I'll text you."

He rattles off the digits. I put them in my phone and then send him a text. The faint *ding* from his pocket tells me he got it.

The rest of the ride back to my resort is silent, and I'm pretty sure it's my fault. Our conversation over dinner was so easy and fun—but my stupid failed attempt to be flirty seems to have killed the vibe. Is he regretting the whole thing? Wondering how he can get out of our date on Thursday?

He turns off the road onto the driveway of the resort, but instead of pulling up to the entrance, he takes the road that loops around the property to the four parking lots and the three other shuttle stops.

"Where—" I begin, but he interrupts me.

"Which is the closest parking lot to your room?"

Oh. He's being thoughtful and saving me the seven-minute (no, I didn't time it—the receptionist told me when I checked in) walk from the main building to the building that houses my room.

"The west one," I tell him, and then we both fall silent again as he skillfully navigates along the deserted, mostly dark road. I rack my brain for something to say. How did this happen? Twenty minutes ago I was one half of an interesting, fun conversation. How did we go from that to awkward silence?

It has to be the idea of dating that's turned us into mere acquaintances with little in common. Right? Until he confirmed that we were on a date, and I asked him on another one, everything was fine. After that, it all went downhill.

Wait… he knew all along that we were on a date. I was the one who wasn't sure what he thought it was. Does that mean this is all me? Am I the reason for the awkwardness?

I'm saved from further introspection (although I suspect it's going to keep me up most of the night) when Derek pulls into the west parking lot and finds a spot at the far end. The lot is pretty well-lit, but back in this corner there are more shadows.

I undo my seat belt. I'm almost desperate to get out of the car and away from this tension, but at the same time, I'm terrified that if I leave it like this, I'm going to get a text from Derek, canceling our date. What can I say to make it all better?

Derek's hand on my face makes me jump.

"Whoa! Sorry, I didn't mean…." He starts to pull away, but I grab his hand and hold it against my cheek. I like having him touch me.

Is this weird? Maybe he was just trying to get my attention and didn't actually want to hold my face.

I drop my hand to my lap, giving him the opportunity to pull back. My face is hot, and I'm thankful for the dim light. He can probably still see that I'm blushing, but not exactly how red I am.

His fingers lightly stroke my cheek.

My breath stutters. I slowly turn to him. His face is closer than I expected, and there's a soft smile on his lips. Even in the dimness of the car, I can see how warm the expression in his eyes is.

I swallow. His smile grows.

"I love when you blush," he says. "It's so—"

"Sweet?" I interrupt acidly. He shakes his head.

"Hot." The word sits between us. Hot? Does he mean literally? Because, yeah, my skin gets hot when I—

Derek leans in and kisses me, and I get it. *Hot.* Derek thinks it's hot when I blush. Really?

Also, man can he kiss.

I gotta be honest, the next few minutes kind of blur out. I'm too focused on Derek's mouth on mine, his hands, his body—because my hands get busy too. The only words I can actually think are adjectives: warm, hard, wet, silky….

I've got my hands in his pants (and can I just say wow?) when it finally occurs to me that as cushy as Derek's car is, it's not roomy enough for us to fuck—well, not comfortably. I jerk back from his kiss. "Not here," I pant. Crap, Kev's likely to be back at our room by now. He was saying earlier that he was exhausted, not having had a day off, and wanted an early night. "Your place?" He's gotta live in Joyville, right? That's what, half an hour away?

Maybe we can get a room. We're at a resort. I'm sure he gets an employee discount here too.

Derek sighs and pulls back, stroking my chest under my polo one last time before drawing his hand out. I miss it instantly.

"You'd better get back to your room," he says. It takes a moment for me to register what he means, and then it's like a slap in the face.

He doesn't want to have sex with me.

I thought our kisses were incredible. I was completely caught up in the moment, in kissing him, touching him. I thought he felt the same.

And he was... what, humoring me? Or is this just another way to show me that I'm not worth anything? If the guys who bullied me all those years ago had been gay, would I have already faced this moment?

My face is hot again, but this time it's with humiliated fury. I don't say a single word as I open the door and get out, my gut churning.

"Trav?" Derek sounds startled, taken aback. I slam the car door, do up my jeans (and damn him, even though right now I *hate* him, I'm still hard, and it's hellish uncomfortable), and stalk in what I think is the direction of my room. I'm not entirely sure, because I've never actually been to the parking lot, but I don't want to delay long enough to look at the signs and orient myself.

Behind me, Derek gets out of the car. "Trav!" Quick footsteps. Is he following me? *Why?* I don't want to continue this, I just want to go curl up in a ball of misery on my bed. It's not fucking fair. I finally begin to think that maybe not all jock-frat-popular guys are basically alike. I finally let one get close, and bam! He proves that I was right all along.

And I really liked him.

I push the thought aside as the footsteps get closer. I am not going to run. I am not going to let him see he got to me.

He grabs my arm and turns me toward him. "Trav, hey, aren't you going to say good n—" The words stop sharply as he sees my face. "What's wrong?"

What. A. Douche.

"What's wrong?" I'm actually pretty proud of myself for the way I sound—cold, disdainful.

"Yeah. Are you... mad?" He seems confused, and that cracks my anger a bit, because of all the things I've thought Derek to be, when I first met him, when I was crushing on him, and right now, I've never thought he was stupid.

So… could I have jumped the gun here? Maybe misunderstood?

"I…." I really don't know what to say. If he's playing me, I don't want to give him more ammunition. On the other hand, if he's genuinely interested and I've somehow got the wrong end of the stick, I don't want to push him away.

I don't want to push him away.

I don't know him well, but nothing I've seen or heard indicates that he'd play this sort of cruel game.

Fuck. Time to be brave.

"I am mad," I confess. "I thought we were heading"—toward a fuck? That sounds crass—"um, I thought we were…." Oh my God, I've lost my words. Where is my ability to construct a sentence?

Fortunately, Derek seems to get what I'm trying to say.

"Oh. Yeah, me too. But then I started thinking about the logistics. You have a roommate, right? And my place isn't that close… and to be honest, I've been up over twenty hours and I need to be up again at six, and… this sounds kind of dumb, but I don't want our first time to be half-assed when I'm tired." He winces. He's right, it does sound kind of lame, like something out of a rom-com, but it's also… nice. It makes my stomach flip and my chest tighten.

He wants it to be special when we have sex the first time. And even though I'm still so hard I'm standing funny, I want that too. Derek's awesome. This isn't a one-nighter. And if he's tired, he's not going to be able to appreciate my best moves. I'm a dancer, I'm really flexible, and I don't want to bring my A game if—

Wait.

"Did you say you've been up over twenty hours?" I look at my watch. It's nearly one. "What the hell for?"

He waves a hand. "Work crap. It's been a crazy couple of days."

Looking closely at his face, I can see the signs of tiredness. How did I miss them before? Probably because he was smiling so much. Animated. Happy.

To be with me.

I really can be an ass sometimes.

I kiss him quickly on the mouth, not letting myself linger even though I really want to. "Go home," I say firmly. "Get some sleep. I'll talk to you tomorrow."

He smiles at me again, his real smile, and predictably I feel all warm and mushy.

"Good night, Trav." He turns and goes back to his car. I stand there and watch until he drives away, waving at me.

It's not until I turn toward the direction signpost to orient myself that I realize.

Oh, crap.

I'm living out a sappy rom-com.

CHAPTER EIGHT

Trav

I WAKE on Wednesday morning with a smile on my face, due entirely to my incredible dreams. Derek played a starring role in all of them, and some had nothing to do with sex.

That actually makes me a bit nervous. I hardly know this guy, but already I feel more than just attraction for him. Part of me is tempted to end it all now, before I can get in too deep, because if I'm already feeling this much now, how much more involved could it get? And how much would it hurt when it all ends?

Because it's going to end. That's not me being negative; it's me being practical. I'm a Broadway performer. I live and work in New York—this is actually the first time I've ever toured with a show, and my contract is only until we finish the run here at Joy Universe. Rick begged me to come along, but I wasn't willing to commit to more than six months away from the city. My agent is already lining up potential parts for me to start rehearsals later in the year. The best place for my career is New York—or maybe London, but I've never seriously considered moving to England. Either way, Joyville, Georgia, doesn't compare. My career is my priority, and I've never made any secret of that, even if my last two boyfriends didn't believe me when I first told them and consequently left me because of it.

Derek, on the other hand, has a great job here. Really, "great" is an understatement. He reports directly to the director of the whole of Joy Universe, who in turn reports directly to the chief executive officer of Joy Incorporated, which has a revenue of tens of billions of dollars every year. Joy Universe itself produces nearly a third of that, and Derek is directly responsible for a big chunk of Joy Universe's current success.

In case you're wondering, no, Derek didn't tell me this. I was so wound up last night that I did some googling from my trusty iPhone.

It's shocking how much information is out there if you take the time to search for it. I now know more than I ever thought I wanted to about Joy Incorporated, Joy Universe, their corporate hierarchy and finances, and Planet Joy, which, it may interest you to know, is the most profitable of all the parks here at Joy Universe. Derek's name came up a few times as well. There have been articles about him in several business magazines, the first three years ago when he was promoted to his current job. Apparently he was the youngest ever person to fill the role. It doesn't surprise me, but it does speak to how committed he is to his job and career—not that I didn't know that, after everything I've seen and heard this week.

An article from earlier this year focused on the revenue and profits of various theme parks and entertainment complexes around the world, and of course Joy Universe featured, since it's the second-largest globally. Derek's name came up several times, because apparently the properties he's responsible for are the most profitable in Joy Universe, and Planet Joy is the second-most profitable theme park *in the world*. That's right, the only theme park that makes more profit than Planet Joy is the Magic Kingdom. The author of the article speculated that Joy Incorporated's executive management and board would eventually transfer Derek to California to work for the parent company.

So what it comes down to is that he's not likely to want to quit and move back to New York.

My train of thought is broken by the quiet beep of my phone. I reach through the dimness—the room is only lit by the tiny bit of early morning sun that can get around the blinds—and snag it from the nightstand, checking the time. Just before seven.

The text is from Derek, and a stupid smile stretches my mouth. Kev's asleep still, and nobody can see, so I let it.

Just wanted to let you know I plan to take advantage of that maybe.

It takes me a second to realize what he's talking about, and when I do, my whole body goes hot and tense. I guess I'm not as terrible at flirting as I thought last night. Or if I am, he at least understood what I meant.

But now I need to text him back, and I have no idea what to say. I want to ask if he slept well. I want to sound flirty and sexy and make sure he's excited about dating me. And maybe set up a time that's not a lunch break for us to get together. At his place. Preferably in his bedroom, although if he has a comfortable couch, I'd be okay with the living room.

Can't wait. Sometime soon, I hope.

I stare at the phone after I send the text, wishing I could take it back. It's not terrible, exactly, but I could probably have come up with something better. If I had six hours, a creative team, and a couple of reference books about the art of flirting and sexting.

Ugh.

My phone rings in my hand and I jump. Derek's name is on the screen, and I swipe to answer as I glance over at Kev, who predictably hasn't woken.

"Hold on," I whisper, throwing back the covers and hightailing it to the door, stopping only to grab my room key on the way.

Outside, the sunshine is already bright despite the early hour. I sit on the steps that lead down to the garden, the same place I sat just two days ago when I was talking to Rick, and lift the phone to my ear. "Hey." I keep my voice as casual as I can, but I can't help the frisson of excitement that runs through me.

"Good morning," Derek says in that voice that *always* does interesting things to my insides. "Did you sleep well?"

I remember some of those dreams, and even though he can't possibly know what I'm thinking, I blush hotly. "Very well," I say, and then clear my throat. Wow, was that my voice, all husky?

There's a slight pause, and then Derek clears his throat as well. "Good," he says.

"Did you sleep well? More to the point, did you sleep enough?" It can't be good for him to get so little sleep. He's not exactly a teenager anymore.

"I did, on both counts. It took me a while to drift off, though. I— er... missed you." That last bit sounds both sheepish and sultry, and I have no idea how he manages to pull it off.

"I missed you too." I assume he's referring to the fact that we were both as hard as steel posts when we parted ways. "Do you have a big day today?"

82

He sighs. From the background noise, he's in the car and driving somewhere—probably to work. "Big enough. We're still catching up after everything that happened on Monday. It was not the best ever start to a week."

I snort. "I'm sure, although it worked out pretty well for me." I nod politely at an older couple strolling past, although the woman glares—probably because I'm only wearing boxers. I'm decently covered, though, nothing hanging out that shouldn't be, so she'll just have to get over it.

"Anyway," Derek goes on, "I called for a reason. Well, mostly because since you were awake and I'm not at work yet, I wanted to talk to you instead of just texting." *Awww.* "But also because I figured you might need the car sooner rather than later, so if you let me know what time is good, I'll arrange for someone to run you out to my house to pick it up."

I hesitate because it feels to me like he'd need to go to a lot of trouble to organize that. "I don't want to put you out," I say slowly. "It can wait until you're not working." As soon as I say it, I realize how dumb that is.

"Trav, I'll probably be here tonight until seven, and I'm guessing that by then, you'll be getting ready for your show, yeah? And I don't want to waste our lunch hour tomorrow driving out to my place and back when we can just be enjoying each other's company. This is no hassle, I swear." He sounds eminently reasonable, and he's right, so I give in.

"If you're sure it's no trouble, that would be great. Um, but I can organize a cab or something. You don't need to send someone."

"It's fine," he says dismissively. "Why should you pay for a cab when JU has a bunch of drivers and cars on call for guests?"

I'm guessing he means VIP guests, but hey, he did say on Monday that those of us who helped out were going to get some special treatment.

"Okay," I agree, because riding in those chauffeur-driven cars was very cool and very comfortable, and I'm okay with doing it one more time. "I want to go for a run and get some breakfast, but I can be ready by nine. Does that work?"

"Perfect." The note of satisfaction in his voice is impossible to miss. "I'll have someone waiting out the front of the resort." His tone shifts to something a little more intimate. "If I don't talk to you again today, can I call you tonight, after the show?"

I feel that buzz again. "Yeah," That husky note is back. "Um, I should be done and back in my room by eleven." It's a little earlier than I'm usually back, but I'd much rather be talking to Derek while Kev's still out than hang around backstage with people I work with every day. Although… Derek needs to be up early, and he could probably do with catching up on sleep. "Is that too late?"

"No." He's smiling, I can tell. "Not too late."

I want to stay on the phone with him, but I also don't want to be the giant dork who keeps him on the phone talking when he has a ton of other things to do, so I say, "Cool. Okay, I better let you go if I'm going to have that run. I'll talk to you later." I'm actually pretty impressed by how normal I sound, because there are a ton of butterflies in my stomach when I think about talking to him tonight.

"Yeah, I'm just about to get to the office, so I really do have to go." He sounds reluctant, though, and I just love that.

It takes us a few more moments to actually say goodbye and end the call. I sit there on the steps for a bit longer, not willing to break the spell. I'm happy. Really happy. Like, I feel stupid about being this happy just because a guy I've been on one date with wants to talk to me at the end of the day. And I'm scared that if I leave this little bubble of happiness here on the steps to one of the many buildings in this resort, it'll burst. Something will change, and I won't be able to get this feeling back again.

But I can't stay here forever. I have to get on with my day.

At least the passing hours will bring me closer to that phone call.

THE DRIVER waiting out the front of the resort passes a bulky envelope back from the front seat before he starts the engine.

"What's this?" I turn the envelope over before it hits me. Duh—I'm going to need a key to drive the car. The driver shrugs.

"Dunno—I was just told to give it to you." He drives down the resort driveway toward the road.

"Thanks. Uh, you know where we're going, right?" Because it's just occurred to me that I don't have a clue.

He rattles off an address, and even though it's all Greek to me, I say, "Great," and settle back in my seat. The envelope seems a bit full to just have a key fob in it, so I rip it open, and the key and a garage door opener fall out.

Huh. I don't know why I just assumed that the car would be parked on the street, or in the driveway, but I did. "Am I supposed to give this back to you?" I ask the driver. He flicks a glance over his shoulder and shrugs.

"Nobody said anything to me."

I pull out my phone and text Derek.

Do you want me to send the garage opener back with the driver?

It takes a few minutes for him to reply, but not so long that we've left the complex yet. Seriously, this place is huge.

Nah, just hang on to it until I see you. It's a spare.

I'm still digesting the trust behind that gesture when another message pops up.

Or if you have time you can bring it to me at the office and we can have coffee? I have a gap between meetings at 10.15, and the coffee cart in the lobby is good.

I don't even hesitate.

How do I find you?

Does that seem too eager? Too bad. I am eager.

I'll send you a link to a map. Give me a few minutes to find it.

K.

I'm grinning as the car finally leaves Joy Universe and turns onto the highway, and yes, I'm still grinning like an idiot when my phone dings with Derek's map and instructions on where I'm going, and yes, the grin is *still* there when we finally pull up in front of a really nice house with a wide porch and a double garage.

The driver puts the car in park. "I'm supposed to wait and make sure you get the car okay."

"Okay, thanks." I get out and close the door behind me, then point the opener toward the garage and hit the button.

The door opens. *That's a good start.*

There's only one car in the garage, which makes sense because Derek would have taken the other one to work. But this car isn't the old banger I was envisaging—although knowing what I do about Derek, I have no idea why I was envisaging a banger. His current car is a Mercedes. It's unlikely the old one would have been a thirty-year-old rust bucket. What's waiting for me is a Lexus.

I've never driven a Lexus before. Admittedly, I've never driven much, because I live in New York, but all my driving has been in much more standard cars. I guess this will be something new.

I walk up the driveway and stop just inside the garage, then look at the key fob. There's a button with an open padlock on it, which I'm guessing is the unlock one. I press it, and the car lights flash—another good sign.

Before I do anything else, I glance quickly around the garage. I'm not being nosy, exactly, but... yeah, I am. In my defense, I don't go poking around in anything; I just let my eyes explore. It's a nice garage, tidy, with storage shelves along one wall and a door (presumably into the house) opposite. Just looking doesn't tell me a lot about Derek, though, except that he's neat.

I get in the car and take a second to orient myself. It all looks straightforward enough, so a moment later I start the engine, kind of relieved when it actually starts. I don't know why, but a tiny part of me was worried that it wouldn't.

I back out of the garage and pause on the driveway while the garage door closes. No way am I risking leaving it open for anyone to wander into. I'm trying to impress Derek, not get him robbed.

Behind me the JU driver beeps his horn and drives off. The garage door closes, and I check the map on my phone again. Getting back to JU should be pretty easy, but after that it might be tricky, so I decide to rely on Google Maps. I program the address in, and it comes back with an ETA of 9:50 a.m.

On impulse, I change my destination to the local community theater. I'm going to be spending some time there in the coming months, so I may as well get the lay of the land. I reverse onto the street and follow the easy directions to downtown Joyville.

It's a really pretty town, but it's not that big, and I'm soon cruising down Main Street toward the community theater. I take in the shops and public buildings. The town isn't that old, relatively speaking, since it was built when Joy Universe was, but I guess the benefit of a town being designed and planned instead of growing organically is that you can choose a style. Joyville is pure Americana, like every small town in every '50s sitcom, except with some modern franchises. I like it.

I pull into the parking lot attached to the community theater and turn off the engine. There's not likely to be anyone there, but I'll walk around the outside of the building, see if they have any posters up by the door. I don't even know what the show will be—or even if it's a play or musical theater. I should have asked, but I always had other things on my mind.

I'm just approaching the front door of the building—after carefully making sure I locked the car—when a woman comes out of the pharmacy next door and intercepts me.

"Excuse me, can I help you?" There's a distinctly wary look on her face, and I mentally revise my idea that the inhabitants of small towns are always open and friendly.

"No, I was just looking around," I assure her. "I'm going to be volunteering with the community theater, and I just wanted to get the lay of the land."

That doesn't seem to assuage her wariness, and she glances over my shoulder toward the car. "Isn't that Derek Bryer's car?" she says pointedly.

Does she think I stole it?

Nah. Why would anyone steal a car and then drive through town in it and park in front of the community theater?

"Yes, it is. He's being nice enough to lend it to me so I have transport while I'm here." It's more information than I would usually give to a stranger, but hey. Small town, right? Be friendly. Volunteer in the community.

I also look over my shoulder toward the car. *Can I leave yet?*

Just as it looks like she's going to say something else, a man comes out of the pharmacy waving a cell phone. "Tracy, it's all right! Derek says he lent him the car."

Oh. My. God.

She did think I stole it. Was she just keeping me here while they checked with Derek? Small towns are creepy. I miss New York.

Sure enough, Tracy is now smiling. "That's so nice of Derek, just the kind of thing he would do. So you're going to volunteer with the theater? That's great. They do some wonderful productions."

I paste on a smile. "Yeah. I'm… excited about it. Sorry I can't stay and chat, but I have to get back. Nice to meet you." I'm backing away before I even finish speaking.

"Oh, you never said your name!" she calls, and I stretch my smile even wider. Times like this I wish I had a fake smile like Derek's.

"It's Trav," I tell her. "Bye!" I get into the car and resist the temptation to check that the doors have locked. That's an overreaction, of course—Tracy's probably a perfectly nice woman who was doing the neighborly thing by making sure Derek's car hadn't been stolen. Still, the lack of anonymity is unlike anything I'm used to.

I pull back onto Main Street. Tracy is standing on the sidewalk, smiling and waving, so I wave halfheartedly back. *People are nice, Trav. Be social.*

WHEN I walk into the lobby of the JU administrative building, Derek is already there. Mind you, so are about a hundred other people, so the fact that my eyes go directly to him is another indication that I have a serious infatuation.

He's standing by the coffee cart, chatting with the vendor as he makes coffee for one of the half-dozen people in line, but as I cross toward him, he looks up and spots me. The wide, natural smile that breaks out makes me smile back.

"Hey," he says as I reach him. "Great timing—Jack was just finishing my coffee. What do you want?"

"Um…." I glance at the line. The woman at the front laughs.

"Don't worry, Derek already waited in line. He even let three people go first."

"Oh." Awww. "Um, I'll have a soy chai latte, please."

Jack winks as he gets to work. "No problem."

Supremely aware of our audience, I dig Derek's garage door opener out of my pocket and offer it to him. "Thanks. And thanks again for the car. Uh, I'm sorry about driving it through town." I can't think of any other way to say "I'm sorry the townspeople here are so nosy and bothered you at work."

He takes the opener and pockets it, raising an eyebrow. "Isn't the whole point of you borrowing it that you need to drive through town?" he teases. I wish I could be annoyed, but that actually gets a smirk out of me.

"Yeah, I know," I concede. "I just didn't expect a welcoming committee—that wasn't very welcoming at first." It's kind of funny, in retrospect. Okay, it would have been funny at the time if it hadn't been happening to me.

"It would have been even more unwelcoming if John had listened to Tracy and called the police before he called me." Derek wiggles his brows. "I would have had to come and bust you out of jail."

Oh. My. God. I smother a shudder. "Well, we can be glad John doesn't listen to Tracy," I say weakly. Because being arrested would have been so much fun.

"Here you go," Jack says cheerfully, handing me my drink. I take it, suddenly desperate, even if it isn't scotch.

"How much do I—"

"Derek took care of it," he tells me, and turns to take the order of the nice woman who's next.

I smile at Derek. "Thanks," I murmur. "The next one's on me."

His face lights up. "I'm glad there's going to be a next one." He leads the way across the lobby to a seating area. "After John and Tracy, I was worried you were going to leave town as fast as you could."

That gets an actual laugh out of me as I sit beside him on a plush sofa. "I won't say I didn't think about it." Because I *did.* "I even started to get directions to the airport from the GPS. But then I decided taking the car to the airport would probably just lead to a dozen more people calling you at work." I deliver the last part with a completely straight face and am rewarded by the stunned look on his.

"You… ohhhhhh." He gets it at last and starts to chuckle. "Crap, Trav, you actually had me going there."

It's nice to sit there with him, sipping my drink and chatting about nothing in particular. I'm amazed by how relaxed I am with him now, when as recently as last night I was still uncomfortable in his company. The shift in our relationship dynamic wasn't dramatic, but getting things out in the open made a huge difference—and I love it.

The minutes fly by, and before long Derek's phone chimes. He groans as he pulls it out and looks at it. "It's Dimi. I asked him to nudge me if I wasn't back by now, because I have a meeting soon."

I glance at my watch and see that it's ten forty. "I need to get going anyway," I say reluctantly. "I have some stuff to get done before the matinee today." I look him full in the eyes, mostly because they're a really pretty blue and I like to look at them. "I'll text you later with plans for lunch tomorrow, yeah?"

He smiles, and little crinkles form around his eyes. Laugh lines, and they suit him. "Yeah. And don't forget I'm going to call you tonight."

Cue romantic sigh, right? We had a date last night, spoke this morning, just met for coffee, have a date tomorrow, and he still wants to talk to me again tonight. No fairy-tale hero was ever so awesome.

Chapter Nine

Derek

I CHANNEL surf idly through what looks like a bunch of mediocre TV shows as the clock ticks slowly—so slowly—closer to eleven. Truthfully, there are probably some good shows in there that would normally interest me, but right now nothing can hold my attention. All I want is to talk to Trav again.

It's been a long time since I've felt this way, this adolescent giddiness and desperate longing for contact with my crush—in fact, I don't think I've reacted like this to a guy since college. All my relationships since then—not that there have been so many—have been much more adult and reasonable and… boring. No, that's not true. Well, not entirely. But while they had attraction and lust and mutual liking and respect, they were all lacking that incendiary spark, that feeling that I *must* see/speak to/be with *him* as often as possible. To be honest, I always thought it was just that I'd grown up, that the volcano of feelings and hormones I experienced in my teens—and right now with Trav—was just a teenage thing, and that adult relationships were less emotional and volatile.

Turns out, I was just dating the wrong people. Now I'm thirty-seven years old and I feel like a teenager again. I haven't been able to stop thinking about Trav all day. Even when I was focused on work, he was always at the back of my mind, ready to step forward and consume my thoughts if I gave him the chance.

And I love it.

I love feeling this strongly. I love that every time he pops into my head, I grin. I love that Dimi and Gina have already started chuckling at me when I get that stupid, besotted grin on my face.

Okay, that last bit probably confuses you. It started when Trav texted me the details for our date tomorrow. Dimi, Gina, and I were having a lunch meeting—which basically means eating sandwiches in

91

my office while we review whatever it is that needs it—when my phone went off with the tone I assigned for Trav's texts. Yes, I assigned him a special tone. That's what you do when you're being all adolescent. Most importantly, it means that no matter what I'm doing or who I'm talking to, I know the text is from him. So I stopped talking pretty much midsentence, put down my sandwich, and pulled out my phone.

And of course, I was already grinning like an idiot before I even opened the text.

Lunch tomorrow, 1.00pm, the Gator Gate Café. Want me to come and pick you up?

Before I could type a reply, another message popped up.

Oh, you should know there's going to be gossip about us. When I booked, I told them I was eating with you but they were NOT to apply your discount.

My grin got wider, which in retrospect I'm surprised was possible. I texted back quickly.

There's already gossip about us. Lots of it. You've just fueled the fire. Pick me up, I want to feel pampered ;-)

I looked up from my phone. Dimi and Gina are staring at me with mouths agape. "What?" I asked.

Gina pointed accusingly at my phone. "Who is it? Who's the person who makes you look like a drooling idiot?"

Seriously, she said that. She called me a drooling idiot. I admit I spent a second rethinking my plan to promote her.

"It's Trav, isn't it?" Dimi interrupted. "The rumors are true?"

"What have you heard?" I knew people were talking about us, what with our date last night and the coffee break this morning, but I wasn't sure how far it went. My phone buzzed in my hand with a new message, and I couldn't resist looking down at it.

Really? People are already gossiping about us? We haven't even been dating 24 hours!

"There it is again!" Gina exclaimed. I raised my head in time to see her turn to Dimi appealingly. "You see it, right? He looks like he belongs in a lunatic asylum!"

Ahhh, the love my subordinates feel for me. Heartwarming, isn't it?

"I think it's sweet," Dimi defended me, but his lips were twitching. "So, is it Trav? Because I haven't gotten in on the betting pool yet, but if it's true I'm going to."

That's right, folks. The loving and supportive Joy Universe family is betting on my love life.

"What's the pool?" I asked, partly because I was actually curious and partly because it would make a great story to tell Trav. And then I texted him.

We closed down a restaurant last night, had coffee this morning, I lent you a car, you booked another date. That's enough for them to have us married with three kids and a condo at the beach. They've even set up a betting pool.

"Bets are on whether you and Trav are dating or just friendly. Then there's a bet that you knew each other in New York, and the reason he was hostile on Monday was because of your bad breakup. There's also a side bet on whether one of you cheated, and who it was. And then there's a ton of bets about what happens next. So... you're dating Trav, then?"

"Someone bet that I cheated on my hypothetical ex-boyfriend? Charming." I made up my mind as my phone buzzed again. I didn't mind some gossip, but this sounded like it was getting out of control. "Hold on."

OMG! They're BETTING on us? Suddenly a lot of things make sense. I think the pool has already spread to the performers at the village, because people here are being super weird.

I cast my mind over the events of the morning. Some of the people I'd spoken to had acted a little oddly. I did think it was because they'd heard the gossip about me dating Trav, but I was a bit creeped out they might think I cheated on my boyfriend... who never existed.

Same. Listen, I've gotta go, but I'll talk to you tonight. If anyone asks if I cheated on you before I moved here, ignore them.

I set my phone aside just as a return text appeared.

???????!!!!!!!

It made me grin, but I ignored it for the time being and looked squarely at Dimi and Gina. "I don't care if you guys want to bet, but I don't like that it's casting aspersions on my and Trav's characters. So here's the deal: I will give you some information to take back to everyone and close down some of those bets, and then you can bet however you like on anything relating to the future. How's that sound?"

"Like a plan," Dimi affirmed. "Spill."

Gina leaned forward, her phone in her hand. I wouldn't have been surprised if she started taking notes or live-texting everything I said.

"Trav and I met for the first time on Monday. I reminded him of someone he dislikes, and that's why he was terse at first." Nobody needed to know more than that. "We had a date last night, and we have another tomorrow. This morning we had coffee when he brought back my garage opener—which I gave him so he could borrow my car, Dimi. So far things are going well, but obviously it's very early days. And that's it." I made my tone firm because I know what the gossip mill is like at JU, and if I gave them an opening, they'd ask all kinds of personal questions.

In fact, Gina looked like she had a list of them ready to go, but after a glance at my face, she closed her mouth and just nodded.

"Thanks, boss," Dimi said jauntily. "Don't worry, we'll spread the word."

Huh. Fancy that. I was supposed to be pleased that people were spreading gossip about me.

My phone chimed with Trav's tone, and I glanced at it, the smile already forming in what was quickly becoming a Pavlovian reaction.

Can't wait to talk to you later.

Dimi and Gina started to laugh.

"What?" I looked up.

Gina's chuckles were too strong for her to answer, so Dimi did. "Every time you look at a text from him, you get that besotted expression. We can tell who's texting you just from your face."

I was torn between mild embarrassment and not caring because I felt so good. "Did you really just use 'besotted' in a sentence?" I heckled, but Dimi just grinned.

The alarm on my phone brings me back to the present. Yes, I set an alarm to alert me when eleven o'clock rolled around—just in case I wasn't staring at the clock. Lucky, huh, since I was off in a daydream.

I snatch up my phone and silence the really annoying alarm. It's time to call Trav.

That stupid grin spreads across my face.

As I drive to work, singing along to the radio as usual, I'm barely able to contain my enthusiasm for this gorgeous Monday morning.

Exactly a week ago I had no idea what the universe (the regular one, not JU—although everything did happen at JU, so....) had in store for me. I had no idea that I'd spend my morning dealing with a murder and a staffing crisis, and that I'd meet a man who, just seven short days later, is already a pivotal part of my life.

Trav.

I always smiled tolerantly at those people who told me that when you meet "the one," you just know. I'm still not convinced it's true for everyone. And to be honest, I don't think that just meeting "the one" is enough—sometimes it won't work out even if they are "the one," because life can be a real bitch. But after only a week with Trav in my life, I *just know* that he's meant to be there, and that I'll work damn hard to keep it that way.

Our second date was just as great as our first—in fact, I lost track of time and ended up being late for a meeting. Lucky for me Dimi is as amazing as he is and had the foresight—once he learned about our date from the gossip mill—to reschedule the meeting for half an hour later than originally planned, so I was only fifteen minutes late, not forty-five.

I really have to do something about finding another job for Dimi. He's ready for more than just an assistant's role, even if being assistant to a JU AD is a demanding and prestigious job.

Since that second date, I've seen Trav three times. We sneak in quick meals and coffee breaks, and of course we text pretty much all day long and talk on the phone at least once a day. Total adolescence, right?

This week has been a pretty good indicator of what a relationship between us would be like, though. I work (mostly) regular business hours. True, I rarely finish at five, but even if I did, Trav and I would only have a few snatched minutes together before he had to head off to work. His evenings are taken up, and he works on weekends too—which actually isn't a problem for me, since I often find myself at Planet Joy or one of the resorts over the weekend.

The thing is, though, that even with such limited time available to us, we've managed to see and talk to each other more in five days than my previous boyfriend and I did in three weeks—and we were both working the same hours. What it comes down to is motivation, and when it comes to Trav, I have it in spades. He seems to feel the same. Even when I asked about the no-leading-roles thing and he fobbed me off with "let's not talk about that now," I got the impression that he'd tell me one day.

My head's not in the sand. I know he leaves at the end of July. But we've only known each other a week—I think we can take some time to explore things before we start fretting about the future.

And tonight the exploration continues. It's Trav's day off, which means tonight he's all mine, all night long. We have plans—you know the kind.

That's right, we haven't had sex yet. We could have, I guess—he could have come out to my place after work one night, or yesterday morning, when neither of us had any commitments, but honestly, that didn't feel right. Most days he has two performances, and by the time he finishes for the night, he's tired—and so am I, since I'm up by six every morning and put in a pretty full day myself. It seemed wrong that our first time together was going to be a halfhearted effort when we were both worn out. As for Sunday morning, we went to breakfast and then to Planet Joy. I know, that's pretty much just what I do most days, but Trav said he hadn't actually been to the park as a guest since he was a kid. He intended to while he's here but hadn't got round to it yet. So we went for a few hours before he had to do the matinee, and it was fun. Usually when I'm at the park, I'm all focused on work, or on assessing the guest experience, but I wanted Trav to have a good time so I closed my eyes to all the stuff I'd usually be paying attention to, and we just enjoyed ourselves.

It was especially cool—although if you tell anyone I said that, I'll strangle you—when some of the impromptu performers recognized us both and went off-script to take us prisoner. The guests watching loved it so much that I think I'll talk to Mandy and Pete about planting some of our performers as "guests" to be taken prisoner for all future shows.

In case you're wondering if my district's catastrophes from last week are all resolved, they mostly are. All performers were free from symptoms by Thursday, but at my insistence, they all had to come in and see medical to be cleared before they could return to work. Most started back over the weekend, and the last of them should be reporting for duty this morning. I also spoke with Maya yesterday, after Trav went to work. She ended up breaking down in tears, because she really wanted—in her words—to "get out of this damn house and get back to being useful," but she didn't want to ever have to go into a guest room again, and since she's a housekeeper, she figured that would mean she'd have to quit.

Um, hell no.

I interrupted Link's Sunday, and between the three of us, we found a back-of-house job that would suit her. She's now going to be managing inventory, which was actually a huge relief for Link because the woman currently doing that job is going on maternity leave for six months at the end of the month, and the guy who was training to take the job decided he'd really rather move to the coast. That gives us six months to find something more permanent for Maya. I also told her that if she wanted to move to one of the other resorts, she had only to say the word, but for now she wants to stay at Tiki with all her friends. She comes back to work this morning too, and while I'll be keeping an eye on things with her, she seems like a really strong woman, and I don't think I need to worry.

As far as how the murder investigation is going… well, the police have officially charged Kylie Rutherford with the murder of her husband. A bail hearing has been postponed pending psychiatric assessment due to the way she behaved after the murder. The cops finished all their crime scene investigating late last week and advised us that the bungalow was no longer a restricted area. I'm still not letting anyone stay there yet, if ever. Link and I agreed that only senior staff are to have access to it, and we got a specialist cleaning team out from Jacksonville on Friday to scrub the place from top to bottom. This week I'm (reluctantly) allowing guests to use the bungalows on either side, although I insist that the guests be advised before they check in that their bungalow is next door to a murder scene and offered alternate accommodation if they prefer. I need to decide soon if I'm going to bulldoze it.

So things are pretty much back on track. This week should be normal—the monthly status meeting is this morning, and that's going to be a bit of a trial, since last week hit the budget hard, but we're enough into the black that we can handle it. Then I also have to meet with Toby and Elise from evarketing about next year's plan for the park. They seem to have been hard at work for the last week, so fingers crossed they'll have something exciting to show me.

And I need to sneak out and meet up with Trav as often as possible. Because I can.

I SETTLE into one of the comfy chairs around the conference table in the boardroom and reach for my coffee. These meetings are pretty dull. Anything that comes up that is out of the ordinary usually calls for a special meeting, so all we do at the monthly status meeting is review the budget and anything that might need to be tweaked in the operating plan—which most of us are aware of before the meeting. Not Ken, though, since he never reads any of the information we send him. Today should be no exception.

Grant sits beside me and leans over with a smirk on his face. "I've been hearing all sorts of interesting things about you," he murmurs.

The stupid grin spreads across my face. I can't help it; every time I even think about Trav, it blindsides me.

"What kind of things?" I stall for time. It's not that I don't want to talk to Grant about Trav, but first I need to make sure he's not just trying to get fodder for the betting pool. And before you can judge him based on that—that's what I'd do.

I mean, he's not to know that things between me and Trav are more than casual. Why shouldn't he think it's all lighthearted and fun, and a great way to make some extra cash?

"Things like you have a hot dancer keeping you company."

Yeah. That's true.

"And that every time someone talks about him, you look like a drooling moron."

"Hey!" Damn it, someone needs to gag Gina. Across the room where the assistants are talking—likely exchanging gossip—Dimi looks up and casts me a guilty glance.

Maybe not Gina, then.

"How much are you paying Dimi to feed you information?" I ask tartly, and Grant laughs.

"Please, like Dimi would tell me anything that wasn't already public knowledge. I offered him a hundred bucks to tell me when your next date is, and he refused."

Possibly because he doesn't know. Trav and I have already moved beyond the initial stage of dating formally, and now we're just spending all our free time together.

Fast, right?

"So this guy is something special?" Grant presses, and damn it, the grin is back. I've really gotta work on that.

"Yeah."

Ken strolls in then, five minutes late as usual. He takes his seat at the head of the conference table as the assistants scurry to take their seats at the other end. Yeah, that's right, Ken won't let our assistants sit with us, even though that's obviously where they'd be of most use. Just another douchey thing he does.

The meeting is as boring as I expected—until Ken turns to me and says, "Report on the events of last week, Derek."

Lucky for me, I was prepared for him to ask, and luckier still, I've been thinking about this shit so much that I could talk about it in my sleep. I run down exactly what happened, what actions we took, how much it cost, and what the situation is at the moment. He's actually got all of this information—remember, I was supposed to report to him until it was all resolved? I have been, of course, or rather Dimi's been preparing the reports and I've been signing off on them. But I told you he never reads them.

It's probably a good thing to let the other ADs know how I handled the situation, though, in the event that it comes up again and they find themselves in the same position. It's always better to reuse a tried-and-true process than forge a new one by the seat of your pants. God knows I would have loved to be able to use someone else's expertise when it all went down. I actually see Margo and Grant taking notes, which I appreciate.

"And what effect has this had on profit?" Ken asks sternly, as if I've done something wrong.

I grimace, making sure I look downcast even though I want to smirk. It's not good news, but it kind of is. "I met with accounting late last week, and we are definitely going to take a substantial hit. The forecast we did in December indicated a 5 percent increase on profit for April over this time last year. We had, of course, hoped to substantially beat that, and all indications year to date were pointing in that direction, but accounting thinks, and I agree, that the month will likely only show a 2-3 percent increase in profit over last year." I keep my face absolutely neutral as my words fall into the silence. *That's right, people; that's how it's done in my district.* Casting a glance down the table, I see that Dimi is also resolutely straight-faced, while the other assistants look like someone just smacked them.

Grant clears his throat beside me. "Can I clarify, please... you had two major crises within a few hours, which led to a large amount of unplanned additional expenditure, blowing out your weekly budget by"—he glances at the notepad in front of him—"nearly 15 percent, but the result is that you're not only still posting a profit, but an increase on last year's profit?" He says it as though it's the most normal thing in the world, as if I haven't just pulled off the feat of the fucking century, but when I look at him there's laughter in his eyes and a twitch at the corner of his mouth.

This is why Grant and I get along so well. It would look really dickish for me to make a big deal about this, so he's going to rub it in everyone's faces for me.

"That's right," I say simply, restraining myself from jumping up on the table and doing a victory dance. However, I can't help adding, "It's not an ideal result, but it's better than some of the alternatives." I keep my smile under wraps. Not an ideal result, my ass. I know for a fact that at least one of the other districts will be barely posting a profit this month, much less an improvement on last year's, and things have been all smooth sailing for them.

"It's an outstanding result," Ken says, and I turn my head so fast that my neck cracks and I swear I give myself whiplash. If everyone was surprised before, there's no word to describe the level of stunned they are now. Ken doesn't give compliments. Not ever. If he says "good job," it's the equivalent of any other boss getting down on their knees and worshipping you. My "not ideal, but better than alternatives" comment was taken from something he said in a past meeting where the situation was a hell of a lot better than what happened last week.

I literally do not know what to think. Is he drunk? Or maybe he's having a stroke? That causes unusual behavior, right? Should I do one of those FAST tests?

I suddenly realize he's looking at me expectantly. Right, I haven't said anything. I should say something. *Humble and appreciative, Derek. You can do it. Then maybe ask medical to check on him.*

"Thank you, Ken. The team worked hard to make it happen. This is a real credit to them." I mentally pat myself on the back. *Perfect.*

"And to you," he says, and really, is he a doppelganger? Did aliens land over the weekend and do something to him? "As you know, one of our primary focuses here at Joy Universe is the guest experience. We spend a lot of money on things that bring no direct revenue"—he's right about that, the nightly fireworks display being a great example—"purely because they add to the overall guest experience. Derek's expenditure last week was so large it frankly would have sent some of the other districts well into the red for the month, but PR sent me the customer satisfaction index, and in Derek's district, it dropped only one point. That is so unexpected as to be shocking."

While I'm sitting there with my mouth hanging open—although the small inner part of me that's still able to function is doing a jig, because I was scared to look at the CSI this morning, just in case all my effort was for nothing—he picks up his tablet and taps the screen.

"One of the guests who checked out of Tiki over the weekend left this comment on their feedback survey: 'My sister called and told me there had been a murder in my hotel. I didn't know. The staff obviously did a brilliant job of making sure it didn't affect us. Good job, Tiki Island Resort and Joy Universe—we came here to get away from the real world, and you made sure that happened.'" He taps the screen again while I make a mental note to find that survey and ensure it gets to Link and his team. "PR also got an email from a woman who visited Planet Joy last Monday. 'We were disappointed when we found out the *Joy versus the Asteroid Monster* show had been canceled for the morning. Our day had been planned very carefully, and that ruined it. Linnie at Information helped us rearrange our schedule so we still did everything we wanted to. It was also really nice to get free refreshments as an apology without even having to make a complaint—it shows that Planet Joy actually does care whether we have a good time, and not just that we paid for our tickets.'"

I actually know who Linnie is—Don has her earmarked for a managerial position as soon as she gets a bit more experience under her belt. It's great to have our confidence in her reinforced.

I'm pretty sure I need to say something again, but I'm kind of at a loss. Ken's never done this—not just the compliment, but passing on positive feedback. Normally if customer feedback is shared in this meeting, it's of the "how do we keep this person from suing" type.

"I'll pass that on," I say finally. "The staff worked really hard to keep things operating smoothly, and they'll be thrilled to know how successful they were." There. That sounded reasonably intelligent.

"I spoke with corporate this morning," Ken went on, because *he's still not done.* What the hell is going on? "They're very pleased that things have turned out so well. Of course, it's not good that JU has been linked to a murder, but I suppose you can't be blamed for that."

And he's back. *That's right, Ken, I can't be blamed for the murder.* Around the table, there's a slight shift, a sense of relief and relaxation. I don't think I was the only one completely thrown by Ken's weird personality shift.

"They also said"—oh, he's not done. Really? When will this end?—"that they'd like a full analysis report submitted to them. They're keen to see how your process can be applied to future crises across the business."

I wait for a few seconds, but he finally seems to be finished. "Not a problem," I tell him. It isn't, since Dimi and I have been diligently documenting and reporting on everything for the past week—which Ken would know if he ever read the reports we send him. By the way, when he says "corporate," he means Malcolm Joy and Seth Holder, the nephews of our late founder, Edwin Joy, and Joy Inc.'s CEO and CFO, respectively. Ken reports directly to Malcolm, although I'm pretty sure if Seth ever gave him an order, he wouldn't say no. "I'll have it on your desk by the end of the day." It will mean rearranging some things and working through lunch—since there's no way in hell I'm going to work late tonight—but since we have the bones of the analysis and all the information ready, it's doable.

Ken nods curtly, and then gets up and strides out in his usual meeting dismissal. His assistant scurries after him, and the rest of us sit there for a moment trying to pull ourselves back together.

"Well," Margo says finally. "That was the weirdest status meeting I've ever been to." Since she's been attending these meetings for about eight years, that's really saying something. "Was he high, do you think?"

Grant, who was sipping from his water bottle, chokes while the rest of us laugh. I pound him on the back.

It's a good day.

I MAKE it home about half an hour before Trav is due to come over. That's a little later than I planned, but still gives me plenty of time to get dinner started. I thought about going out somewhere, but yesterday while we were having brunch, Trav said the food was almost as good as homemade, and then it came out that he misses home cooking. I'd never thought about it, but I guess the performers at the village do get the rough end of the stick in that regard—they have to live for months out of a hotel room with no kitchen. Sure, they get discounted meals at all the excellent JU restaurants and eateries, but eating out can become tiresome after a while.

So tonight I have plain, at-home food on the menu. Trav doesn't eat heavy food except as the occasional treat, since he has to be in good shape for his job. Really good shape. Like, his abs are amazing. I tried to think of a meal that isn't boring, but also isn't complicated and fattening, and boy, it was *hard*. In the end I settled on lemon-pepper steak, roasted Mediterranean vegetables with brown rice, and salad. For dessert we're having fresh fruit with Greek yogurt and honey. Simple and healthy, but pretty damn yum—well, I think so, anyway.

I hadn't realized until now, but I'm actually nervous. How dumb is that? I just want everything to be perfect tonight. I want Trav to be delighted by the meal, even if it is nothing special. I want our first time together to be all moonlight and roses and that other romantic crap you see in Hollywood movies, many of which are made by Joy Inc. And I want this to be the beginning of something important.

Wow. That's a bit intense. Sorry. I forget sometimes that people aren't interested in hearing my innermost thoughts and feelings.

Anyway, I get started on dinner. The veg needs the longest to cook, while the steak doesn't need to go on until Trav arrives. I open a bottle of wine too. Trav doesn't drink a lot, but he mentioned the other night that he's particularly partial to several reds. Maybe I went out and bought one of his favorites. It's a special night, after all.

By the time the doorbell rings, I'm back in control of myself and my runaway emotions and fears. I'll bet you're glad—I know I am. I open the door, and that stupid smile pops out. I can't help it—Trav looks edible. Normally when I see him, he's in sweats and a T-shirt—after all, he spends a lot of time either rehearsing or in costume. Otherwise, his "uniform" seems to be jeans and—you guessed it—a T-shirt. Tonight, though, he must have dug into the bottom of his suitcase, because he's wearing chinos and a collared shirt, open at the neck and with the sleeves rolled up. It's a mint-green color that really flatters his eyes. I wonder if that's why he chose it. Probably, right? I mean, that's why I chose the shirt *I'm* wearing.

I hope he notices that the cornflower-blue cotton makes my eyes look awesome.

"Hey." I lean forward and kiss him, partly because I've really missed him over the past thirtyish hours and partly just because his lips are right there, looking all soft and pink and inviting.

"Hi," he says when we finally pull back from the kiss. I had intended for it to be just a light hello peck, but you know what they say about good intentions and the road to hell. Trav's face is slightly flushed now, just the way I like it. I smile at him—thankfully not that stupid goofball smile—and step back, gesturing for him to come in.

I close the door and turn around. He's studying my house avidly—well, what he can see of it. He hasn't been here yet, and I have to admit I feel a little thrill about getting to show it off. That's why I spent most of yesterday afternoon cleaning. Not that it was dirty to begin with—I have a weekly cleaning lady—but I'd let it get a bit untidy since I didn't spend much time at home last week.

There's a gift bag hanging from one of his hands.

"What's that?" I point. He blushes.

"Nothing, really. Just… my mom always made a big deal about not going to someone's place for dinner empty-handed." He hands me the bag while I fight back the urge to say "awwww." He looks vaguely embarrassed and a little flustered as I take it and peer inside.

There's a bottle of wine and a small box of gourmet chocolates, and I smile and start to thank him—but my eye is caught by something else. It's mostly under the chocolates, but it looks like…. I reach into the bag and push the chocolates aside as Trav groans and mutters something. Excitement coils low in my abdomen, and my dick goes partly hard.

Because it's a brand-new tube of lube.

It's not that it's a surprise, exactly. We both knew what the plans were for tonight—hell, I checked that I had supplies before I left for work this morning. But him buying lube and giving it to me as a gift feels like a declaration. It makes me feel special, like I'm worth the effort he went to.

Here I go again, talking about feelings. Sigh, right?

I look up. Trav's biting his lip. It's too much to resist, and I grab his hand, tug him closer, and kiss him.

I love the way he tastes. As his soft lips move against mine and our tongues tangle, we move closer together, body to body, and we fit perfectly, hard muscle against hard muscle. I love the warmth of him pressed against me. I've gone from semihard to pretty much all the way there, and so has he.

I wrap my arms around him and conk him in the back with the gift bag. He makes an *oof* sound, and we break apart, breathing heavily.

"The chocolates aren't that nice," he pants, and I laugh. How did I get this lucky?

"How hungry are you?" It'll take me all of thirty seconds to turn off the oven. The vegetables should keep okay until later.

He grimaces. "I'd say 'not very' and tackle you to the floor right here in the entryway, but I'm afraid my growling stomach will give me away."

You know that fight against the urge to say "*awww*"? Yeah, I lost. I lean over and plant a short kiss on his mouth. If you could see it, you'd understand why—it's all puffy from our kiss, and I swear it's calling me. "Come on." I lead him toward the kitchen. "You can keep me company while I do the steaks."

"Steak? Yum," Trav declares.

DINNER'S EATEN (it was a hit, by the way), the dishes are loaded in the dishwasher (mostly because Trav insisted we not just leave them), and Trav and I are snuggled on the couch. Ostensibly we're watching TV, but neither of us have so much as glanced at the screen for about an hour. We're too busy tangling ourselves in each other. We both lost our shirts a while ago, and I managed to wiggle Trav's pants down over his hips before I got distracted by his nipple. Sucking on that led to kissing my way back up his chest, to his mouth, and then I had to spend an appropriate amount of time worshipping it.

Trav pulls back, gasping slightly. "This is amazing, but it's also heinous torture," he says. "Here or the bedroom?"

Huh. I pause to consider, absently stroking his abs. He shudders.

"Here." The couch is comfy enough, and I don't want to let him go even long enough to get to the bedroom. But crap, we need supplies.

While I'm mentally calculating which would take less time, me dashing to the bathroom for condoms and then back, or Trav and me both going to the bedroom via the bathroom, Trav lies back on the couch, pushes down his pants and underwear, and starts stroking himself.

Breath seizes in my chest, and my jaw drops. I've seen a lot, but somehow this is sexier than anything.

His green eyes fix on me. "Condom?" he asks, and I start breathing again on a gasp. In seconds, I'm off the couch and on my way to the bathroom.

By the time I get back, Trav has stripped off his remaining clothes and is stretched out on my couch like an offering to some long-forgotten pagan god. If you've ever wondered, I can tell you that dancers are

fucking ripped. All that lean, defined muscle covered by pale skin...
ungh. I want to take a bite.

I toss the box of condoms—didn't want to waste time getting one
out—and the lube onto his chest and start pulling off my clothes. We've
talked about sex before, so I know we're both vers, but....

"You do me," I tell him. He grins and grabs the condoms.

CHAPTER TEN

Trav

IT'S BEEN a little over six weeks since I met Derek, and just on six since we started dating. We're well beyond that now, even though only a short time has passed—I've practically moved in to his place.

I can almost hear your surprise and judgment. *But, Trav, it's only been six weeks!* That's what my sister said when I told her on the phone this morning—I held off on telling her earlier because I knew she would. The truth is, after that first night Derek and I spent together, I never really went back to staying at the resort. I've showered there a couple times, picked up and dropped off clothes, and hung out during the day when Derek was working—until he realized I was doing that and told me to treat his place like home—but all my nights have been spent at his place.

Can you blame me? He's there. Why would I want to share a hotel room with a coworker (even if it is Kev, who's a friend) when I can be snuggled up to the man I'm falling for?

I'm still sticking with "falling for" right now, even though I strongly suspect I'm kidding myself and the falling has been over and done for a while. As long as I don't admit it, we're still in the getting-to-know-you phase of the relationship, right? And I don't have to think about the long-term, and how we can possibly be together when he works here and I work in New York.

So for all intents and purposes, I'm living with Derek. Kev's thrilled—it basically means he gets a room to himself. He's dropped quite a few broad hints about how I should call first before dropping by, even though technically it's still my room too and I have a key. I told him if he's doing anything I can't walk in on, he should stick the Do Not Disturb sign out, but otherwise he's shit out of luck. I guess I should just officially move out of the resort… but. Yeah, I'm too chickenshit. It feels like that would jinx the whole thing. Being with Derek, our whole relationship, has been kind of perfect. Even the few arguments we have, or that misunderstanding when I thought he didn't want me, are all just little hurdles that make things between us better after. And other than those, we just fit together so well. He's more of a people person than I am, but he doesn't need to be constantly surrounded. We balance each other there—he encourages me to be a bit more social, and I give him a space where he doesn't need to be "on" all the time. We both love the theater—he can give me a real run for my money on theater trivia, but I have him beat on gossip—and we're both fairly well-read. There have never been any lags in conversation between us.

But I'm absolutely petrified that if I actually admit things between us aren't just casual, if I move out of the resort officially, it will all come tumbling down. I already feel so much more for him than I ever have for anyone else I've been with, even my last boyfriend, who I lived with for nearly two years. How can I risk that?

So for now I'll just keep pretending to myself that we're having a fling, and I'll hang on to my resort room key, even if I haven't been exactly sure where it is for the last few days. It'll turn up, probably when I do some laundry.

I wander in through the backstage door earlier than usual. Mark, our lead, got called back to New York with a family emergency in the wee hours—they thought his dad had a heart attack, but it turned out to be angina. Mark's going to stay and make sure he's settled at home with everything he needs but will be back in time for Friday's shows. His understudy can handle it for a couple of days, and normally there would be no drama, but—and here comes the drama—Phil, who was Mark's understudy and had done the role several times when Mark had time off, ran off with his best friend's girlfriend last week. Yep, that's right, they took off for Vegas, no warning, and got married. Since he didn't warn anyone he was going, just didn't show up for work, it's unlikely Phil would have had a job to come back to, but it's all made worse by the fact that Phil's best friend is Mark.

Mark's having a really bad couple of weeks.

Anyway, the new understudy has never actually performed the part for an audience, so we're all going in early to do a run-through of blocking etcetera. It's only three shows that Jim—the understudy—has to cover, and he's been with us since New York, so it should be a piece of cake.

THE RUN-THROUGH goes great. I mean, we don't perform the whole show, but Jim has the blocking and choreography down and is spot-on with the lines we do. He has a good grasp of the character and seems to get it.

But, oh God, as soon as the curtain goes up, he just falls apart. I see it happen. He freezes, misses a cue, and when he finally gets his line out, he's so *wooden*. Worse, it just keeps happening—he seems to be getting it together, and then he freezes, misses a line, uses the wrong line, mixes up some choreography... it gets worse and worse. Audience members are actually walking out. To give the kid credit, he sticks it out, keeps going until the last curtain falls—but it might have been better for him if he hadn't.

What a fucking nightmare.

Backstage is absurdly quiet. Usually after a show, even when we're dog tired, there's a cacophony of sound. Cheer if it was a good performance, the occasional shouted conversation, and the usual chatter of a lot of people getting things put away and reset for the next show.

Not today. The quiet is heavy, as if we're all afraid to speak. The only other time I've ever felt anything like this was three years ago, right after a show where someone was pretty seriously injured. Thank God, nothing like that happened today, but... I feel so very, very bad for Jim.

If I knew him a little better, I'd be going to talk to him, because he's gotta be feeling like utter shit right now. We all know that Rick authorized ticket refunds for anyone who requested them.

I finish changing and look around. It's seriously like a morgue back here, and I can tell everyone is freaking out about tonight's show. I'm worried myself. What the hell are we going to do? There's no way Jim can go on again—even if Rick and John, our director, were inclined to let him, from the look on his face when the curtain came down to boos, he wouldn't do it.

"Trav? Got a second?"

Rick beckons me from the doorway of the little room he and John use as an office.

"Sure." I go to join them, and Rick closes the door behind me. The room is cramped with the three of us in there, as well as a bunch of other crap that's somehow managed to migrate in over the last couple months we've been here.

"Have a seat," John offers, pushing over a folding chair. He's perched on one himself, and Rick takes another. We sit in a kind of wonky circle and just stare at each other before Rick blows out a breath.

"So, that was a catastrophe," he says, and I grimace.

"Yeah. Poor Jim. Have you spoken to him yet?"

John shakes his head. "He went and locked himself in the bathroom right after the show, and we figured we'd give him some time to get it together. Poor kid's probably kicking himself."

"I think it was just the pressure," I say honestly. "Especially since Mark is actually not here, not just having the afternoon off. Jim's good, but his first time in the spotlight…." I trail off, because they know. Shit like this happens. It doesn't mean Jim won't eventually grow into a great headline performer, but this is definitely a setback.

"Meanwhile, we're stuck," Rick confesses. "He can't go back on, and there are two more shows until Mark comes back."

I run my mind over the cast list. Who've we got in the chorus who could handle this? "Tony might be able to do it," I suggest. "He's—"

"No," John says firmly. "I'm not risking someone inexperienced again. Not two shows in a row."

"That doesn't leave you with any options," I begin, and then I catch sight of the pleading look on Rick's face.

Oh no.

Fuck, no.

How could I not have realized this was what they were leading toward?

How am I going to get out of it?

Wait. Don't jump the gun.

So I wait. I sit there with my mouth shut and wait for them to say it.

Only it seems like they're waiting for me to speak first, and the silence is excruciating. Surely they can't think I'll volunteer? I've only worked with John once before, but Rick and I have worked together tons of times, and he knows there's no way in hell this is happening.

Finally John sighs.

"Trav, please. Everyone knows you're not interested in lead roles, and we wouldn't ask if we had any other options. It's only two performances."

"No." That's it. Just one word. I don't trust myself to say more, because if I start making excuses, they might be able to talk me into it.

They exchange glances, and Rick leans forward. "Trav, we're desperate. We have to come back with a great performance tonight, show that this afternoon was a one-off, or ticket sales are going to tank. We've got six more stops after we leave here, and if rumors start going round that the show sucks, some of 'em are probably going to get canceled. It's two performances. We both know you know the part. We know you could do it with your eyes closed. Just give us these two performances, and we will owe you big. If you ever want a part in any show I'm involved in, it's yours."

"It would be mine anyway," I scoff. That's a little more egotistical than I usually go for, but it's not untrue. Rick likes working with me, and I'm *good* at my job. I wipe my sweating palms on my legs.

I just don't know if I'd be any good in a lead role.

That's the crux of it. I'm afraid I'll completely tank it.

"True," Rick concedes. "I'm begging you, Trav. Do me this favor."

I want to say no again and walk out, so badly that I can taste it. But I also feel really guilty for not already having said yes, gut-churning guilt. It's not like they're asking me to donate a kidney, after all.

"How would this work? I'm not saying yes," I caution, when John's face lights up. "Just… walk me through your plan."

"You take the lead," John tells me. "We put Jim in your role."

My eyebrows shoot up in surprise, and he nods.

"I know, but you're right; he's good. We want him to get used to a role with a lot of lines, but less pressure than the lead. If he still sucks by the end of the first act, he goes back to the chorus, and Tony will finish out the performance in your role—but that doesn't leave this room. We don't want to add more pressure."

I turn the idea over. It's practical and considerate of Jim's feelings. The only problem is that I would have to perform the lead role.

I really don't want to. Just thinking about it makes me feel sick.

My hesitation must go on too long, because Rick and John exchange glances again, and when they look at me, their expressions have changed slightly. There's a hardness there, and an air of resignation, and I know what they're going to say. My contract has a clause in it that requires me to step into any other role if necessary. It's standard to pretty much any contract I've ever signed, and although I once asked my agent if we could have it removed, he told me it wasn't worth the effort—and the gossip it would generate. I had to concede the point, and it's never come up in all my years performing.

But Rick and John are desperate, and they're going to use it. I can tell they don't want to—after all, forcing me to do something I don't want to is not a good way to foster fond feelings, especially since Rick is still trying to get me to agree to keep touring with the show.

I sigh. "Fine. Two performances only."

CHAPTER ELEVEN

Derek

DIMI AND I are in my office Wednesday afternoon, reviewing the almost-finalized plan for next year from evarketing, when my door bursts open.

To say we're startled is putting it mildly. We both leap to our feet, and Dimi grabs the stapler from my desk—what he plans to do with it, I couldn't even guess. Throw it?

We'll never know, because the intruder is just Toby, and although I haven't forgotten his comment about poisoning my coffee, he's never struck me as a violent person. Anyway, I could take him.

"Derek, how excited are you? You must be thrilled! I know you haven't been together that long, but still!"

I blink and look back at the plan on my laptop screen. It's a good one, much better than I was expecting given the time constraints, but I wouldn't say I'm thrilled by it, or even particularly excited. I'm about to tell him so—diplomatically—when the last part of his outburst sinks in. Who hasn't been together that long? Me and the plan?

Thankfully, I have Dimi on my side.

"What's going on?" he asks Toby, with just the right amount of enthralled curiosity in his voice, even as he shoots me a confused and weirded-out look. He's actually a pretty good actor.

"Trav is taking on the lead role in *Day Dot* until Mark Aston gets back from wherever he is."

"New York," I supply automatically. Trav told me this morning that Mark—who's a really great guy; I met him a couple weeks ago when Trav brought me to drinks with the cast—had to go home to his dad for a few days. He was racing to get ready because he had to go in early so the understudy could practice, or something, because of the drama last week—and wasn't *that* some delicious gossip? "What happened to the understudy?" I ask stupidly, then shake my head. *Seriously, Derek, who cares? Trav's in a lead role!*

"He bombed during the matinee," Toby announces, with a little too much glee for my liking. I can see from the way that Dimi's mouth tightens that he agrees.

"Poor guy," he says pointedly, and to give him credit, Toby looks a little shamefaced.

I flash my megawatt smile, the one Trav told me he hates and I never use on him but that works so well on everyone else. "I guess I should scrounge up a ticket for the show tonight—and give Trav a call." I'm itching to pull out my phone. Why didn't Trav call and let me know? That article I read when I was cyberstalking him, the one that said he's turned down starring roles before, plays in my head. Could he be unhappy about this? Is that why he hasn't called me, all excited? After that one time I asked him and he said he didn't want to talk about it yet, it hasn't come up again, and now I have to wonder if maybe this isn't a good thing after all.

"I thought you might need one, so I got it for you." Toby whips a ticket—an actual paper ticket, which means he's been down to the box office at the village—out of his pocket and presents it like it's a priceless diamond. He's fishing for gossip, of course, but that doesn't change the fact that he's done me a favor, so I keep smiling and thank him.

Between us, Dimi and I manage to move him along—finally—and as Dimi closes the door behind him, he shoots me a glance over his shoulder. "Give it a few seconds for him to get out of sight, then I'll go and you can call Trav," he says. "Congratulate him for me. I'm going to see if I can grab a ticket myself." Dimi and Trav have become pretty close over the past month. Trav's really getting into his consulting job at the community theater—he's there every Monday evening and Saturday morning.

I smile—gratefully this time, not my public smile. "Thanks, Dimi. Have a look at the comp list and grab one from there if there are any left." We get a certain allocation of comped tickets for the shows at the village, ostensibly to use for promo packages and give to VIPs. Because the shows themselves aren't run by JU, we can't just comp tickets and absorb it into the cost center—well, we can, but we have to pay full price for them.

He grins at me and slips out. I slide my phone from my pocket and dial Trav in fewer seconds than it's ever taken me in my life—and then I have to wait *four rings* before he answers.

"Hey."

Uh-oh. That is not the voice of someone who is thrilled to receive a brilliant opportunity.

"Hi," I say, wondering if I should wait for him to mention it. *Fuck it.* "I hear congratulations are in order."

"Yeah."

Man, he sounds like he's about to cry. I'm genuinely worried now, because even if he doesn't want to be a Broadway star, the idea of doing a couple of performances in a lead role shouldn't make him this depressed.

"Trav, you okay?" I ask hesitantly. I don't want to stir things up, but I can't pretend this is normal.

There's a long silence. His breath hitches.

"No."

Fuck. "Where are you?" I hit a key on my laptop and the JU app pops up.

"At home."

Despite my concern, a warm buzz shoots through me when I hear him say "home." It's nice that he thinks of it that way. A few taps on the keyboard sends a message to Dimi that I have to go, and he should handle whatever else comes up today.

"I'm coming, baby. Let's have some quiet time together, yeah?" I close my laptop and snag my keys.

"You're busy," he protests, but it's halfhearted.

"Never too busy for time with you," I assure him as I stride out of my office. Dimi is hurrying toward me, a concerned look on his face. I flash him a smile and shake my head, and he stops, nods.

He's got my back.

"Put some music on while you're waiting," I instruct Trav as I hit the stairwell. "I'm going to lose signal, but I'll be home soon."

I just hear him murmur an assent before the call drops out. Trav, not surprisingly, loves music and dancing. After the third time he asked me if it was okay for him to play music while he was hanging out at my place, I told him to feel free to just blast it whenever he wanted. And he does. He's got really eclectic taste in music—the show tunes were expected, but he mixes it up with club music, rap, top forty, classical, jazz, occasionally country, though he says he has to be in the right mood for that. What surprised me was his love for cheesy '80s power ballads. And when I say love, I mean obsession. I've seen his playlists, and he has many of them dedicated to the power ballad. He plays them often, loudly, and belts out the lyrics with enthusiasm and emotion.

It's adorable. It's endearing. It's captivating. I don't understand why he loves them so much, but when I watch him singing along and dancing around, my heart feels too big for my chest, and I want nothing more than to keep watching for the rest of my life.

Heavy stuff, considering we've known each other less than two months.

I DON'T exactly speed all the way home, but I am walking through the door from the garage in good time. I could hear the music before I even got out of the car, but it's only as I walk through the kitchen toward the living room that I realize it's one song on repeat.

"If I Could" by 1927.

It's one of Trav's favorites—it might actually be *the* favorite. He plays it all the time. This is a big deal because he has literally thousands of songs in his playlists, and I've been introduced to titles and artists I've never even heard of. There are only a few songs I've heard him play more than once, but this song gets played at least three times a week—and that's only that I've heard.

I asked him about it after the first couple of weeks, on a lazy Sunday when he'd played it three times.

"What's your obsession with this song?" I teased as the opening notes played, but I was genuinely curious.

His face went deliciously red, and he shrugged. "I just like it." He reached for his iPhone. "I'll change it."

I stayed his hand. "No, leave it. You like it, that's all that matters. It just…. You're always so practical, and then I discover this secret fetish for power ballads—"

"It's not a fetish!" he protested, and I leaned over and kissed him.

"Share this with me," I murmured, kissing my way down his neck. "Tell me why you love this song so much."

His breathing got heavy as I nibbled on his collarbone, and he wrapped his arms tight around me, sliding his hands over my bare back.

"I just…." He gasped. His hands roamed down toward the waistband of my sleep pants. "I… it speaks to me." He shoved down my pants, and we got a little distracted for a while.

Later, lying in each other's arms on the couch, "If I Could" long over and another playlist blaring through the speakers, he turned his head toward me.

"I know the power ballads are dumb," he began, and when I started to speak, he shook his head. "I know they are, Derek. But they're so… honest. And power is the key word. They're all about feelings being amped up and belted out there. I like that. I like that there's no hiding, no pretending. You can't sing one of those songs quietly. You have to put it all right out there."

I'd never thought of it that way. To me, power ballads were just one more aspect of the '80s to make fun of, along with big hair and shoulder pads. It'd been a long time since I'd actually stopped to listen to one—probably since my childhood.

"I can see that," I said slowly, stroking his arm. It was so nice to have my hands on him, just touching. "So why 'If I Could' specifically?"

He hesitated. "The lyrics just speak to me. I want to be someone's favorite star too." He kissed me then, and I was too preoccupied to think about it anymore. Later, I'd looked up the lyrics and found the line he was talking about. It made sense to me—doesn't everyone want to be the center of someone's universe?

Now, though, listening to the song play again, I wonder if I misinterpreted what he meant. Maybe it has to do with his job? A more literal stardom?

Shaking off the introspection, I go to find him. He's lying on the couch in the living room, staring at the ceiling, face blank.

"Trav?" I call quietly, and he turns his head.

"Hey."

I cross to the couch and sit beside him. "What's up?"

Tears well in his eyes, and something twists in my chest. "Oh, hey. It's okay. Tell me what's wrong, and I'll fix it." I can't stand to see him cry.

He makes a sound somewhere between a sob and a laugh and sits up. "You can't fix this. Don't worry, I'm just being stupid."

I grab his hand and squeeze. "Not stupid," I say firmly. "Your feelings are never stupid. Tell me."

He avoids my gaze and sighs. "How'd you find out? That's a dumb question," he says on a brittle laugh. "This place is a hotbed of gossip."

"It really is." I don't know what to say. Should I push him? Or just let him tell it in his own time—if he even wants to.

He leans against me and sighs again. "I'm good at my job," he says quietly.

"I know," I reply, just as quietly. "I've seen you. I googled you, remember?"

He lifts his head, grins at me, and I'm relieved. "I googled you too," he confesses, and then the grin dies. "That's right, you saw the feature with Laurie Henderson."

"Yeah."

"It's true. I have turned down big parts."

I hesitate. "This is probably a bad time, but just out of curiosity, how many?"

This time he laughs outright. "Seven."

Wow. My guy is awesome. "I'm so proud of you," I say impulsively, and he pulls back, looking at me in surprise.

"Why?"

I shrug. "Because you're awesome. That's it."

He blushes hotly. "Um. Well… thanks. Anyway, I'm good at my job, and I *do* a good job. I try to be reliable and always give my best. But I don't do lead roles."

He stops, and I get the feeling he wants to say more but needs encouragement. "Why not?" I squeeze his hand again. I can give encouragement.

He takes a deep breath, and I smile. We worked out not long after we started seeing each other that it's a habit we share, so I know he's preparing himself for something.

"I'm scared." The words are almost soundless, just a whisper. I wait because I don't understand. He takes another deep breath. "I…. You know… I told you that I used to get bullied."

I nod slowly, trying to work it out. Did someone bully him at work? No, wouldn't he have said so, when he told me about the bullying? "Yeah," I say, mostly because he seems to be waiting for verbal acknowledgment.

"I… It was always worse when I was… when I didn't hide. If I sort of crept around at school and didn't speak up in class, they all seemed to… forget about me, I guess. But when I was… confident, for want of a better word, it was like I had a target on my back. I've never been an outgoing person, but it started to seem better—safer—if I just… hid."

Ding ding ding. Something clicks in my head. If he didn't feel able as a teenager to be himself, to put himself out there, that explains the attachment to power ballads—right? He said it himself, what he likes about them is the no-hiding element of putting it all right out there—loudly.

"So you tried not to attract attention."

He sighs, rubs his forehead, and nods. "Yeah. It didn't make it stop completely, but it was… easier. And it tended to be more physical, which wasn't great, but it was worse when they…. I got so sick of being shoved around, but sometimes I hated it more when they just used words. They… they always went with the same theme."

"The gay thing?" Trav hadn't come out to the world until college, but I didn't figure that would have mattered to his classmates. A kid who openly took dance lessons and was involved in theater plus never had a girlfriend would have been an obvious target for bullies.

"Some," he admits, "but that didn't bug me as much. I was okay with being gay—it was probably easier for me because I knew I wanted to work in theater, and that's an industry where homosexuality is almost expected. It was more when they told me how worthless I was. No, not even that—more that I just wasn't any good at anything." He stops, takes another breath. "It was worse when I was actually doing stuff. The school play… I used to go out for it every year, and I always got a part. I loved it, but the bullying was always worse then. They'd say things like how I wasn't as good as I thought, that people were laughing behind my back, that when opening night came, I was going to make a fool of myself."

I open my mouth to utter an outraged denial, but he's shaking his head.

"I know it's not true, Derek. I *know*. The logical part of me knew even then. I'm a good dancer. I'm a good actor. I can sing well. I never got any part for any reason other than that I'm good at what I do. I know this. But… there's a tiny part of me that always worries that maybe they were right. The part that's purely emotion, with no logic. And it's dumb, but when I went to college, the bullies hit the exact same spot—I was no good, I thought I was special, but I wasn't. One day I would see what a fool I was making of myself."

He sucks in another deep breath, and this time it's shaky. My chest aches from holding in everything I want to say, and my arms ache to wrap around him, but he needs to get this out. I can't take this from him.

"That tiny, illogical, emotional part of me started to think that if two unconnected groups of people both said the same thing, there had to be an element of truth to it." He holds up a hand to stop me. "I know there isn't. I knew then, but it still bugged me. My folks could see something was worrying me, and they kept asking until I told them. We talked it out, and they pointed out everything I already knew. They even took me to see a therapist. I haven't struggled with this alone, and I know nothing they said to me was true. But I can't stop that tiny part of me from thinking it is."

He takes another deep breath and flops against the back of the couch, closing his eyes. I study him for a moment. I can see now where this is going, but I think he needs to say it out loud.

"Are you scared every time you perform?"

My words feel heavy, and part of me wishes I hadn't said them, but Trav opens his eyes and looks right at me.

"Yes."

"But you do it anyway."

He sits up, leans against me. "I have to. I love it so much… I can't imagine doing anything else with my life. When I'm too old to dance on stage, I might try going out for plays only, or I'll find another way to stay in theater."

"And you're good at your job. You know it's true. That's not me saying it because I love you; other people in the industry obviously think so too."

It's only when the silence drags out that I realize what I've said.

Fuck.

Is it too soon?

It's definitely not a good time.

Is this going to make things harder for him?

"Trav, I—"

His arms wrap tightly around me, and he buries his face against my neck. "I love you," he whispers. I close my eyes. Everything in me relaxes as I put my arms around him too. This is right. This is how it's supposed to be.

We sit there for a while, just holding each other. I don't know what my future will bring, but I know Trav will be in it. There's no fucking way I'm letting him go. Maybe I'll make that a physical reality as well as a metaphorical one—I'll just sit here holding him all night—

Except Trav has to work. He has to perform. In a lead role.

I swallow hard.

"Trav?"

"Mmm?"

The contented sound is a balm to my soul. I love knowing I can make him sound like that when not long ago he was so upset.

Too bad I have to wreck it.

I rub his back, a few long strokes, then let go. "Trav, I love you, but we need to finish this."

He sighs, squeezes me, then lets go and straightens. "I know." He meets my gaze, and there's something in the depths of his green eyes that wasn't there before. He's... more settled. Calmer.

More confident.

He's beautiful.

"I love you too," he tells me. "I'm not just saying it because you did. I've been... thinking about it for a while."

I smile at him, take his hand, lift it to my mouth, and kiss it. I want to kiss his mouth, those soft, pink lips, but I'm afraid if I start, I won't stop.

Then I drag the elephant back into the room.

"You're good at your job and you love it, even though you're afraid every time you go on stage."

"Yeah. For a long time, I used to throw up every time I had to perform. I was so convinced I'd make an idiot of myself, that I'd freeze or just plain suck and ruin the show for the audience, for the rest of the cast, for everyone. I… convinced myself that even if I did end up sucking, I was such an insignificant part of the show it wouldn't matter. That worked really well when I was just in the chorus. When… when I started getting better parts, I had to tell myself that as long as I wasn't in the spotlight, as long as I wasn't the star of the show, it didn't matter if maybe I fucked something up. And… that works for me."

"But you've basically convinced yourself you can never have a lead role, ever," I protest. He nods.

"I know. And now tonight I have to, and I'm screwed." Tears fill his eyes again. "I don't want to be a laughingstock, Derek. I don't want to let everyone down. I don't want them all feeling sorry for me because the audience walked out and Rick has to give refunds."

Well, just fuck that.

"Travis—" I stop. "What's your middle name?"

He gives me a weird look. "I don't have one. My name's not Travis, either."

I blink, sidetracked. "It's not? Is it just Trav?"

He shakes his head and swipes away a tear that's rolling down his cheek. "Traveon."

"That's unusual." I kiss the spot where the tear was, and he smiles shakily at me.

"It's Welsh. My dad's dad emigrated from Wales when he was a kid, and my parents decided to give us Welsh names as a reminder of our heritage."

That's pretty cool. I didn't know his grandfather was Welsh, and I'm about to ask him about it when I realize exactly how far off track I've gotten. I clear my throat.

"Traveon Jones, I can't believe what I'm hearing!"

He looks confused. "You can't believe I'm part Welsh?"

I laugh. I have to. I mean, come on, you did too. After a second Trav joins in.

"You know what I meant," I chide. He huffs, but nods.

"I know."

"You know that Rick wouldn't risk another show like this afternoon."

"Rick doesn't know I'm a risk," he points out, and I leap into the opening.

"That's right; he doesn't. Rick's a professional who's worked in the industry for… how long?"

Trav can see where I'm going with this. "Twenty-five years," he mutters, looking at his hands.

"And in twenty-five years, he's probably worked with a lot of people. *Day Dot* won awards, didn't it?"

He nods.

"So if Rick, who's been working with good performers for twenty-five years, doesn't think you're a risk, maybe that means something."

He heaves a sigh. "Derek, you're trying to appeal to logic, and that won't work. I'm not an idiot. I know I have the ability to do this. But knowing doesn't change the way I feel, and I'm terrified that feeling this way is going to fuck it all up."

What the hell do I say to that? "I guess there's only one way to find out."

His head jerks up, and he stares at me. I keep my hard-ass face intact. I want to hold him and tell him everything will be okay, but that's not going to help.

"Will you be there?" he whispers. I'm not sure what he wants to hear, so I go with the truth.

"Yes," I say firmly. "And if it looks like you're fucking it all up, I swear on all that's holy that I'll find a way to stop the show. I'll… hell, I don't know. I'll start a fire in the men's room so the fire alarm will go off."

He laughs again, and that smile warms my insides. "You will not," he scoffs.

I hold his gaze. "I will if it matters to you this much."

We sit there staring at each other. I can see Trav working through his fears, see the thoughts processing behind his gaze. Finally, he nods.

"Okay. I think I might vomit, though."

I'M NERVOUS as hell as I wait for the theater doors to open. In the end, I drove Trav to work, telling him I'd grab some dinner while I waited—but there's no way I could eat. I know he has the ability to do this, but I'm terrified that he's convinced himself he can't, and that it's going to be some kind of self-fulfilling prophecy. If he bombs this tonight, he's never going to get past this fear—and I'm worried it's going to affect his self-esteem in other ways, maybe damage his career.

So, food? Not tonight. Not until the curtain comes down on a great performance.

I'm pacing by the doors when I hear my name. That's not uncommon—incestuous community, remember? Plus, there's only so much to do in Joyville, and the shows at the village are a big component. It's a relief to see Dimi when I look up, along with a couple of the performers from JU who volunteer at the community theater with Trav—Sam and Parker, if I remember right.

I force a smile. "Hey. You came."

"Wouldn't miss it," Sam says enthusiastically. "Man, I'm so stoked! This is awesome for Trav."

Parker's grinning from ear to ear. "Kind of puts paid to my fledgling plan to convince him to stay here, though. Once he's had a taste of being a star, no way he'll be happy with theme park performances."

Uh…. "You were going to convince Trav to stay?" Wow. Surprised? Me? I mean, don't think I haven't thought of it, because I have. I even talked to Pete about it, on the down low—I know he's been thinking about retiring in a few years, and I figured Trav could perform until then and then move into a coordinator-slash-choreography role. He's good at it, so…. But in the end Pete and I agreed that Trav probably needs more than that. After all, most of our performers are just starting out—they're all so *young*, like Sam and Parker. They move on to jobs like Trav's—if they're lucky. This would be a huge step back for him. So even though I haven't given up on him moving here just yet, I haven't worked it all out.

The other option, of course, is for me to follow him to New York. With my experience and track record, I could get a job pretty easily. I'd hate leaving JU, but I think I could do it for Trav. It's a backup plan, though, because I'd *really* hate leaving JU, and I think Trav's starting to love it here too.

Parker shrugs. "Yeah, of course. He's a great performer, really fantastic as a volunteer, and a lot of fun. He's got you here, and I figured...." He shrugs again. "Why not give it a go, right?"

"Right," I say, making a mental note to tap Parker for ideas if I can't come up with anything myself.

"Is Trav excited?" Dimi asks. From the way he's looking at me, I can tell he knows everything is not all sunshine and roses.

"That's one word for it." Excited can mean worked up and on tenterhooks, right? It doesn't strictly have to be happy. I think.

The ushers start opening the doors into the theater, and my heartbeat picks up. "Where are you sitting?" I ask, mostly to prevent myself from rushing inside. The show isn't due to start for another twenty minutes or more, so I'm not going to be any better off in there.

Dimi pulls his ticket from his pocket and flashes it at me. Their seats are not far from mine. Is that a good thing or bad?

I mentally smack myself. Am I seriously wondering if the location of their seats is important? I'm in an even worse state than I thought.

"You guys want a drink?" I hear myself say. "On me. Come on, let's hit the bar." I usher them in that direction, and they come willingly enough—Sam and Parker seem pretty eager, actually, and hey, free drink, can't blame them—but Dimi looks a bit surprised.

The drink helps. These guys are pretty cool—I already knew Dimi is awesome, but we don't really hang out outside of work, and I barely know the other two—and they're a great distraction. It's not long before the bell is chiming for us to take our seats.

I settle in, breathing so deeply that there's a very real danger I'll hyperventilate. You'd think it was me who had to get up there and perform from the way I'm behaving. It's just... I can't stand the thought of Trav being hurt by this.

As the music begins to play and the curtain goes up, I shut my eyes, then force them open. I'm going to be with him for every second of this.

My nails bite into my palms as he and the guy playing his usual role— that Jim kid who fucked up this afternoon—wander out into the office set. I'm close enough to the stage to see their faces clearly. Jim looks hella nervous. Like, I think he might vomit any second. Trav looks fine, calm, relaxed, completely in the role... to someone who doesn't know him. His tension isn't overt, but I can see it, and as he opens his mouth to deliver the first line, I hold my breath.

It goes fine.

So does the rest of the opening dialogue. Not brilliantly—I wouldn't say they set the stage alight—but fine. Jim's voice shakes a little at first, but after a minute he settles. Trav seems to relax a bit too.

Just as well, because if I remember right, in a second he's going to need to sing and dance, and the first number is pretty full-on.

Sure enough, the music starts softly. Trav and Jim are still bantering, but the music is ramping up slowly, building....

Trav bursts into song, leaping across the stage. I'm not gonna lie, it's a little shaky. Definitely not as smooth as he usually is, and I wonder if this is when it all ends. Is he going to lose confidence?

No.

In fact, I should be ashamed of myself for even thinking he might. It's like the music imbues him with poise and assurance. By the end of the song, his usual stage charisma is back, and as the scene progresses, he *owns* the show. Oh, he's not perfect—he hasn't performed the role before, and there're a few slips—once he opens his mouth to deliver a line that would usually be his—but nothing show-stopping, and it all gets smoother as time passes.

Thank God.

I settle into my seat and let myself enjoy the performance. Even Jim seems to be doing better. Although I don't know him, I'm glad, because it would be really soul destroying to bomb out in two consecutive shows.

When the curtain comes down for intermission, I'm grinning. My boyfriend is fucking amazing. I knew that, of course—I've seen him before. But with the spotlight focused mostly on him, he *shines*. Most important, he's relaxed. That tension is gone.

The lights come up, and I bound to my feet. I'm energized, excited—and I have a plan. We have to celebrate. Trav and I both went into this thinking it could be a disaster, imagining how we'd need to recover from the night, and neither of us considered what a triumph this is for him. His first performance in a lead role! A champagne supper—whether with friends or just the two of us will depend on what he wants—and flowers. It might seem stupid, but he's going to get flowers tonight if it kills me.

I'm already scrolling through my contacts as I inch with the crowd toward the lobby. I've never actually sent flowers here before—I send them to my mom on her birthday and Mothers' Day, but obviously that florist is in New York. JU has its own florist department and outlets in many of the resorts, but not one in the village. I try to work out which resort is closest and most likely to have something nice left *and* be able to deliver to Trav by the end of the show.

"Derek." A hand lands on my shoulder, and I glance back at Dimi. Sam and Parker are right behind him. All three are grinning.

"He's amazing!" Sam enthuses. "He started kind of slow, but he was probably nervous. Isn't he amazing?"

"He is," I agree. "Dimi, help. I need flowers. Where—"

"The Chateau," he says immediately, reaching for his pocket. "Do you want me to—"

"Nah, I've got it," I assure him. "I just wasn't sure where at this time of night. Thanks." I hold up my phone. "I'm just gonna…." They all nod, and I hit the contact for the switchboard at the Chateau, which is one of my resorts, then lift the phone to my ear, plugging the other ear with a finger in an attempt to block out the noise of the crowd as we continue to inch toward the lobby.

I'm smiling the whole time. Today has been *epic*.

CHAPTER TWELVE

Trav

THE CURTAIN comes down after the third encore, and we leave the stage. For the first time all night, I let my grin burst free. I was so scared…. But there was no reason to be. There have been times when I was uncertain of a performance, but this isn't one of them. I killed it tonight, even with the tiny mistakes.

I'm not being immodest either—that's what everyone's been saying all night. During intermission, Rick and John were almost giddy with joy. I refused to let my guard down, though, just in case.

I change into street clothes and have started taking off the makeup when I hear the shouts, and my grin gets wider. I spin around and brace before Parker and Sam crash into me.

"You're fucking awesome!" Parker shouts, jumping up and down and pounding me on the back.

"That was amazing!" Sam grips my arm and shakes it.

"Back off, you morons," Dimi says, somehow sneaking between them and grabbing me in a hug. "Great job," he murmurs. "You were fantastic."

"Thanks, guys." The grin is still on my face. I'm starting to think maybe it'll be there forever. "Is, uh, have you seen Derek?" I kind of expected him to be here by now. I mean, these guys have become pretty good friends, and I'm glad they're here, but….

Sam snorts, and Parker laughs outright.

"He got held up," Dimi says. "He'll be here any second." He keeps a straight face, but his eyes are dancing.

Hmm.

I'm about to drill for more information when someone gasps. I look up…

…and see a floral bouquet with legs.

129

Seriously. There's a massive arrangement of the most amazing flowers in shades of red, orange, and yellow walking toward me.

"I guess he figured out how to get it through the door," Dimi murmurs.

Oh. My. God.

Derek?

"Derek?" I call. There's a muffled curse, some shuffling of flowers, and then his head, his gorgeous blond head, pops out from between two lilies.

"Hey," he says.

I laugh.

BY THE time the curtain comes down on Thursday night, I'm feeling... thoughtful. The last thirty or so hours have been tumultuous, to say the least. I went from being absolutely terrified and lacking in self-esteem to elated that Derek loves me, to nervous and sick that I had to do the performances but secure in the knowledge that I wasn't alone, to cautiously optimistic, to flat-out thrilled. Emotional roller coaster, right? I've been feeling really great today, confident, happy—after all, everything in my life has fallen into place. I gotta admit, I get a real high from being in the lead role. I've loved my career so far, but there's something about being the focus of the scene, of the whole show, that feels incredible.

So why thoughtful now, instead of still floating on cloud nine—or disappointed that my time in the spotlight is over? It's got to do with my future career path. When Derek and I finally got home last night—really late, after a champagne celebration supper with half a dozen people from the show, Dimi, Parker, and Sam—I was still hyper. We wrestled the flowers into the house, I jumped him in the kitchen (because that's a great way to work off energy, plus he bought out a florist for me, plus he's hot, incredible, and loves me), and then we fell into bed. He drifted off pretty much right away—holding my hand, by the way—but I was still kind of energized. I started planning a call to my agent. He's been lining up possible jobs for me for when I get back to New York in August, and I know without a doubt that he'll be ecstatic if I tell him he doesn't have

130

to stick to supporting roles. He's been trying to talk me into a starring part for years.

Did you catch that "if"? Last night, when I was lying in the dark beside the love of my life, flying high on my success and plotting out the course of my career, it was a "when."

Then this morning I woke up when his alarm went off, stretched, and sneaked a cuddle and a kiss before he got out of bed. I watched his bare backside as he walked toward the en suite bathroom, and it struck me: this isn't going to last. When I go back to New York, I won't have the workday mornings. I won't be able to slip in a coffee break with Derek, or lunch if his schedule allows it. There won't be any more lazy Sunday mornings. Even if we decide to do long-distance, those things will be few and far between, and they won't be everyday things. We won't be part of each other's routine. I'll miss that.

Worse, though—last night, when I was dreaming of what my career will become, of my name in lights and some really amazing parts, always in my mind was the image of Derek there with me. Sitting in the audience on opening night, cheering me on. Bringing me flowers. Taking me out to celebrate a brilliant performance. I'd imagined the opening night of the first show in which I had the headline role, and Derek was there.

While I listened to Derek get in the shower, the first threads of thoughtfulness slipped into my mind. Derek and I need to have a conversation about our relationship.

The next few threads appeared just before lunchtime, when Mark called. He'd spoken to Rick and was calling to congratulate me.

"I've been waiting for you to get past whatever it was that was holding you back," he'd enthused. "When you get back to New York, you're gonna take them all by storm! Rick was raving about how great you were. Ha ha, good thing your contract is up in July, or I'd worry about my job!" He was joking, of course, but it reminded me of how very cut-throat my colleagues can be when it comes to the top parts. Sure, there's a lot of competition for supporting roles as well, but that level of ruthlessness isn't there. I've managed to make friends with a lot of star performers who are generally perceived as standoffish, because they know I'm not—wasn't—interested in the top job. They felt more relaxed around me. Is that going to change now?

Still more threads in the early afternoon, when I got a call from Laurie Henderson, the entertainment journalist who did a feature on me for a popular Broadway publication last year.

"I just ran into Mark Aston," he told me. "He says you're filling in for him in *Day Dot*. Is it true? You've taken a lead role?"

"Just last night and tonight," I protested. "Mark will be back tomorrow." I found myself wishing I hadn't answered the phone. I didn't usually have to deal with the press—most of the publicity around shows centers on the stars, with supporting actors only occasionally being called on for interview if the part is particularly interesting. I'd only agreed to do the feature last year when Laurie approached me because my agent thought it was a good idea, and Rick had added weight to that, since *Day Dot* had been about to open.

"Does this mean we can expect to see you in some starring roles when you come back to New York?" Laurie pressed, and that was when it struck me. If I start going for the big parts on Broadway, I'm going to have to deal with publicity a lot more. I'm going to have to do interviews. Journalists are going to want to talk to me.

I fobbed Laurie off and spent the rest of the afternoon mulling it all over. In the end, I decided to do the show tonight and see how I felt after—and then take my time thinking about it. After all, I'm still contracted with *Day Dot* until the end of July. Nothing can happen until then. I don't have to decide anything right away. In fact, I don't have to decide anything until and unless I get offered a lead role.

Now the show is over, and I'm feeling thoughtful. It was an amazing night. I'm lucky in that it's been years since I've had to perform in a show I didn't like—these days, I can be choosy about which parts I go out for because work is steady. So tonight I got to perform the lead role in a show I really like, and it was great.

I change and clean off my makeup, and Derek comes backstage to meet me. He was in the audience again tonight, even though I told him he didn't have to come. We had a really late night last night and he was up at his usual time for work this morning, so I thought he should stay home and take it easy, but he insisted. Still, it gives me a legitimate reason to put off my castmates who want to go out and celebrate again, because I don't think they would have accepted "I'm pondering my career path" as an excuse.

Derek and I chitchat on the way home, but I'm distracted, and I know he can tell. For all I've been telling myself that I don't need to make any decisions yet, I can't stop thinking about it.

I wander into the living room and turn on the TV. I'm pretty sure there isn't anything on that I want to watch, but the noise makes for a good distraction—and I can always pretend to actually be watching it as a cover for thinking. Clever plan, huh? Too bad it didn't work.

Derek turns the TV off and sits beside me. "You're quiet," he says over my halfhearted protest.

I shrug. "Tired, I guess. It's been a crazy couple of days." I smile when I remember for the millionth time that part of that craziness was him saying he loves me.

"Yeah." His gaze is searching, and a hint of something in his gorgeous blue eyes gets all my attention—worry. "But you don't normally go all quiet when you're tired. Uh, I guess you can't wait to get back to New York and start auditioning, hey?"

I lean over and kiss him, mostly because I can and it feels good, but also because I don't like seeing him worried. "To be honest, I'm not sure."

He blinks, and I'm tempted to pull out my phone and take a pic, because I've never seen that stunned look on his face before. He shakes his head as if to clear it. "You're not sure about what?"

Slumping back into the comfy couch, I sigh. "Whether I want to be a Broadway star with my name in lights."

He shifts so he's settled just as comfortably as I am, but facing me. The shocked expression has given way to a considering one. "You don't want fame," he says matter-of-factly, and my smile this time is because he already knows me so well. I point a finger at him.

"Got it in one. Not just fame, though. I love my job, and I've met a lot of great people in the industry, but there's also a lot of backbiting and bitchiness. And the higher up you get, the worse it is." I close my eyes for a second because I *am* tired too. "I never wanted to be famous, not really. Appreciated for my work, yes, definitely, especially by my peers. But not famous. I don't like having a lot of attention on me." I make a face. "And yes, I know that sounds dumb considering I get up on stage every night for hundreds, if not thousands of people to stare at."

He shakes his head. "Nah, that's different. It's not you they're staring at, it's the character. Plus, you're part of an overall production." He looks like he's thinking about what I've said, considering all the angles. I've gotten to know that look. His sharp, analytical mind is part of the reason Derek is so good at his job, and honestly, it's kind of a turn-on to know he's so smart. "But if you could have the lead roles without the fame and politics?"

"I'd be there in a heartbeat," I say promptly, without even thinking about it. "I would kill to have some of those parts. I...." The words stick in my throat, more out of habit than anything else. *This is Derek*, I remind myself. *He knows.* My stomach clenches nervously anyway. I don't know if I'll ever be comfortable talking about this. "There have been a lot of parts over the years that I really wanted. Two of the ones that were offered to me were...." I shake my head. I can't even think of the words to describe how fabulous it would have been to perform those characters. "It really hurt to turn them down. And now I can go for them, and I was—*am*—so excited about that. But I really don't want to deal with the rest of that shit, so...." I shrug. "Maybe I'll just go for the ones I really want. If I'm not consistently in lead roles, it might not be as bad."

"That's a good idea. And it would give you breathing space if you still took the occasional supporting role." He takes my arm and tugs me closer, and I go willingly into his embrace.

I have time to think about this.

CHAPTER THIRTEEN

Derek

I'M AT the park when Kim calls me.

Life's been good—no, *great*. Seriously, the only fly in my ointment lately is that every passing day brings us closer to the end of July and Trav's departure. Well, he doesn't actually have to leave when *Day Dot* does, and he's not going to, but he can't hang around indefinitely without a job—that's not him. I've yet to come up with the perfect solution to this, but I will. I'm working on it. And other than that, the month since we told each other we love each other has been… incredible. I love living with him. I love having him in my life. I love him.

So I'm in a good mood, going along with Don as he does his routine weekly check-ins with his senior staff, when Kim's name flashes on my iPhone screen. I've just wrapped up a conversation with the concessions manager and have a few minutes before we check in with the maintenance supervisor, so I excuse myself to Don and answer.

"Hi, Kim." Maybe my tone is just a bit breezy. It's that kind of day, sunny, with a light wind to keep things from getting too hot—although "too hot" is relative in southern Georgia in early July. How can anyone be unhappy on a day like this?

"Derek, where are you?" Kim's tone is *not* breezy, and instantly I know my day is not going to be happy for much longer.

"I'm at the park. What's happened?" I'm mentally reviewing everything that's happened lately that might make her freak out, and there's nothing. Even if someone is suing—which happens way more than you would think, and usually over dumb shit—that wouldn't make Kim sound like the zombie apocalypse is coming.

"I need you back at your office now for a briefing. Don't talk to anyone, especially the press."

Fuck. I gesture to Don, and he walks toward me.

135

"Kim, give me a hint here."

"Kylie Rutherford has made a statement to the press. I'm sorry, Derek, I have to make a couple more calls. I'll see you ASAP, yeah?"

"Yeah," I manage to get in before she ends the call. I still don't quite understand—what the heck can Kylie Rutherford have said to make Kim panic like that?—but Kim's the best, so if she's worried, I should be too. I turn to Don. "I'm sorry, I've been called back to HQ. I'll try and get back out later in the week to talk to the others." I don't actually have to, but since I've spoken with some of the team leaders, it looks bad for me to leave others out.

"No worries," he assures me, and I take off for the staff entrance and my car.

Twenty minutes later, I'm parking at the main admin building, and I'm seriously worried. My phone's rung twice with calls from enterprising members of the press who managed to get hold of the number. I referred them both to the media office, telling them I wasn't at liberty to discuss the situation. Never mind that I don't actually know what the damn situation *is*.

I stride into the foyer, and the place *hushes*. Seriously. It goes quiet. I can't remember the last time that happened—oh, wait. I do. It was earlier this year, right after JU had to close down a park for a few days. The news went out, and when the AD of that district walked into the building the next morning, everyone shut up. I wasn't actually there, but I heard all about it. Several hours later, he got fired.

I shake that thought from my head as I bypass the elevators and head for the stairs, ignoring all the stares. I could grab one of the bystanders and demand to know what's going on, but that's just going to delay me, and Kim will have the most current and accurate information anyway. Plus, nobody sees me sweat. Always in control, that's me.

By the time I reach my office, adrenaline is pumping through me. I'm ready. Whatever's happened, I'm taking it down.

Gina is standing by her desk, talking on the phone, her face pale. When she sees me, she covers the microphone of her headset and says, "Kim and Dimi are in your office."

"Thanks, Gina." That's a relief. Dimi will have things in hand. I walk in to find them both on the phone—separately—with Dimi also tapping away at his tablet. He looks up, and his expression gives me pause.

This might be even worse than I thought.

He ends the call and scrambles up from his seat. Kim gives me a distracted nod and paces over to the window. "Derek, I need you to authorize this," Dimi says urgently, thrusting the tablet at me. I take it and scan the district-wide memo he wants to send with a red flag. It's the red flag that needs my authorization—I'm the only one who can send those to the whole district at once.

The memo tells me nothing—it basically just reminds all staff that if they are approached by a member of the press, they need to refer them to the media office, and that they are contractually obliged not to discuss anything related to JU with anyone not employed by JU. That sounds innocent enough, right? But Dimi wouldn't be red flagging something like this if the shit wasn't about to hit the fan.

I tap in the code to authorize it, and send the memo.

"Derek," Kim says, finally off the phone. Thank God, because I don't think my nerves can take waiting any longer. "Thanks for getting back here so fast."

"What's going on?" I ask her point-blank, and in response she holds out her tablet. I take it and see what appears to be a press release on the screen. Right. She said Kylie Rutherford issued a statement to the press. I read it.

Then read it again.

And one more time, because I must be imagining it. This cannot be fucking real. I pin Kim with an incredulous look. "She's claiming to have been drugged and forced to kill her husband by JU employees?"

Yep, folks. That's what it said. There's a little more detail than that—according to Whack Job Rutherford, her husband's murder was a JU conspiracy that began with them being advised by a concierge to have dinner at a specific restaurant, then recommended particular dishes and drinks by the waiter there, and ended with her waking from a "dazed, dreamlike state" to find that she'd been arrested and her husband was dead. There's also some lovely editorializing warning people about JU, since clearly the conspirators must have members in high places, perhaps even in senior management, to have gotten away with it. Personally, I think she overplays it a bit with the line where she wonders how often it's happened in the past and been covered up, but it's the sort of thing the press and the public will eat up.

I take a deep breath, hand Kim back her tablet, and take another deep breath. I open my mouth to speak, then close it and take another deep breath.

"Does Ken know?" I finally say, starting to pace in front of my desk.

"Yes," Kim tells me. "I managed to get a copy of the press release before it went live anywhere, but it got out about five minutes after I called you. Ken knows, and so does corporate." She's referring to Joy Incorporated's corporate head office in LA. "Ken was out"—oh fuck, it's golf day—"but he's on his way in. I've got a call in to the local police to see if there's any possible way what she says can be true."

What the FUCK! I turn so fast she takes a step back. "You don't really think—" I begin hotly, but she interrupts.

"No. I honestly don't. And even if by some freak chance it turns out that a couple of employees did conspire to commit murder, there's no way in hell it's as widespread as she says. But, Derek, I have to cover all angles. When we release our statement, and that has to be soon, I need to be able to say with complete honesty that what she claims is impossible. We can't backtrack on something like this later if it turns out she pissed off a server and they slipped a roofie in her drink to get her back, and it all spiraled out of control from there."

I suck in a deep breath, then another. The technique appears to be failing for the first time ever. She's right, but that doesn't stop my anger.

Her phone rings, and we all stop. "This is Kim," she answers, and then her expression changes and she waves at me. "Detective, thank you for calling. Do you mind if I put you on speaker? I have AD Derek Bryer here with me. Thank you." She pulls the phone away from her ear and taps the screen. "Detective Gooding is in charge of the investigation into the Rutherford murder, Derek," she says by way of introduction.

"Yes, we met." I remember him as a tall, thin, balding man with a hard stare. He struck me at the time as a man who didn't care about social niceties and politics so much as getting the job done. "Hello, Detective."

"Mr. Bryer," he says shortly. I seem to remember telling him to call me Derek, but that's not important now.

"Detective, I'm not sure if you've seen—" Kim begins, but she's cut off.

"Our media liaison sent me the press release, and my phone's been ringing off the hook. I know why you called." The words are abrupt, but I hear a slight softening in his tone. "The investigation is closed and charges have been laid, so this is all a matter of public record, but I'll save you the time reading the report. We have the security camera footage of the area around the bungalow where the Rutherfords were staying. It shows them leaving for dinner, a maid entering shortly after, which we were advised was for the requested turn-down service, the maid departing, the Rutherfords returning, neither showing obvious signs of being drugged or intoxicated, and then nothing until the maid entered the next morning. A toxicology screen was performed on Kylie Rutherford and on the remains of Peter Rutherford, and no drugs were found. They'd both consumed alcohol but were well under the legal limit. I just spoke with our toxicology expert, and she confirms that if Mrs. Rutherford had been under the influence to the degree she describes in her statement—that she didn't regain full awareness until after her arrest—the substance would definitely have still been in her system at the time the sample was taken."

My knees weaken, and I lean against the desk. This is good, and his rapid, facts-only monotone is reassuring. I take a deep breath and open my mouth to thank him, but he's not done.

"The psychological assessment found Mrs. Rutherford to be entirely sane. Ruthless, amoral, arrogant, and completely self-serving, but sane. Interviews we conducted with staff at the Rutherford home indicated that in June of last year, Mrs. Rutherford discovered that Mr. Rutherford was having an affair. The staff are aware of this because it was the topic of many screaming arguments for weeks. Eventually the fighting stopped, and Mrs. Rutherford gave her husband the cold shoulder for about six months, ending abruptly in late January, when she became happy again. They will testify to that. Her change in mood coincides with an online order of a custom-made suitcase with a hidden compartment containing a built-in knife sheath, and a credit card charge at a custom knifemaker store. The owner remembers her well and has confirmed that the knife used in the murder is the one he made to her specifications. We have the order forms, and he will testify also. These all speak to premeditation. Even with her very expensive lawyers, Mrs. Rutherford will have a tough time convincing a jury that she was pissed at her husband, bought these items, brought them with her to Joy Universe, but that his death was a result of her being drugged by a magic drug that leaves no traces and coerced by people who were never there."

"So why is she doing this, then?" Kim asks, beginning to pace. Me, I'm still leaning against the desk for support. "I mean, what's the point? It sounds like she never even tried to hide what she was planning, and then she throws out this story?"

Gooding sighs. "I don't know exactly," he admits. "I can tell you that she never spoke a word about any conspiracy or of being coerced while she was in custody, and her attorneys never mentioned it either. Maybe she just wants some media attention? Maybe someone at JU annoyed her, and she wants revenge. Or maybe this is a tactic to sway a future jury in her favor, muddy the waters. She's had a few minor charges laid against her in the past—D and D, minor assault, DUI—and they all went away, either withdrawn by the complainant or dealt with by some expensive lawyers. The impression I got when I interviewed her was that she thought she could throw enough money at this to make it go away, too. She was arrogant beyond anything I've ever seen."

"So we're just collateral damage to her?" I can hear the bitterness in my voice. Even when the accusations are shown to be groundless, this is going to affect us. People believe what they see on TV, and they love to believe the worst of large corporations.

"Sorry, Mr. Bryer."

"Derek," I mutter. It's reflexive, I swear. "Thank you for telling us this, Detective. We really appreciate it."

"No problem," he says, then hesitates. "Look, when I was out there for the investigation, I saw how you run that place. Your staff were as helpful as they could be. Sure, sometimes when I asked for stuff, they had me wait while they got permission, but I never had to wait long, and I never had to jump through hoops. And the service they gave the customers was better than anywhere I've seen. If I can see that without having stayed at the hotel, then people who've stayed in the past will remember it. This is going to blow over."

I grimace. It's supposed to be a smile, but never quite makes it. There's a lead weight in my stomach.

"Thank you, Detective." Kim comes to my rescue. "If you could send me a copy of the police report, I'd really appreciate it. We have a request in, but it's still working through the system." She winds up the call while I stare at my feet, taking deep breaths. I can hear the soft tap-tap of Dimi on his tablet. He's been working away industriously all through the call.

"It's not so bad," Kim tries to reassure me. I give her a flat look. "It's not," she insists. "It's not good, in fact it's terrible, but it could be worse. It could be true."

She has a point.

"So what happens now?"

Kim sighs and sits in one of the visitor chairs. "We release a statement denying it all. It's tricky, because her husband has just been brutally murdered. We don't want to seem insensitive to that."

What? I run the sentence through in my head. Nope, still weird. "Her husband was brutally murdered by her," I point out incredulously. "How sensitive can she be?"

"Allegedly," Kim reminds me. "Until she's convicted, it's all alleged."

My groan is forestalled by a knock. Gina pokes her head around the door. "Ken is waiting for you in the conference room," she says.

I stand. It's going to be a long day.

IT GOT worse, of course. Kylie Rutherford didn't go quite as far as calling a press conference, but she didn't lock the front gates of her megamansion, and when the media came swarming at her door, she opened it and answered questions—selected ones, of course, like "Kylie, did you hear any of your attackers call each other by name?" Amazingly, she *did*—according to her statement, she can't remember exactly what happened while she was "drugged," but she can remember the names used by "attackers" who didn't exist. Do I sound bitter? That might be because the names she tossed out there are Paul, Chris, and Kate, of which we have numerous at just Tiki and the restaurant she frequented that night, *and*…. Derek. Apparently, "Derek" was in charge.

How long do you think it took the gutter press to make a big deal of that? I didn't leave the office until after nine, but my neighbor called me at six to tell me there were reporters on my front lawn. I called the cops on them. I was just glad that Trav had already left for work.

He came by the office as soon as he heard, but I was in meetings all afternoon, trying to hammer out a concrete plan of action. Within hours of the press release, park attendance dropped. People just left. And the word from the resorts is that a lot of people are checking out early, and others have asked whether they would be refunded the remainder of their stay if they had to leave.

It's a nightmare.

It's a disaster. And not just for JU and Joy Inc.—the town of Joyville is mostly populated by JU employees. If this goes on too long and we have to start laying people off, there aren't enough local jobs to employ them all. People will start moving away, and that's going to cause the town economy to collapse.

I know what you're thinking. Don't borrow trouble, Derek. Right? After all, this is only day one, and we haven't actually done the heinous thing we've been accused of—and we have strong evidence to support that.

It doesn't stop me from worrying.

I drag myself out of my car and into the house. It's empty, of course—Trav sent a text that he'd stay home from work if I wanted him to, but since I was going to be working late, I told him not to. And anyway, what could he have done? I'm planning to mope in the dark for a while, and it's not like I could do that with him home. He doesn't need to see me all droopy. After all, who wants a sad sack boyfriend?

Flopping down on the couch, I vaguely realize I'm hungry. Ken's assistant ordered in food for us a few hours ago, but I couldn't eat much. I was too depressed by how very unproductive our meetings were. I mean, sure, the statement got released, followed shortly after by one from the police confirming that there was no evidence to show JU employees had been involved in any way, but the rest of the time we were just trying to work out how to stop the crash. Discount vouchers to encourage people to stay were the big win of the night.

I haven't closed the living room curtains, and the glow from the street filters in, dimly lighting the room. I stare into the gloom, my stomach a tight, hard knot of anger and frustration, and turn the problem over and over in my head. How can I make this better?

The light snaps on, and I blink. What the…?

"Derek?" It's Trav, crossing the room with a worried look on his face. "What are you doing sitting in the dark?"

I shake my head. "I was just thinking." I dredge up a smile. It's completely fake, but hopefully doesn't look it. "You're home early."

The worry ramps up a notch. "No, actually. How long have you been sitting here?"

I look at my watch. Yeah, he's not early. I've been lost in my head for about an hour and a half. I shrug. "Not that long. How was the show tonight?"

The worry morphs to… caution? "Okay," he says slowly. "The theater wasn't as full as usual, but that might be because the run is coming to an end." That's an outright lie, and we both know it. "How were things at work tonight?"

I get up. "Not great, but what can you do? I think I'm gonna hit the sack. Tomorrow is going to be a busy day."

"Wait, Derek." He grabs my arm as I start to walk past. "Are you okay? I heard the news reports. What she said about…. I heard."

I take a deep breath, because he doesn't need to see me melt down. "I'm not thrilled about it," I say honestly. "It's pretty crap, actually. But it's not like I can do anything."

That doesn't seem to satisfy him, really, but he lets go of my arm, and I dredge up another smile. "Are you coming to bed, or are you too revved tonight?"

"I'll be there in a minute," he says, and his smile looks just as fake as mine feels.

CHAPTER FOURTEEN

Trav

I'M TOTALLY freaked out. Since the shit hit the fan at JU on Wednesday, things have just been getting worse and worse. I don't mean there were more "revelations," although on Thursday some conspiracy blogger showed Bitchface Kylie Rutherford a photo of Derek, said "Kylie, this is Derek Bryer, an assistant director at Joy Universe," and she exclaimed with what were very obviously crocodile tears, "He's the one! He was there, the one in charge." My only knowledge of the court system comes from books and TV, but I'm pretty sure that wouldn't stand up. Still, it was another blow, with editorializing nut jobs protesting against JU, and Derek in particular. Honestly, after the fifth diatribe I read/heard, I gave up in disgust. It's pretty clear that these people have no idea, that they're just jumping on a bandwagon, gleeful that they have the chance to drag someone down. I worked once with a dancer from Australia who called it tall poppy syndrome.

It could be worse—it's hard to see past the negatives right now, especially with Derek being directly affected, but it really could be worse. Most of the negative publicity is coming from the trashier news outlets. The more reputable ones covered the initial statement, but their follow-up reports keep stating that there's no evidence to indicate JU was involved. A few of the talk show hosts are openly saying that Kylie Rutherford is just trying to distract the public. But... people love to think the worst, right? Derek's not talking about it much, but from what I can gather, this is hitting really hard at JU's bottom line, even though it's only been a few days.

What worries me the most is that Derek's *not talking about it*. At a time like this, shouldn't he be pissed? Ranting? Unloading all his frustrations? Instead he says, in that nothing tone, that he's angry, but hey, can't do anything, and do I want to add anything to the grocery list/ go to bed/watch whatever-the-fuck on TV?

That's not normal, right? He's repressing his feelings, and Derek is such an open, outgoing personality that it strikes me as intrinsically wrong for him to repress anything.

Or maybe it's just me he doesn't want to talk to?

I know he loves me, but maybe it's not the same love I feel for him. Maybe his love for me is more of a "friends who fuck and have a great time together but aren't meant to last forever" love. That would break my heart, because I'm in this for the long haul. I thought he knew that. *Day Dot* is due to close at the village in just a few weeks, but I've already told my agent to push back any auditions until September, and to turn down any that would need me to start work before January. Derek knows that. We also talked about going somewhere at Christmastime, and when we were looking at flights, they were all departing from here. I hadn't exactly decided to move here, but I was thinking of taking some time off work to sort things out between us, work out what the best path is for the future. There's no work for me here except in the parks, and that would be a huge step back for my career.

I thought Derek and I were on the same page, that we were both intent on working out a way for our relationship to move successfully forward, but... was I wrong? If he won't talk to me about something that's creating such huge upheaval in his life, maybe he's not as invested in us as I am.

Or maybe I'm just making this all about me because of my insecurities, and I shouldn't be. Maybe him not wanting to talk has nothing to do with me at all.

And I've come full circle. Whatever reason he has for bottling everything up, it's not healthy and will just lead to worse problems later.

I let it go on Wednesday night. After all, it had just happened. Maybe he needed time to process. I let it go Thursday, too, because there were some new shocks and... well, I was still waiting for him to lean on me. Yesterday, I stewed about it all day, and finally decided I needed to force the issue... but after a good night's sleep.

Which brings us to now. Bright and early Saturday morning. I'm due at the community theater in an hour, which doesn't give us much time to talk, but Derek's sleeping so peacefully, I didn't want to wake him any earlier. Breakfast will be ready in about five minutes, and I'll wake him them and we can talk over food.

"Hey."

I turn from the stove, Derek's raspy morning voice surprising but welcome. He's standing in the doorway in his boxers, his hair every which way, eyes sleepy. I like seeing his morning muss. He's so perfect the rest of the time that this feels like a real intimacy.

"Good morning," I say, trying to sound casual but supportive and coming off as… constipated? Who knows.

He doesn't seem to notice, just comes over to give me a kiss. It's nice, if a little… perfunctory? Is he losing interest, or preoccupied?

I'm driving myself nuts.

"What's this?" He looks at the pancake in the frypan. It's the last one; the others are already in the warming oven.

"Breakfast." I bend to take out the plate of pancakes and then adding the last one. I turn off the stove and lead him to the table, already set and ready to go. "Do you want coffee?"

He turns back to the counter. "I'll get it. Can I top you up?"

I hand him my mug, and we go through the calming, comfortable process of settling in and dishing up food. I've just taken my first bite when he says, "I thought you had the community theater this morning."

A perfect opening. Guess that means I can't put it off anymore.

I finish chewing, swallow, and put down my cutlery.

"I do, but you've had a rough week, so I wanted to do something nice for you." I watch him carefully as I speak, but he doesn't react at all. "I also wanted some time with you—I haven't seen you much in the last few days."

He flashes a smile, *that* smile, the one I hate, and it makes my heart ache. He hasn't used his megawatt smile on me for months, not since right after we met. Why is he suddenly hiding his real self from me?

"I've missed you." It's the first thing he's said in three days that feels completely truthful. "I know you're busy today, but maybe tomorrow morning we can go out somewhere together?"

Hm. Time to push more. "Wouldn't you rather just stay here and relax? Things have been pretty full-on. If you want to talk about everything, I'm here." That's pretty blunt, right? *Talk to me. Let me share your burden.*

He shrugs, and any hope I had slips away. "Nothing to talk about. It is what it is." He shovels in a large forkful of food, an obvious excuse not to talk, and I suck in a deep breath.

"Derek, just because it is what it is doesn't mean there's nothing to talk about. I know you have to be angry. This is a big deal. Why don't you share that with me?"

He swallows his mouthful. "There's not really anything to share. It's… well, it's all bullshit, but that's life."

My patience snaps. I shove back my chair and stand up. "That's *not* fucking life, Derek. Life is when you talk to your partner about the things that are bothering you!" I grab my keys—damn it, *his* keys, to *his* house and *his* car—and storm out, slamming the door.

There's a sick feeling in my stomach, but it takes second place to my anger. What the fuck have the last few months been about? Have I just been a convenient live-in booty call? Why did he bother helping me with my emotional crisis last month if that's all I mean to him? I mean, honestly, if a guy spends time and effort pulling you out of a mental trap, you're allowed to assume he's committed! But people in committed relationships go to their partners for emotional support when things go to crap, and so clearly Derek doesn't consider me his partner in any way. Couldn't he have mentioned that before I started rearranging my life?

I slam into the car and hit the garage door opener. In just a few weeks, I'll be out of work, and not only do I not have anything lined up, I actually *put things off* because I was planning to stay here with Derek for a bit. I was planning a future with him—and he *knew* that. We talked about it. Wouldn't that have been a good time for him to mention that he's not that invested?

And oh fuck, I've made it about me again.

AN HOUR later, I've taken ownership of one of the seats in the front row of the community theater, and I'm hunkered down nursing my rage—at both Derek and myself. I think it's pretty obvious to everyone that I'm in a shitty mood, because they steer clear. I haven't snapped at anyone, I swear—although that might be because they haven't given me the opportunity. I would probably have tried not to take my mood out on them, though. After all, they haven't done anything wrong. It's not their fault my boyfriend is a closed-off, emotionless moron who's incapable of having a decent relationship, and that I'm so self-centered that I've interpreted his desire not to share as a diss on our relationship.

I really don't know what pisses me off more.

Someone drops into the seat beside me. "Having a bad day?" a sympathetic voice asks. I grunt at Dimi.

"What makes you think that?" Hmm, maybe I should dial down the sarcasm. *Repeat after me, Trav: not his fault.*

"Maybe it's the way you're glaring at the set like you wish it would spontaneously combust," he says drily. "Or it could be because you're using that same glare on anyone who gets within four feet of you. We took a vote, and while we'd really like to just let you stew for a while, we need some advice, so I've been delegated as agony aunt. Tell Dimi all your problems." He sounds way too cheerful, and if I were a violent person, he would likely be in some serious danger.

Lucky for Dimi, the only physical pain I'm capable of doling out is an earache from having to listen to me whine. Which I won't do. My and Derek's relationship woes are personal, between the two of us. It's not anybody else's business that he won't talk to me. That he treats me like I'm just anyone else, not his boyfriend who loves him and wants to—

"What the hell is the matter with him?" I burst out.

Dimi sighs. "Oh. Relationship troubles. I was really hoping for career or family issues."

I ignore that and carry on. It's just occurred to me that I'm talking to the one person who spends almost as much time with Derek as I do, and neither of them sleep during any of that time. "Seriously, Dimi, you've worked for him for years. Why is he so closed off?"

"Before we get any further into this conversation," he says slowly, as if he's choosing his words, "are you sure you want to have it with me? We're friends, Trav, but Derek's been a brilliant boss and mentor to me for a long time. My first loyalty is to him."

I think about that for a second. In a way, I think it's actually a good thing—better than if I talked to Kev or Mark or my sister or any of my friends in New York who would be on my side and probably just say what I want to hear. I know I'm not completely in the right here, and this way I might get information or advice that can help me in dealing specifically with Derek.

"Dimi, Derek and I had a fight this morning because I'm worried about him," I declare. "Since this whole publicity nightmare began, he's become more and more withdrawn. I don't think anybody else even notices, because he still has that big, fake, *fucking awful* smile"—I doubt Dimi misses the loathing in my voice—"and he's still all friendly and helpful and… you know, all the rest of the crap that goes with his golden boy persona." I turn my head to see if Dimi knows what I mean. He's nodding thoughtfully. "But he doesn't talk about anything. He doesn't show stress. He's gotta be stressed, right? His name is being dragged through the mud in the national—hell, *international*—media, his job is on the line, and he's having to watch JU be affected because people think he did something horrible. It's bullying on the worst scale, but he's just internalizing everything! All I want to know is that he's dealing with this, that he has a plan for what he'll do if everything goes to complete crap, but he *shut me down.*" I take a deep breath. My tone is getting hysterical, and Dimi doesn't need to see me break down.

I take another breath.

And another.

Then I look at Dimi again. There's concern written on his face, but when he sees that I've calmed down, it clears.

"I have a theory," he begins. "It's literally just a theory, so I could be wrong, but maybe it will help."

"Go on," I say cautiously, hoping it's not going to be one of those "make peace with the universe and accept that you can't change it" useless pieces of crap advice.

"I've worked directly for Derek for three years," Dimi tells me. "When the last AD of our district retired, so did his assistant. I was working in a pretty senior role in events at the time, and when Derek got promoted, he came to see me and told me I could name my price to be his assistant."

I'm surprised for several reasons. First is because "name your price" is a really generous offer for an assistant job. Derek's talked about how great Dimi is, but clearly I still underestimated him. The other reason is— "You left a 'pretty senior role' to be an assistant?" I asked. I always thought it went the other way.

"Hell yes." Dimi is emphatic. "There was only so far I could go in events before I'd either have to transfer out to another department or leave JU and get a job elsewhere. I'd already started thinking about my options, and I didn't like any of them. Pretty much any department would leave me in the same position. My best bet for a management job was in the parks or the resorts, but those roles are usually filled within the ranks, and I really didn't feel like taking a demotion to work toward my promotion, if you know what I mean."

I cast a thought back over that sentence, and I think I get it. "Right." Maybe.

"Plus, you gotta understand—assistant to the AD is not about getting coffee and picking up dry cleaning. Even if it was, Derek would probably shoot himself before asking me to do that. In this job I— Wait, I've gone off topic."

"My fault. I asked," I admitted. A part of me, the part that is almost scared to hear what Dimi's theory is—what if he thinks Derek needs space?—isn't sorry about the tangent.

"If you're really interested, we'll talk about it over a beer one night," he tells me with a grin. "But getting back to what I was saying, I've worked directly for Derek for three years. Before that, I worked with him occasionally for another two. I—"

"How old are you?" I interrupt. Again, only partly because I'm curious. I thought Dimi was a few years younger than me, but if he's worked for JU for five years, that might not be the case.

The other part is still because I'm scared.

"Twenty-nine," he says, raising an eyebrow and giving me a look that says he knows what I'm doing. Huh. He's actually older than me.

"You look amazing. I pegged you for five years younger," I confess, and he laughs.

"Good genes. New rule, by the way—save all questions until the end." He winks, but it only does a little to mollify my indignation. I fold my arms and slump a little lower in the chair.

"So, known Derek a long time, worked closely for the last few years… right. In all that time, I can count on the fingers of one hand the number of times Derek has talked about anything personal."

I straighten. That's… weird. I mean, I know Dimi works for Derek, that they see each other in a work environment, but they spend a shitload of time together. My colleagues and I spend most of our time together singing and dancing and pretending to be other people, but we still chitchat in snatched seconds here and there. We talk about our families, what we do for fun, relationships…. How can Derek have never talked about anything personal?

"Are you sure?" I venture, and immediately feel like an idiot. *Stupid question, Trav!*

"Yes," Dimi declares. "I know his parents are still alive because last year while Derek was dealing with a crisis, he asked me to find a travel agent who could help him plan an anniversary vacation for them. I found one, gave him the details, and that's it. I don't know their names. It's common knowledge here that he moved from New York to take his first JU job, but I don't know if he was born there or just moved there at some stage. I don't know where he went to college. I don't know if he has siblings. I don't know what his hobbies are. If you ask Derek what he did on the weekend, the answer usually either involves work of some kind, or he'll say something about chilling out. He doesn't talk about his vacations unless—"

"Okay, I get it," I interrupt again. "Derek's a private person. But, Dimi, I'm not a work colleague. Isn't he supposed to share *some* of this stuff with his boyfriend?" Secretly, I'm actually feeling a bit chuffed. I know more about Derek than Dimi does—like where he went to school, that he's an only child, his parents' names and occupations, that he's a native New Yorker, that he played lacrosse… actually, it's kind of thin. Those are all pretty superficial details.

"I'm not finished," Dimi says patiently. "I was just getting to the important bit."

I wave a hand for him to continue.

"He doesn't talk about his vacations unless you ask—and here's the thing, Trav. Not many people ask."

I blink. "What?"

Dimi nods. "Don't get me wrong, when he gets back after a trip, people always ask him how it was, and he'll say 'great,' and *that's it*. He doesn't volunteer any information and nobody ever pushes. Not even me," he admits. "I did once, but he just... I don't know. He told me he'd been to Aruba, it was great, and next thing I knew, we were talking about *my* last vacation. I figured he just didn't like to get personal, but...." He shrugs. "I think what you said before sums it up perfectly."

"Really? What did I say?" I cast my mind back. There was some ranting—okay, a lot of ranting—and then a few attempts to derail the conversation. What does any of that have to do with the fact that Derek apparently doesn't like making friends at work?

Hold on.

"Does Derek have friends?" I blurt, and then wince. God, that sounds horrible. "I mean—"

"I don't think so." Dimi's words hang between us. "Not the way you and I would think of friends. I consider him a friend—or he would be if he wasn't always trying to avoid personal contact. The only other person I would say he's friendly with at JU is Grant."

"He's mentioned him," I murmur. "We haven't met yet." And thinking about it, that's weird. Derek and I have been together for months. He's been out for drinks with some of my friends—cast members from *Day Dot* and some of the people from the theater here, including Dimi—but he's never suggested meeting up with his friends.

"Have you met any of his friends?" Dimi asks quietly.

"No." A pang shoots through me. "Maybe he just doesn't want me to because I'm not here permanently." Or he doesn't really think I'm special enough.

Not about you, Trav.

I hope.

The look Dimi gives me says more clearly than words ever could that I'm a moron. "Or maybe he doesn't have any because he's friendly with everyone but not that close to anyone. What you said before about him being the golden boy—he really is. People love Derek, but none of

152

them know him beyond the big smiles, the helpfulness, the great boss and efficient administrator. I've never seen anyone really try to get to know him. My theory is that it's always been that way for him—people see the surface, and don't bother to get to know the man underneath, so he… I don't know. The theory goes wonky there. I haven't really thought it all the way through. Honestly, though, I think you need to tell him you want to know this shit because you care about him and you want to support him. Be persistent and be patient."

I turn that over a few times in my mind. Derek does rely an awful lot on his fake smile. I'm just as guilty as everyone else of only seeing the surface—if he hadn't had his ego bruised by my initial attitude toward him, we may never have gotten beyond the superficial relationship he has with everyone else. Now that I've seen his real smile, though, and gotten to know the real him—even if it isn't as much as I'd like—he's so much more amazing than golden boy Derek could ever be.

"Thanks, Dimi." I really want to leave, go back to Derek's place, and hammer—metaphorically—at his stubborn head until I crack it like a nut. But he's probably gone to work, like he always does to hide from the world, and I made a commitment here that I'm not doing a great job of fulfilling. Plus, I need to stew on this a bit, work out the best approach. Make sure that when I talk to him, it's about him and his problems and not me and my insecurities. "Did you say you need me?"

He smiles. "Yeah, we could do with your input. All good?"

I nod firmly. I got this.

I COULD have called in sick to work and gone back to Derek's place to talk, but I was pretty sure—no, I was certain that he would have gone to work himself. If not to the office, then to the park or to one of the resorts. He would chat to the staff and guests, observe, and just generally make sure everything was going as smoothly as it should, keeping his eyes open for any improvements that could be made. I guess Derek is a workaholic, but the fact is that he loves his work. It's not a chore for him. He really is a social person, and he loves seeing the joy people feel here at JU. That friendly, charismatic exterior isn't something he just puts on. It's genuinely a part of him—but it's not *all* of him.

I'm not a huge fan of what I call his golden boy persona, but that's mostly because initially it reminded me of the guys who used to bully me, and now it feels like a wall he's hiding behind—hiding from me. Keeping himself from me. And I hate that he doesn't feel he can share all of himself with me—or that he doesn't want to. There's still that insidious voice in my head telling me that Derek probably knows he can do better, and I hate that too.

So I don't call in sick. Tomorrow's Sunday, and Derek doesn't need to get up early for work. After tonight's show, I'm going to go back to his place, and we're going to have a calm and rational conversation. If neither of us gets upset—and by "neither of us," I mean me, because Derek doesn't get upset, he just shuts down—then nothing can go wrong. Everything will be resolved, and we'll move forward in our relationship.

I keep telling myself that. While I'm getting ready, all through the matinee show—I nearly miss a cue because I'm so busy mentally chanting "It'll be fine, it'll be fine." The break between shows is murder. I end up talking Kev and two others into joining me at the cinema in the village to watch some stupid movie I can't even remember the name of while I'm sitting in there watching it.

By the time the final curtain comes down on the evening performance, I'm a wreck. The scared part of me, the part that is so desperate not to lose Derek that it would do anything to prevent that, is getting louder and louder.

Why are you trying to change him? He doesn't want to share his feelings—he has the right not to.

It's not wrong. Derek does have the right to bottle up his feelings and not tell me about them. But… I don't think that's healthy. I honestly believe that will ultimately lead to destructive behavior—bottled-up emotions don't just go away, and over the years it takes more and more to dull them, push them down. I don't think I could watch that happen to him. If he genuinely isn't ever going to be able to be completely open with me, if we can't have a relationship that's based on give and take, then maybe we're better off apart.

The thought rips me in half.

Are you crazy? You love him! How can you think you'd be better off without him?

How can I be in a relationship where my partner doesn't want to share his burdens with me? Would that then lead to me feeling unable to share mine? What would we be sharing, other than sex and companionship? I want more than that from my boyfriend.

And honestly, I believe Derek wants more too. Now that I've spoken with Dimi, especially, I think him being closed-off is more about having been taught to be that way rather than a desire for it.

I clean off my stage makeup, change into street clothes, and grab my stuff. I'll find out soon enough, won't I?

I LET myself into Derek's house. There's a light on in the living room, and as I head in that direction, Derek appears in the doorway. He looks surprised.

"I wasn't expecting to see you tonight," he says softly.

My stomach clenches so hard I think I might throw up. "Do you want me to go?" I ask, and then clear my throat, because my voice is all husky.

He shakes his head sharply. "No! I just… thought you might still be mad and want some space." He takes a deep breath. "I always want you here."

All of a sudden, the fear is gone. Derek loves me. We're going to fight—it's a rare couple that doesn't—but there's no reason we can't work out our issues.

"Derek, do you know why I was mad?"

He opens his mouth to answer, and it hits me that we're really having this conversation in the hallway. I hold up a hand. "Wait—let's go sit down. This is important, and it might take a while."

That makes him look a little nervous, but he turns and goes back into the living room. I follow, and while he stands awkwardly in the middle of the room, I sit on the couch and pat the spot next to me. He sits, and I take his hand.

"I love you," I start, and his head snaps up.

"But?" he interrupts, his whole body practically vibrating with tension.

I blink.

"What do you mean? There's no but. I love you."

The tension drops away, and he sags against the couch back. "Oh. I love you too. I thought that was the beginning of a breakup speech. 'Derek, I love you, but we need to be apart.'"

I try to keep my face blank, because… I don't want things to go in that direction, but who knows?

"Do you know why I was mad this morning?" Time to get things back on track.

"Because you wanted to talk about what's happening at work, and I didn't," he replies promptly.

Huh. That's kind of a simplistic take on it. "Yes and no." Is he being evasive, or does he really not get what this is about? "I— We've talked a bit about my family." I decide to take another tack. "But I don't think I've told you that my parents were really big on just getting things out there. Nobody ever gave the silent treatment or sulked in our house. We did a lot of yelling, we told each other exactly what we thought and how we felt, and then we got over it. And if we had problems, we'd talk about those and come up with solutions. Or if there was no solution, at least by sharing, we weren't dealing with it alone. My mom and dad tell each other everything—the only secrets they ever keep are what they're buying each other for their birthdays. I guess what I'm trying to say is that I was raised to believe that couples are completely open with each other and share everything. When you keep your feelings and your troubles to yourself, it makes me wonder if maybe you're not as committed to this relationship as I am." I wince, because that last part sounds like an accusation, like he needs to change to prove his love, and that's not what I want. "I don't mean you need to do anything you're uncomfortable with," I rush on. "I'm just telling you how I feel and why I got mad. Mostly it was because I'm scared. I also want you to know that if you ever want to share anything, I always want to hear it." I stop there, because really, what else can I say? It's his turn now. If he leaves things there, says "thank you" or "okay, let's go to bed," I'll have to try again, but maybe he won't. Maybe he'll give me a response we can work with.

You know how people sometimes say that silence is loud? I never really got that—it always seemed stupid to me. I mean, silence is silent, right?

This silence is screaming.

Finally Derek takes a deep breath, and it startles me so much that I jump. I'm so relieved he's broken the silence that I almost burst into tears.

"That's…." He pauses, clears his throat. "Uh, that's different from how I was brought up. I, uh…. You know my parents are very cerebral." I do. His dad's an entrepreneur, and his mom is an academic. From what he's told me, his upbringing was very much focused on achievement. I never got the impression that he was unhappy or neglected, though, so I'm a bit worried about what he'll say next. "It's not that I was ever told not to talk about my feelings… it's just…. Damn it!" He leaps up from the couch and starts pacing. I watch him warily, not sure if he's angry or just struggling to verbalize. "I don't know how to say this!"

Well, that answers that. I keep silent. If I rush in to help now, he'll never get the hang of expressing himself.

He stops pacing, swings around to glare at me. His sunny, friendly façade is gone now, replaced by a real man who's hurting. My boyfriend.

"People don't want to hear about my feelings, Trav. Nobody really gives a shit what's going on inside anyone else. If you have a problem that's solvable, yes. People like finding solutions. If it's some existential crisis, then no. That's just whining." I feel the words like a punch to the gut, but he's still talking, so I push the pain aside and listen. "It's fine to say you're mad or sad or whatever, but talking about it in detail doesn't achieve anything. You say you're mad, you do what you have to do to get over it, and you move on. People don't want to hear it!"

He stands there, fists clenched, panting, still glaring at me, although his stare has lost a lot of its intensity and there's something behind it now that tugs at my heartstrings.

I swallow hard. I take a deep breath. "I don't want to fight," I say as calmly as I can. "I'm not asking this because I want to fight. I'm asking because I genuinely want to know." I have to pause, to screw up my courage because I have never been more afraid in my life. "When we talked about—about the bullying, and how it made me feel… about how

I was afraid to take a lead role… were you wishing I would just shut up and get over it?"

The genuine shock on his face is a balm to my wounded heart.

"Trav, no!" In two quick steps he crosses to the couch, sits beside me, and seizes my hands. "No, of course not. That was something really important to you. I hated hearing how they hurt you, but knowing you trusted me with it and that I could do even a little… bit…." He falters to a stop, a stunned expression taking over.

"I love you," I tell him again. "It hurts me to know you're hurting, and, Derek, I know how much you love your job, how much pride you take in it, so even without you telling me, I know you're hurting. I want to help. I want to share your burden, and even if there is literally nothing we can do to solve this problem, maybe in sharing the load I can help just a little bit."

Derek looks overloaded, like he can't quite process what's happening. His eyes are flicking rapidly from side to side. I keep tight hold on his hands, anchoring him to the moment—to me.

Finally, he takes another deep breath, and this time it doesn't startle me. I find it reassuring. If he's got enough presence of mind to know he needs that moment to settle himself, then he's coming back from the shock.

"I never thought of it that way," he admits. "I… It didn't occur to me that… I mean…." He stumbles to a stop, but I know what he's trying to say.

"Derek, you're such a warm, charismatic person. People gravitate toward you, and they love to… to… I don't know, to *bask* in your presence. You're friendly, you're fun, intelligent, good-looking. For a lot of people, you're what they dream of being." He starts to protest, but I shake my head. "No, let me finish. That's not on you, what others see and expect. You're being yourself, and that's all you should ever have to be. But it doesn't change that in today's society, you're an ideal—attractive, successful, personable. And people don't like to see their idols as anything less than perfect, so while they were happy for you to listen to their problems, they never wanted you to share anything that would tarnish their image of you. I think." I make a slight face. "I'm mostly guessing here, based on what I know of you and what I've seen and heard while I've been here." I decide to keep my conversation with Dimi to myself for now, until Derek has had time to process. I think Dimi could be a really great friend for Derek, not just a colleague, but that's something that needs time to develop.

He leans back against the couch, still holding my hands, and sighs. "I don't know what to think," he admits. "It's—all just going around in my head." He meets my gaze, and those normally cheerful blue eyes are a haze of confusion.

"That's okay." I feel much more in control now, much more confident in the situation. Derek loves me. He's not shutting me out because he doesn't want to share with me, because he doesn't want me in his life forever. I knew that, of course, but that part of me that doubted just couldn't be silenced. It's okay, though. He just doesn't know how to share, isn't confident that people care.

So I need to show him I care. That I'll care no matter what.

"It can be hard dealing with feelings," I continue. "Sometimes it's easier to ignore them, lock them away and pretend they don't exist. But I can tell you from experience that they won't go away, and I'm here, Derek. I love you. I always want to listen to you, I always want to take part in your life. I want to share the good things *and* the bad things, because anything I can do to make your life easier, or better, or *anything* is what I want." I lean back against the couch, beside him, pressing the length of my body against his. He's warm and solid, and just feeling him beside me is a comfort after the stress of the hellishly long day. "Why don't we go to bed, cuddle, get a good night's sleep? Tomorrow is a new day, and everything will seem different. You have a lot to think about and I think you need to give yourself some time to decompress."

He slumps against my shoulder, turns his head, and kisses my neck, but otherwise doesn't move, doesn't say anything. Have I pushed too far? Should I prod him? Just sit here with him in silence, or get up and leave him to have some alone time?

I'm in an agony of doubt, wishing my old therapist were here to give me some advice, when Derek whispers, "I can't lose this job."

I close my eyes, swamped with relief but at the same time aching for him.

"I know," I whisper back, but don't turn. His face is still against my neck, and I figure it might be easier for him this way—an illusion of privacy.

"I love it here, Trav. Really love it. I love my park. I love my resorts. I could work in hospitality anywhere, for any company, but that's not what I want. I want the dream come true. I want to see the little kids have a magical experience, and to see the pride their parents feel at being able to give it to them. I want to see the adults who always wanted to come here, who spent years planning and saving to give themselves this experience, and then get here and finally get to take part in the magic *after wanting to all their lives*. I love knowing that what I do makes all that possible. I love knowing that my staff are the most productive, that they have the highest satisfaction index, that my district is the most profitable and has the best customer feedback rating. I love knowing that I work damn hard"—his voice starts to rise—"but that it's *worth it* because it makes people *happy*. And I *hate* that some stupid bitch who murdered her husband thinks she can shit all over that to distract a fucking jury, and *worse* is that it's working and she's fucking with people being happy, with *me* being happy, with my fucking life!" There's anger in his voice now, and he's almost shouting, but I can also feel the hot wetness of tears against my skin.

I turn then, not just my head, but my whole body, curling into him and wrapping my arms around him. A sob breaks from his throat as he presses harder against me. I hold him, kiss his hair, and hide my own tears from him. "Stupid bitch" is right, and I wish with all my might that Kylie Rutherford will be sent to prison for the rest of her life. I also make a mental note to talk to a lawyer. I want to sue her for what she's putting Derek through; I want to strip away any last remaining iota of dignity she might have left after her criminal trial.

Derek and I stay cuddled together like that for a long time, so long that I begin to wonder if he's fallen asleep, and feel a little drowsy myself. It's been a long day, both in terms of hours and emotional wear and tear.

Eventually he shifts, lifting his head and sitting up. I inch back a tiny bit, a silent offer of space if he wants to take it, but he captures my hand and hangs on.

"Thank you," he says, his voice a little rough. His eyes are slightly puffy and definitely red-rimmed, and he looks tired and worn-out, but there's a sense of lightness to him that's been missing the last few days. "I… never realized how good it could feel to…." He doesn't finish the sentence, but this is one he doesn't need to. I nod.

"I know. And you know I'm here, right? I'm right here."

He sighs, squeezes my hand. "I know. I'm sorry I put you through this." I open my mouth to protest, worried that maybe he didn't get it quite as well as I thought he did, but he shakes his head. "Not that you listened to me, Trav. That you had to push so hard. That we had to fight. That you spent the whole day stressing over it—because you did, didn't you?"

He knows me so well. "Yeah," I admit. "But you didn't do this on purpose, babe. This was something you had to learn to do, and I'm so glad I could help you do that—just as I'm glad to share any burden you carry."

He smiles softly at me, and it feels like the sun's just come out. Then he sighs again. "It feels better, knowing I'm not alone… but it doesn't fix anything, does it?"

"No," I concede. "But it's not like you can fix a lot. The cops said there's no question about the park or any employee being involved, right?" He nods. "And Kim heard from her friend of a friend of a cousin or whoever that the bitch's lawyers dumped her after that statement, right, and she had to hire new ones?" Another nod. "So it looks really bad now, but this case is going to be in the media spotlight for a long time. Eventually she's going to be convicted, and it will show her for the lying, conniving, murdering fiend she is—and people will realize that not only did she murder her husband, she then tried to throw the investigation off by dragging one of the most beloved vacation destinations in the world through the mud. Already there are rumblings in your favor. We just need to hold tight. It's horrible, but not insurmountable. And I really don't think you'll lose your job because of unsubstantiated allegations."

"That's true," he agrees, surprising me. "They won't fire me because of her stupid lies. I've done nothing wrong. But, Trav, I've never in all my time at JU had to post figures as low as last week's. People are canceling reservations because of this. If it continues, they'll fire me because my district is underperforming."

Fuck. I didn't think of that.

"There's nothing we can do about it tonight," I finally say. "It's been a really, really long day. Let's go to bed, and we can look at this with fresh eyes tomorrow. And if nothing can be done," I add, forestalling him, "then we'll consider our options. I know this place is your dream come true, but I'll bet it wasn't always, right? You didn't spend your whole childhood imagining yourself as a theme park administrator?"

"No," he concedes reluctantly.

I stand and tug him up with me. "Exactly. So if we have to, we'll find your next amazing dream. But we may not have to."

CHAPTER FIFTEEN

Derek

WHEN I walk into the office on Monday morning, I'm exhausted. Letting your emotions out really sucks the life from you. And man, it's like punching a hole in a dam! I spent more time fighting back tears on Sunday than I ever did in my life.

But Trav was there. He was there, and that pinched look he had last week was gone. I was so afraid that look meant he was disgusted. That he thought I was a loser, incapable of managing my own life.

Instead, he was just worried about me. Worried that I wasn't telling him my feelings because I didn't want him.

As if that could ever be true.

Things are good between us now. We spent a lot of time talking, and that was exhausting too. It's so much easier to just smile and brush things away than it is to think about how they actually make you feel, to let yourself feel them, and harder still is talking about them. Sometimes I couldn't actually think of the right words. Trav's amazing, though, and as hard as yesterday was, as tired and emotionally drained as I am today, there's a part of me that feels settled and confident that I will survive this. And now that I know how… safe it can feel to share my feelings, I think I maybe need to think about building some closer relationships. One of the things Trav and I talked about was how none of my friends are particularly close to me. There was nobody I felt I could confide in, not even *after* my breakdown, when I realized it was okay to talk about my feelings.

So while I'm not my usual bouncy Monday morning self, I'm okay. It's going to be okay.

Even if I do have to face the monthly status meeting today.

Dimi sticks his head around my office door. I waved to him as I arrived, but he was on the phone, and we didn't speak.

"All good?" he asks, which is strange.

"Yeah, why?" Is there something going on I don't know about?

He gives me a pointed look, then comes in and shuts the door. "Last week was a shitstorm. I would have said nothing could be shittier, but then I saw Trav's face on Saturday morning." He holds up a hand. "Not my business, I know. I just want to know if you're okay, or if I should run interference and get you some time out of the office today."

Those damn tears I've been fighting for the last thirty hours prick the backs of my eyes again, and I swallow hard. "Dimi, I'm okay. Trav doesn't have that look on his face anymore, and no matter what comes out of last week's debacle, I'm going to be okay. Thank you, though. You've been a good friend to me." It's true, I realize. I've always been so careful to keep things "work friendly" between us, but Dimi has been more of a friend to me than any of my so-called high school and college "best friends."

He gives me a level look, as if assessing whether I'm bullshitting him, and I grin. Suddenly I just want to laugh. "Dimi, I swear, it's all going to be okay. I know things look rough, but even if I get canned for underperforming—"

"What?" He sounds startled, and the expression on his face matches. It surprises me, because Dimi's not dumb—well, you know that. I've been telling you all along how brilliant he is. So he's gotta know it's not a good thing when profits drop.

I wait for him to catch on. Eventually it'll all click together what I'm talking about. I hold his gaze and wait.

And wait.

Any second now.

We're just staring at each other.

It's getting kind of awkward.

Why isn't he catching on?

Why am I just staring?

I shake my head sharply, breaking the stare. "C'mon, Dimi, you know how things work here. Profit is king. Sure, we need strong guest-satisfaction ratings, but profitability goes hand-in-hand with that—and right now, our district has neither."

He nods. "Sure, but I doubt corporate will fire the entire JU management team at once. This is clearly a JU issue, not a district one, and it's temporary."

Come again?

He must see my confusion because he whips out his ever-present tablet and taps away as he crosses the office toward me. "You obviously saw our figures for last week," he begins.

"Of course." Even though I didn't want to, I made myself check them. They were just as abysmal as I'd thought they would be. I get up from my chair and join him where he's standing beside the desk. He turns the tablet toward me.

"Did you look at the figures for everyone else?"

The words hang in the air between us as I stare at the numbers on the screen. I didn't look at the figures for the other districts—that's unusual for me, but at the time I couldn't bear to see the difference between us and everyone else. I definitely hadn't looked at the ranking. Normally my district is at the top. If one of the other parks or resorts has a killer promotion on, I might come in second. But since the seventh month after I was promoted to AD, my district has not been out of the top two positions.

And it still isn't.

I blink at the screen. My throat is suddenly tight. Last week's figures are abysmal... for all of JU. This is not about my district. This is not about me. This is about a stupid woman who murdered her husband and is trying to muddy the waters. I can't believe I didn't realize that. I can't believe I let myself get so fucked-up that my business brain stopped working.

My knees give out, and I drop into an undignified heap on the carpet. Dimi makes a strangled noise. "Are you okay?" He crouches beside me.

I focus on him, slightly dazed. "Trav said it. He said this wasn't on me. And logically I knew he was right, but... he's right. This is not a management issue. This is an external influence."

Dimi tilts his head and looks at me, then leans back slightly so he drops to sit on his ass. He crosses his legs in front of him like a schoolkid. "That's right. This is an external influence. It's up to PR and legal to spin this. Our job is to keep things running the way they always do."

Confidence surges through me again, but this time there's no exhaustion behind it. My mind is clear, completely clear for the first time since I got that damn call from Kim nearly five days ago. I'm still who I've always been—damn good at my job, confident, capable, and now I have a secret weapon in the form of Trav. I've totally got this.

"Thanks, Dimi." I scramble up off the floor and offer him a hand up. "Numbers are down because of this bullshit. PR and legal will do their bit to neutralize the damage, but in the meantime, we need to be looking at ways to attract new guests—maybe ones who wouldn't have come under normal circumstances." Repeating it makes it real, solid. I feel energized. This is my forte.

Dimi grins. "Do you want a brainstorming session?"

I nod as I pace over to the window. My view is out toward the park, but I can't actually see it—just parking lot and trees. "Yeah. For early afternoon, I think. Ask evarketing—"

He shouts with laughter, and I belatedly realize what I've said.

"Oops." I shoot him a sly glance. "This stays between us, right?"

He wipes moisture from his eyes. "Of course. But… how long have you been calling them that, and why did I never know?"

I shrug. "Not that long. And it's not exactly good form to rename departments, so…." I spread my hands, then grin. "It suits them, though, doesn't it?"

He's tapping at his tablet, grinning broadly. "It really does. Okay, I'll ask the *events* and *marketing* teams to send reps."

There's a hard knock, and we both turn just as the door is shoved open and Gina rushes in, slamming it closed behind her. Her face is pale and she's wild-eyed.

Fuck.

"Gina, what's wrong?" I ask, crossing to her.

"Corporate's here," she gasps. I feel a momentary twinge of worry, but it's overtaken by confusion. I exchange a glance with Dimi.

"Okay. Well, it's not shocking—there's a lot going on, and it's not unusual for them to send someone out when we have a big legal issue. I was kind of surprised they didn't come last week." I take her arm and lead her toward one of my visitor chairs. "Sit for a minute. Do you want some water?" Is something else going on with her that I've been too preoccupied to notice? Gina is normally a rock in the midst of a storm, but she seems really shaken.

She pulls away from me. "*Not* a rep. Not someone from legal or PR. *Corporate*—Malcolm Joy and Seth Holder. And some others."

Oh.

She's staring at me expectantly now, and my mind is racing.

"It's okay," I say finally. "It just means they're giving this more weight than we expected." *Or they're planning to fire the entire management team.*

I shake that thought away. I have no reason to believe it's true.

"Where are they now?" I ask Gina. She seems to be settling down a little in the face of my calm.

"Boardroom. They went straight in with Ken as soon as they arrived."

"Has anyone said anything about the monthly status meeting?" Dimi asks. Most of his attention is focused on his tablet—he's probably checking for any relevant memos... or gossip. The JU staff app is supposed to be for work, but it functions well for circulating "news."

Gina opens her mouth to answer, but her words are drowned out by the buzz of the phone on my desk. We all turn to stare at it. I literally cannot remember the last time it rang—nobody uses the landline anymore, when we all know the quickest way to reach each other is via cell phone or the app.

Dimi pulls himself together first, crosses to the desk, and snatches up the cordless receiver. "Derek Bryer's office," he says briskly. "Yes. Absolutely. No problem. Thank you." He puts the handset down as I wonder when he lost the ability to speak in full sentences. I mean, really, would it have hurt him to repeat some of the caller's comments, give us a hint?

"Well?" Gina demands, clearly thinking along the same lines as me.

Dimi turns to face us. He's maybe a *little* bit pale. He has pretty fair skin naturally, so I might just be imagining it. I hope.

"You've been called to attend a meeting with corporate and the rest of the executive management team," he says. "I'm to clear your schedule for the rest of the day."

Well, fuck. But—

"The whole exec team?" I ask. "Not just the ADs?" This might just be corporate taking an interest in how we plan to handle this whole situation.

He shrugs. "She said the executive management team." He hesitates. "That's a good sign, right? They're not going to fire the entire exec team."

"It's a great sign," I tell them both firmly, even though I'm still not convinced. "Did they say if assistants are invited?"

Dimi makes a face. "You're welcome to bring your assistant if you choose."

I raise a brow. "Do you not want to come?" That surprises me. Dimi has always been of the opinion that knowledge is power.

"I guess I'm just a little nervous about this whole thing. We've never had so many bigwigs from corporate here at once, and I don't think both Joy and Holder have been here at the same time since I've been working for JU." He shakes his head. "But if I don't come, I'll regret it. Get down there before it looks like you're stalling or something. I need five minutes to clear the rest of your day, and then I'll join you." There's a determined set to his jaw now that makes me feel… proud?

"I can do it," Gina volunteers. "Go, both of you. I can cancel or reschedule all your meetings." Dimi looks like he's going to protest, but she shoos us toward the door. "Dim, this is a great opportunity for you to meet the bosses. Don't be the doofus who strolls in late and interrupts."

"I don't think it's so great to meet anyone in the middle of a crisis," Dimi points out, but allows himself to be shooed. I check my pocket for my cell as we're ushered out the door.

A few harrowing minutes later—harrowing because everyone we pass in the halls seems to know exactly where we're going and either avoids eye contact or gives us sympathetic, mock-cheerful looks—we're in the boardroom and taking seats at the table. It's worth noting that Ken definitely isn't in charge of this meeting. I can tell straight away, because assistants aren't relegated to the far end of the table.

Most of the exec team, including the other assistant directors, are present, but the "meeting" hasn't begun yet—we seem to be waiting for Margo and Toby—so everyone is talking quietly to their neighbors. From across the table, Kim shoots me a wink. I smile and nod back. She looks just as in control and confident as always, despite the pressure that must be on her and her team, and I murmur as much to Dimi.

He chuckles. "So do you, and we both know you're only half as confident as usual."

I drop my gaze to the table. Huh. Maybe I'm not the only one who pretends sometimes. I let my attention wander to the head of the table, where two men are standing, deep in discussion with Ken. I've met them both, briefly, on separate occasions—Dimi was right when he said Malcolm Joy and Seth Holder haven't both been here at the same time for years. They're both tall, well-dressed men in their late sixties, and there's a pretty strong family resemblance. The man and woman sitting nearest to them I recognize from pictures—Malcolm's daughter Samantha and Nicholas Carrow, both senior execs, both slated to step up when Malcolm and Seth retire. A quick glance around shows that two board members are also here, chatting by the window.

On the plus side, nobody looks especially grim. I mean, no one is laughing with joy (no pun intended), but that's to be expected given we have a major situation on our hands. I'm not seeing the "oh shit, I have to fire everyone in this room" expression, though.

Not that I've ever seen that before.

Margo and Toby come in together with their assistants right then, and someone closes the door. People who were standing take seats, including Malcolm and Seth, which settles the room.

In fact, you could say the silence is deadly. The weight of expectations hangs in the air.

Am I being dramatic? Sorry, I'll stop. It's not like me, anyway, and it feels kind of weird. The moment just seemed to need something more than "we all shut up and waited for the big bosses to speak."

"Thank you all for rearranging your day on short notice," Malcolm says. He has a truly amazing voice, really deep and just a bit gravelly. I can understand why he's been in demand as a speaker for the past few decades, even disregarding his incredible business acumen. "Things have been a bit unsettled here for the past few days, and we'd like to plot out a clear course of action."

Well, that's straight to the point.

"You all know what the situation is. You know that JU bears no fault whatsoever in the murder of Peter Rutherford. The legal system will determine the rest—it's not our problem. However, in response to Kylie Rutherford's patently false allegations, Joy Inc. will be suing, on behalf of both the company and the individuals who were accused of taking part." His gaze meets mine. "Derek, we have the utmost confidence in you and your people. You've worked hard and tirelessly for Joy Inc. for the last ten years, and we're not going to let your reputation be tarnished."

I swallow hard. It feels like I've been punched in the stomach, but I manage to pull myself together enough to say, "Thank you." I was sure it would come out thready or croaky, because my throat is so dry, but it actually sounds strong, so I follow it up with a small smile. "I appreciate that." And I do, oh hell, I do. Those few words mean more than I'm willing to let anyone see.

But I'll tell Trav about it later.

Malcolm nods sharply. "The details are in the hands of legal, of course, but their instructions are to go hard." He looks down the table at Jeff, who heads up the legal team for JU. "Head office has been in touch with you?"

Jeff nods. "Yes, sir. We've forwarded all the information we have, and a teleconference has been set up for later today."

Malcolm's gaze shifts to Kim. "If you haven't already, you'll be receiving a memo on this, Kim," he tells her, and her smile is almost evil.

"I have it," she says. "And I can't wait to get started."

His nod this time is approving. "For the rest of you, Kim's instructions, and the line everyone at Joy Inc. will be taking from this point is that Kylie Rutherford deliberately set out to kill dreams." He pauses. "That sounds a bit dramatic, but essentially we no longer intend to remain neutral, or to claim that she's mistaken, confused, or grieving. Our standpoint going forward is that she deliberately chose to kill her husband here at JU, and to then accuse JU employees of being complicit, with the full knowledge that she would be tainting one of the places millions of children dream of visiting."

Wow. As the others around the table stir, I turn that over in my head. It's a hard line to take, and if it takes, it's going to turn the tide of public opinion very firmly against Kylie Rutherford.

I can't say that upsets me much.

The noise settles, but there's an air of excitement now. It's like the knowledge that we're going to hit back has energized everyone, and I can't blame them. It's certainly brightened my day. That awful, heavy weight in my stomach is gone, and I don't feel like I have to "just get through" anymore.

Malcolm's not done. "This is in the hands of legal and PR now, and I know you all agree that they're very capable hands. That's probably not going to stop some of you from worrying"—he shoots a look at me. Am I really so obvious?—"but we ask that you keep your focus where it belongs, on the running of this complex. And on that note, I'm going to hand you over to Seth."

Seth smiles and picks up the remote for the huge TV on the wall. I glance over as he turns it on and see that he's got his laptop hooked up to it. The screen comes to life with the image of a financial chart, and a quick look shows that it's not a good one. The red line plunges pretty drastically. In fact… I frown at the chart. That can't be right.

"I'm not going to go into a lot of detail here," Seth begins. "You've all seen the numbers, and you all know they're not good. But I want to show you why this management team has my and Malcolm's—and the board's—complete trust and confidence. The graph you're looking at was compiled by a team of top analysts. You may have noticed that the figures don't correlate with last week's. That's because this chart isn't about what happened last week. I gave that team the last twelve months' figures for Derek's district, right up until the week before the murder. I gave them an outline of exactly what happened that week—murder, staff crisis—and asked them for a projection. This"—he waves toward the screen—"is what they projected should have happened to Derek's profit center. This"—he lifts the remote and hits a button—"is what actually happened." A blue line appears. The only place it touches the red line— or comes anywhere close to it—is right at the beginning, where the chart is dated Sunday. "This graph only shows that week, but the projection was for three months, and I can assure you that reality is much better."

He hits another button, and a new graph appears. "This is the projection the team did for me after last week's crisis." The red line on this one is even worse. The numbers this time are for all of JU, not just my district, and it's a pretty catastrophic downward plunge. I skim along the time axis—this one is for three months, and although it shows some recovery, the numbers are nowhere near what they should be. I fight the urge to sink dow— Wait. Hang on. Those numbers aren't quite right. I frown at the screen again.

"And here are the actual figures," Seth says. The blue line appears again—not for the whole graph, since it's been less than a week—and a ripple goes around the table. The blue line is plunging, sure, but not as much as the red line, and it seems to be leveling off a little—it's hard to tell with the scale of the graph.

"Seth, could we see that on a shorter time scale?" Grant asks. He's leaning forward in his seat, eyes fixed intently on the screen.

Seth smiles and hits a button. Another graph appears, this one with both lines already visible, and showing only a two-week period. And yes, the drop definitely slowed over the weekend.

"It's still early days, of course," Seth cautioned, "but when I spoke to the analysts again this morning, I was told that no public relations gimmick, no statement we issued last week could have caused this result. This, I'm told, is the return we get on long-term hard work and excellent reputation. There was the initial shock at the accusation, but now people are starting to think about it, and they can see it doesn't make sense. We expect things to continue to stabilize organically and believe that our next steps will boost that even more. This *success*"—he looks around the table—"because it is a success in the face of adversity, is entirely due to the excellent team in this room and the people you have working for you. You should all be proud."

Those damn tears sting my eyes again, and I focus on holding them back. It's all kind of sappy, right? Maybe Malcolm and Seth have been watching too many of Joy Inc.'s movies, the ones where the good guys always win and there's at least one inspirational speech.

Although, hell, if the people who make those movies can't live them out, who can? And I sure as shit like being told I'm a success who should be proud. Seth's right, we work damn hard here, and it's nice to see that recognized.

"So," Seth says in a summing-up kind of voice, "what we're going to do moving forward is act from a position of strength. Marketing has put together a proposal for heavily discounted vacation packages to attract people"—he nods to Elise—"and while that would be the usual strategy in this situation, Mal and I have decided not to go ahead with it. Instead we want small rewards for guests who are already here—discounted meals and services, freebies in the parks, that sort of thing. Employees should be prepared to be spontaneous about giving things away—we want guests kept on their toes, not sure what they might get or when. Accounting is already working up a special budget for this. Otherwise, let's keep it business as usual on the operational level. We don't need to discount vacations here, because we've done nothing wrong, and people are going to see that."

I lean back and think about it as Margo asks a question. It's ballsy. He's right that the usual strategy would be to get people in even if it's at a loss—after all, nothing looks worse than a partly empty vacation destination, and *some* money is better than *no* money and empty rooms. But I think I like this idea. It's flipping the bird at all the people who turned on us.

I tune back in as Malcolm starts to speak. "The next stage of our genius plan is to announce something big—something strategic for the complex. Make it seem as though not only are we so unaffected by this that we're not going into crisis mode, we're actually moving forward with expansion."

Also ballsy, and really kind of clever. "What are we announcing?" I ask. A new park, maybe? That could work, although I have no idea what theme they'd go with.

Malcolm shrugs, and Seth smiles sheepishly. "No idea. That's why we had you clear the day, for brainstorming. You're all on the ground here—what do you think?"

Silence.

"Actually," Toby says. We all turn to look at him. His expression is a cross between excited and nervous. "I've been working on a proposal that might be what you're looking for."

Malcolm makes a "go on" gesture; Seth leans forward slightly.

"It's, uh…. Well, as you know the village has seven full theaters. My department keeps them booked with all the best shows, and it hasn't exactly been hard—most production companies are happy to plan a run in a place with a captive audience, so to speak, and not a lot of competition. A lot of the time they approach us, rather than the other way around. The challenge is maintaining a balance of shows to appeal to all our guests. Last year, for example, I really thought we'd have to leave one of the theaters empty for a three-month stretch because my choices were limited to sad, dramatic productions only, and we already had four of those in the lineup. I managed to find something else, but I remember thinking at the time that it would be so much easier if we had complete control over the productions ourselves. Then Tr— Uh, I started thinking about it again a month or so ago"—his gaze flicks in my direction, and suddenly I know exactly where he's going with this—"and…." He spreads his hands. "When I looked at the numbers, it actually seemed feasible."

Malcolm and Seth look thoughtful, but Ken's face is confused. "What seemed feasible?" he barks.

Yep. Barks. He didn't get his job because of how he treats his employees.

"A production company," Malcolm says, and Toby nods.

"Small to start," he adds. "One theater, one show at a time. That would allow us to get a feel for it with minimal risk. We have a pool of performers already employed by us—I thought we could enlarge it a little, and let them audition for the roles, rotate through the theater the same way they do the parks. Most of our performers move on after a relatively short while. As a rule, they're quite young and just starting out. But the opportunity to get experience in a full-length production might entice them to stay. Especially if we bring in a seasoned director."

My heart is in my throat. I'm not joking. I want to speak, to leap in and seize this incredible chance, but I can't. Did I ever say a bad word about Toby? I take it back. He's my new best friend.

Dimi nudges me, and then I guess he realizes I'm paralyzed, because he says thoughtfully, "It might be an idea to hire an experienced performer to be attached to the company. Someone who's been on

Broadway, for instance, and can act as both a creative guide for the production and a mentor to the other performers."

I love Dimi. He and Toby are neck-and-neck for best friend status.

And suddenly I know what I'm going to do with Dimi, career-wise. I turn the idea over, examining it for flaws, but it's perfect.

My attention is drawn back to the group by Toby. "I was thinking something along those lines," he agrees, and his gaze is on me.

Seth clears his throat. "Derek, do you have a secret past in the theater that we know nothing about?"

We all laugh, although Toby's cheeks are a bit pink as he chuckles. "Sorry, that was a bit obvious, wasn't it? Actually, the reason I started thinking about this again was—" He stops abruptly. "Do you mind?" he asks me, and I shake my head.

"Go for it. All of JU already knows; why not Joy Inc.?" I smile to show I'm kidding, and he grins back.

"Right, well, a couple months back Derek started dating one of the performers from the village. Things between them seem to have gotten quite serious, and I was thinking what a shame it is that there's not really any avenue for his career here... and that brought me to the idea of a production company."

Malcolm raises an eyebrow at Dimi. "So when... it's Dimitri, isn't it?"

"Dimi, please," Dimi says, and I'm so proud of the casual confidence in his voice. I'm also hella proud that Malcolm knows who he is—assistant to the AD isn't exactly a junior position, but Malcolm has a lot of executive names to remember already without adding assistants.

"So when Dimi suggested an experienced performer be attached to the production company, and you agreed, Toby, you were both thinking specifically of Derek's boyfriend?"

"Yes, sir," Dimi replies, while Toby nods.

"Is he at least good? What's his name?"

I decide to hold off on being offended, because Trav *is* good, and nobody can say otherwise.

"Trav Jones, and he's excellent, sir," Toby assures him.

"Oh, I know that name," Nicholas Carrow says, speaking for the first time. He turns to Malcolm and Seth. "You know my youngest goes to drama school in New York. She's always talking about Trav Jones—if she wanted to go into musical theater instead of film, he'd be her idol."

I make a mental note to find out where she goes to school and send her something. No, wait, that's creepy, right?

Malcolm looks somewhat mollified to know that if we hired Trav, it wouldn't just be because he's my boyfriend. "Well, it's early to be considering staffing," he concedes, "but it's a definite possibility. How far along is your proposal?"

"It's only an outline." Toby shrugs. "It wasn't a priority, and I was mostly working on it in my own time."

"It's a priority now. Take whatever resources you need to get it done ASAP—we want to see a draft on Wednesday morning." Toby looks a little overwhelmed but nods. Malcolm sweeps his gaze around the table. "I like Toby's idea. I like it a lot. It's probably what we'll go with. But I've got you all here now, and you've all cleared your calendars, so let's brainstorm anyway."

CHAPTER SIXTEEN

Trav

DEREK'S BEEN squirrelly all week, but it's okay. I know it's okay because he told me. Oh, not in that "I'm fine" way that worried me so much last week. He actually came home from work on Monday night and said to me, "Trav, there's something new happening at work that's got me preoccupied. I'm not ready to talk about it yet, but if I seem distracted, that's why. It's not bad, don't worry." Since he's been trying really hard to be open about his feelings about everything else, I can only trust that he'll sort this out in his head and share it when he's ready.

It's been a tough week, although a lot better than I feared. I spent Monday morning working myself into a lather about Derek going to work after our very difficult and emotional weekend. Then I turned on the business news (because I wanted to torture myself by checking for updates on Joy Inc.'s market status) and a panel of "experts" was discussing the situation. It made me want to vomit at first, but it actually wasn't that bad—not the business side, because they all agreed that profits had dropped—but their analysis of the situation. The only woman on the panel said this was a rough patch that wouldn't last because all evidence pointed toward JU being "simply collateral damage in the Rutherford murder." They also had some nice things to say about Derek, although one guy said something that seemed more like a backhanded compliment than anything else: "I don't believe Derek Bryer was involved in anything like that. He's too diligent a businessman to not know how it would affect his bottom line."

Um. Okay? I guess respect for human life comes after the almighty dollar in his world. Still, it made me feel better overall that people are recognizing what's actually going on.

Derek texted after lunch to say he'd be a bit late home. The big bosses were in town, and his time was being taken up meeting with them. Luckily, his text also said that his job was safe; otherwise, I might have *died* waiting for him to get home and reassure me.

I'm really glad Joy Inc. is going to sue Kylie Rutherford, because it saves me the trouble and expense. Plus, they can afford much better lawyers than I can—the kind of lawyers that aren't happy until their opposition is crying tears of blood.

Derek's also optimistic about his financial forecast. He says the worst seems to be over, and he's spent a lot of time this week encouraging staff to make sure things are fabulous for the guests who haven't abandoned ship. It's now more important than ever that the JU experience is a wonderful one.

The other reason the week's been tough is because *Day Dot*'s run at the village is winding down. In two more weeks, it'll close and move on to… I think it's Orlando, but to be honest, I'm not exactly sure. Since I didn't plan to stay with the tour after the first six months, I never checked the whole schedule. We've been here for over three months, though, and that means we've all had time to almost put down roots. We've certainly collected a lot of crap, and now everyone's trying to offload it before they have to pack their bags. I'm going to miss this cast—I've been working with many of them for almost a year now, and of course Rick is one of my favorite producers to work with. Plus, once the others leave, I have to face my future. Last Sunday while we were wallowing in feelings, Derek and I revisited my plans for after the show closes. We wondered if maybe I should go straight back to New York and find a part that started soon, since we thought he might be looking for work too—and God knows there are more jobs for him in the city than in Joyville. But then on Monday when he came home and told me Joy Inc. was going to bat for his reputation, we decided to stick to the original plan. I'll look for work starting next year, and we'll take the next five or so months to assess our relationship and consider our options.

That's the sensible plan, right? It makes it sound like neither of us are rushing into career decisions that would affect the rest of our lives.

In reality, we're both all in; we're just procrastinating because we know there's no easy solution.

So now it's Friday, and I've got the night off. I talked to Rick and John, who of course know what's been happening, and they agreed to let my understudy perform tonight so Derek and I can have some time together to just chill. I thought about hitting the grocery store after the matinee and making a special dinner, but ordering pizza or something seems like a much better idea. We both deserve some sloth and calories.

I slouch farther down on the couch. Derek should be home any minute, and while I wait I'm watching... something on Netflix. I can't actually remember what it's called, and it doesn't exactly have me on the edge of my seat, but it's letting my brain switch off, and I don't think I need anything else from it.

The buzz of the garage door opening cuts into my mental fog, and a few minutes later, it buzzes closed. The door into the house opens, and I smile. He's home. Should I get up and go say hello? Nah, he'll come looking for me—he knows I have the night off—and I really can't muster the energy.

Sure enough, a moment later he appears in the doorway from the kitchen... and I sit up, my lethargy forgotten. Something's happened, and I think it's good. He's got this air of excitement, a silly grin that's only half repressed....

"What?" I ask. Whoops. Should I have led with "Hi"?

"It's okay to say no," he blurts, and I blink.

"Say no to what? Do you have some kinky sex thi—"

"No!" He pauses. "Well, maybe, but that's not...." He sighs. "I think we need to start again." He comes over, drops onto the couch, beside me, and leans over to kiss me. "Hi."

I smile. "Hi. You look happy about something."

"I am." He nods. "You know that thing at work I was preoccupied with? I'm ready to talk about it." He looks so proud of himself that I can't stop a grin.

"Okay, tell me. This is good news, I'm guessing?" I lay a hand on his thigh. I love touching him.

He nods again. "I think it is, and I hope you will too, but it's okay if you don't."

That's the second time he's said something like that, and it's no clearer than it was before. I wait somewhat impatiently for him to get started.

"So, I told you that Malcolm and Seth wanted things to be business as usual instead of trying to do damage control, yeah? And that they wanted an idea for expansion."

"Yes," I say, because he seems to expect a response.

"Right, so we brainstormed a bunch of ideas, and they asked for proposals on the three they liked the most, but one was always a front-runner. The proposal draft was green-lighted on Wednesday, and since then Toby and his team have been refining the details... and this afternoon Malcolm and Seth gave it the go-ahead. The press release will go out Monday morning."

I frown. I'm still not sure why he's so excited. "Isn't that kind of fast? To go from concept to approval in a week?"

"It's very fast," he agrees. "Ridiculously fast. This whole project will be fast-tracked, though, because part of the reason for it is to serve as a distraction. That it's a great idea and projected to be highly profitable is just a bonus."

Meh. Not my area, and really nothing to do with me. "All right, so what is it, and why are you so worked up about it?"

"A production company at the village," he says, and even before I fully take that in, something in my brain must grasp the implications—the possibilities—because every muscle in my body tenses. Derek's watching me closely.

"What kind of production company?" I manage to ask. Oh God, oh God, could it really all just fall into my lap like this? A fabulous man who loves me in a great town where I've made friends and have an input in the community, and a job in my chosen field?

No one's that lucky, I warn myself, tamping down the excitement.

But as Derek talks, explaining how the company will work, a little bit of the excitement dies off naturally. I enjoyed the two days working in the park but rotating between that and real theater work is not what I want for my career. Still, this is a better option by far than anything else we've come up with, and let's face it, I'm an experienced performer at the top of my career—it's unlikely I'll often be beat out at auditions by the kids working in the parks. Some of them are really good, but they don't have my background in theater. I force myself to keep smiling and pay attention, because this is *good*.

"… and they haven't worked out yet how it's going to be managed, whether it'll be part of the village district or events or entertainment or its own department, so the interview will be with Ken, Malcolm, and Seth. They're coming back on Monday to do it—I told them that was best because it's your day off. But if you don't want to, tell me now and I'll tell them not to bother." He finishes on a slightly anxious note. Have you even seen a puppy desperately waiting for you to throw a ball or stick? That's what the expression on his face reminds me of right now.

I should have been paying closer attention, because it seems really weird that the CEO and CFO of Joy Incorporated would fly out from LA to interview a performer. Also, what interview?

He must see the blankness on my face, because he sighs, then pats my hand where it's resting on his thigh. "Where did I lose you?"

"Right after auditions and rotating," I admit, and he laughs.

"You missed the best bit! The part where I said there would be one performer permanently attached to the production company to help the others ensure continuity—someone with a lot of theater experience, since most of our other performers don't have that."

The hope that I've been carefully tamping down explodes out in fireworks. I swallow hard. "And, um, did I hear something about an interview?" Oh my God oh my God oh my *God*!

He's grinning widely now. "Monday at ten. Entertainment usually interview performers, but because this role probably won't report to entertainment, and also because Toby blurted that he basically came up with the idea because of you and Malcolm and Seth are now curious, you get to interview with the big bosses." He leans forward and kisses me. "Just between you and me, I think it's pretty much in the bag. They went to see the show last night and googled you this morning, and then asked me about a million questions."

Oh my GOD!

"So…." I stop and swallow again. "So what you're saying is that I could have a job here?"

"If you want it."

I study his face. That slight anxiety is back, mingling with his excitement. He's so handsome and charismatic—I don't think I'll ever not notice that—but now when I look at him, I also see his kindness, his bone-deep desire to please, to make people happy.

"I want it."

Epilogue

Derek

I SING loudly to myself and anyone who might be listening as I drive to the airport. My musical repertoire has expanded since Trav came into my life, and I'm not ashamed to admit that the song I'm belting right now is a power ballad—"Glory of Love" by Peter Cetera. Trav's right; there's something extremely satisfying about putting all your energy into those lyrics.

In six months, my life has changed, and I couldn't be more thrilled. If someone had asked me at the beginning of the year if I was happy, my answer would have been a resounding "Hell, yes!" And I was happy. I had everything I wanted—until I met Trav and realized I needed him more than any of it.

Before Trav went in for that interview a couple months back, he asked me rather anxiously what we'd do if he didn't get the job. We'd both been putting off making permanent decisions because it was just too damn hard, but right at that moment, looking at his face that I love so much, I knew the only decision that mattered was the one to stay together. So I told him if he didn't get the job, I'd quit mine and move back to New York.

And I meant it. After he left, I even went so far as to make a few calls, see what was out there, and not once did I feel uncertain. Because as much as I love JU, I love Trav more, and I could never be happy again without him.

But in the end, it was a moot point. Seth and Malcolm both thought Trav was—is—perfect for the job. They offered it to him on the spot—I think the interview was a formality. Trav found out later that they'd already reached out to some contacts in New York to ask about him. He accepted the job, of course, and we celebrated all night long, if you know what I mean. That's right, if you could see me right now, I'd be winking at you.

Things moved into high gear pretty much straight away, and the plan is for the company to begin performances early next year. The first show has been selected, and auditions will begin as soon as a director is hired, which hopefully will be next week. Trav's superexcited—he had a huge part in deciding which show to open with, and he's going to be the lead. He won't always, but for this first one, he can't resist. He still has trouble believing everything worked out so well—this is his dream come true, the opportunity to perform pretty much any part he wants without having to deal with the Broadway hype. And he has me. Do I sound smug? I feel smug.

Right now, like I said, I'm on my way to the airport. Trav went up to New York last week to start packing up his apartment, and I'm going to help him finish up. We'll also introduce each other to our respective parents and chat to a director Toby is convinced would be perfect for us. Keep your fingers crossed that he is, because we really need someone soon.

Oh, you probably want to know what's going on with JU and the whole murder thing, right? Well, profitability still isn't where we want it, but it's close. By the end of the year we should be back to normal—and we're definitely in a better position than the experts projected. That was probably helped when a really well-respected crime journalist did an investigative report. She was extremely thorough, extremely factual, and completely ripped Kylie Rutherford's claims to shreds. That report was syndicated across the world, and the reporter has made guest appearances on some popular talk shows to discuss it. So that helped spread the word.

It also helped when Joy Inc. sued. For some reason, people assume that suing means you're in the right. Both the criminal and civil cases are awaiting trial, but I've been assured that given the overwhelming evidence for both, it would take a miracle for her to get away with it. Meanwhile, the word is that she's afraid to leave her house. Society has snubbed her, and people jeer at her in the streets.

I'm okay with that.

I've got a pretty great life. A job I love, friends I get to see nearly every day—because yeah, I'm working on building closer friendships—and in a few hours I'm going to be with the man I love.

We've got this.

LOUISA MASTERS started reading romance much earlier than her mother thought she should. While other teenagers were sneaking out of the house, Louisa was sneaking romance novels in and working out how to read them without being discovered. She's spent most of her life feeling sorry for people who don't read, convinced that books are the solution to every problem. As an adult, she feeds her addiction in every spare second, only occasionally tearing herself away to do things like answer the phone and pay bills. She spent years trying to build a "sensible" career, working in bookstores, recruitment, resource management, administration, and as a travel agent, before finally conceding defeat and devoting herself to the world of romance novels. Louisa has a long list of places first discovered in books that she wants to visit, and every so often she overcomes her loathing of jet lag and takes a trip that charges her imagination. She lives in Melbourne, Australia, where she whines about the weather for most of the year while secretly admitting she'll probably never move.

Website: www.louisamasters.com
Facebook: www.facebook.com/LouisaMastersAuthor
Twitter: @AuthorLouisaM
Instagram: @AuthorLouisaM
Email: louisa@louisamasters.com
Subscribe for a free novella! http://bit.ly/subscribeLouisaM

DREAMSPUN
DESIRES

THE ATHLETE
AND THE ARISTOCRAT
Louisa Masters

Sometimes love takes balls.

Sometimes love takes balls.

Newly retired championship footballer Simon Wood is taking on his next challenge. His plan for a charity to provide funding for underprivileged children to pursue football as a career has passed its first hurdle: he has backers and an executive consultant. Now it's time to get the ball rolling.

Lucien Morel, heir to the multibillion-euro Morel Corporation, is shocked—and thrilled—to learn his father has volunteered him as consultant to a fledgling football charity. Better yet, the brains behind it all is heartthrob Simon Wood, his teenage idol and crush.

Although Simon and Lucien get off on the wrong foot, it's not long before they're getting along like a house on fire—sparks included. But with the charity under public scrutiny, can their romance thrive?

www.dreamspinnerpress.com

DREAMSPUN
DESIRES

THE BUNNY AND THE BILLIONAIRE

Louisa Masters

Spending their fortunes and losing their hearts.

Spending their fortunes and losing their hearts.

Hardworking Australian nurse Ben Adams inherits a substantial sum and decides to tour Europe. In Monaco, the home of glamour and the idle rich, he meets French billionaire playboy Léo Artois. After getting off on the wrong foot—as happens when one accuses a stranger of being part of the Albanian mafia—their attraction blazes. Léo, born to the top tier of society, has never known limits, and Ben, used to budgeting every cent, finds it difficult to adjust to not only Léo's world, but also the changes wealth brings to his own life.

As they make allowances for each other's foibles, Ben gradually appreciates the finer things, and Léo widens his perspective. They both know one thing: this is not a typical holiday romance and they're not ready to say goodbye.

www.dreamspinnerpress.com

Made in the
USA
Middletown, DE